Monty's Coming of Age
The Grand European Tour

Eustace Hope-Langmore

Preface

Monty's Coming of Age is the first of three books I have initially planned for this series.

Written somewhat tongue in cheek, the story commences in the dying days of the nineteenth century and offers a glimpse into the gilded life of a young man born into a world of Victorian privilege and entitlement.

Set to the backdrop of his erotic awakening, and increasingly erotic endeavours, the reader will journey in the footsteps of the aristocratic young men and women of the Grand European Tour.

More particularly, they will follow in the footsteps of Montague Finch-Morton III as he prematurely journeys toward manhood, maturity, and social eligibility.

Primarily a work of fiction, I have also interwoven this tale with certain real-life figures, places, and events.

Where appropriate, and where I have felt it necessary to enliven the story, or its characters, I have also exercised a considerable dash of artistic licence, and French *joie de vivre*.

Neither of these liberties should be taken altogether too seriously.

If you enjoy reading this book, I would be delighted if you would be so kind as to leave a review or rating on the platform of your choice.

With my kindest regards,

Eustace Hope-Langmore

11 April 2022

Eustace Hope-Langmore

Contents

Prologue

For a young man born into a world of privilege and entitlement during the glory years of Her Majesty's vast and illustrious empire, one might almost describe that station in life as something akin to saying, "Breaking the bank in Monte Carlo."

And so it was for me. At the time of my birth, Her Majesty Queen Victoria, by the Grace of God, presided over the largest empire in history. Larger even than the famed Roman, or Persian empires, our glorious queen held sway over a quarter of the earth's population, its lands, its beasts, and of course, its immeasurable natural resources.

With a realm stretching as far afield as Canada and New Zealand, Her Majesty's flag, and her ambassadors effortlessly garnered the willing and undying adulation, loyalty, and respect of its indigenous populace.

Her armies, navies, and gunboats were, of course, always on hand to ensure the safety, security, and peace of mind of those self-same lands, and peoples.

Such was Her Majesty's impact in bringing desperately needed governance, education, and religion to those previously savage, and uncivilized lands. It was only fitting for parliament to award her the additional title of Empress of India in 1878.

Fitting, of course, but also highly appropriate when one might rightly consider India to be the brightest of all jewels in the weighty crown of her glorious empire.

And for a courageous, and ambitious young man of noble birth unafraid to set forth into the as yet unexplored vastness of her colonies, protectorates, and dominions, there lay an unrivaled opportunity to make a name for himself, whilst heaping further glory on his family, queen, and empire.

I should point out, however, noble birth isn't simply adventure, glory, and privilege. It also entails a significant chunk of self-sacrifice, and public service.

Service to one's family. Service to one's God, and the church. But most importantly of all, service to one's country, and one's monarch.

As you may well then imagine, the path in life for a young man of my generation and pedigree was more or less preordained, even from before my loving conception in the hallowed surroundings of the family estate, Morton Hall.

Indeed, until the age of ten, a young man of my social class might expect to receive his first formal education from a full time governess, employed to teach the basics of the three "R's" (reading, writing, and arithmetic).

Dependent on family circumstance, he may also receive private instruction in classical literature, British and world history, geography, and the arts. In addition to schooling in world languages, including Italian, French, German, and Latin.

All are subjects which will serve him in good stead during his eight to nine years as a full time boarder at Eton, or Harrow college.

Dependent on his chosen career path, he may then move up to Oxford, or Cambridge, or like me, he may choose to take his place at the prestigious Royal Military College, Sandhurst.

Schooled in the finer aspects of military tactics, musketry, sword play, etiquette and horsemanship, a bright young man of promise may expect to graduate Sandhurst as a well-rounded, highly polished, eligible Victorian gentleman.

From here, one might reasonably expect a first appointment overseas as a junior subaltern (Second Lieutenant) in one of Her Majesties premier regiments of the line. In my case, this would be my father's, and my grandfather's regiment before him, the Twenty-First (Empress of India's) Lancers.

An illustrious regiment, they were originally raised in 1858 by the East India Company, for service during the Indian Rebellion.

Barring death or disablement, an officer engaged in a short service commission would then serve for a minimum of ten years at home and abroad. During which time, he should make every effort to climb the ranks, and distinguish himself on both the field of battle, and in the advancement of the empire and his monarch through exploration, science, and diplomacy.

He may then opt to extend his military engagement in the hope of regimental command, or continue his overseas service with an appointment to the Foreign Office, or the Diplomatic Service, before semi-retirement and natural accession to the House of Lords in the Palace of Westminster.

He should, of course, also marry well while still young and virile enough to sire strong and healthy male heirs to carry forth the family name and legacy.

This last point is made all the more urgent by the perilous nature of overseas service. The irony of which is not lost on me.

And so it was that I myself walked that gilded and predetermined path until just a few months shy of my eighteenth birthday.

It was, in fact, just a few days into the first term of my final year at Eton when news came of an event that would change my life forever.

And in ways I could never have imagined.

The Right Honorable
Montague Finch-Morton III
Eighth Earl of Benfleet.
Captain, Twenty-First Empress of India's Lancers
12 March 1905

Chapter One

Eton College – 7 September 1898

The senior housemaster, Mr. Davenport, is reciting a lengthy, and somewhat tedious extract from Homer's Iliad in Latin, when he is rudely interrupted by a flustered, and out of breath young messenger boy barreling unannounced into the classroom.

For my part, I barely give the greasy young oik a second glance. I'm far more interested in the view from my window, and the action on the rugger field outside. I pay no heed to the boy, until the portly Mr. Davenport loses his patience and demands, "Well, boy, are you mute as well as ignorant? Is there a reason for this intrusion?"

"Um, yes. I mean yes, sir," the child blusters. "I was told to bring a message. A telegram, sir. And a note from the headmaster."

Davenport leans forward in expectation. The messenger looks bemused and unsure of himself.

"Well?" Davenport barks impatiently. "Hand them over, boy. You do still have them, I presume?"

The sniveling young fag* now looks close to wetting his breeches. I should, of course, be embarrassed for him, but I'm not. We've all been there, and instead, I snigger along with the rest of my classmates at his growing discomfort.

His face now resembling an overripe strawberry, the boy nervously fumbles in his pockets before offering a trembling hand. Growing ever more impatient, Davenport snatches the two small buff-colored envelopes, before angrily shooing the boy away like some bothersome insect.

*Fag/Fagging – a traditional practice in British public schools, whereby younger pupils were required to act as personal servants to the eldest boys and masters.

Peering across the top of his wire-rimmed spectacles, Davenport inspects the front of each envelope before returning to his desk.

"You boys should continue to read the same passage in silence until told otherwise. And no slacking off. I'll be watching you all."

Happy for this unexpected, but welcome respite from the tedium of Latin prose, I check the time on my pocket watch before turning back to the window.

I'm so engrossed with the match outside, I don't hear my name the first time it's called. Rising to his feet, Davenport loudly clears his throat, and sarcastically repeats, "Are you with us, Finch-Morton? Or is there something more exciting than Latin recitation outside?"

"Um, yes, sir. I mean, no, sir," I splutter. "I was just. I mean, I was—"

I'm cut off mid splutter, and Davenport sarcastically sneers, "You were daydreaming, boy. Which is precisely the reason you will never amount to anything. But no matter, I have important news to share. Come here."

Confused and unsure, I ask, "Me, sir?"

Dumbfounded, the house master slowly shakes his head before saying, "Well, I don't see any other Finch-Morton's in the room. Do you?"

Ignoring the muffled titters of my peers, and faced with my obviously blank expression, he then angrily snaps, "Yes, boy, I mean you! Come now, we haven't got all day."

Blushing, I scurry to the front of the class where Davenport turns me to face my classmates. Still standing, he takes a sip from a glass of water before loudly clearing his throat for a second time.

"Now boys, as you all know from recent dispatches, a combined Anglo-Egyptian force under the command of Major-General Horatio Herbert Kitchener were victorious in inflicting a crushing defeat on the self-proclaimed Mahdi, and his fanatical hordes at the battle of Omdurman in the Sudan."

As victory's in battle go, this one has done more than most to bolster national pride. For most in England, it is a long overdue, and much needed comeuppance to avenge the defeat, and what most see as the murder in 1885 of Major-General Charles Gordon at his residence in Khartoum.

For myself, however, the main source of pride comes from knowing of my father's involvement in the Sudan campaign. Other boys at Eton have fathers serving with Kitchener, but none in a regiment as glorious and feted as the Twenty-First Lancer's.

I'm glowing with pride, but am still pondering why I, in particular, have been singled out from amongst my peers, when Davenport proudly holds aloft a small slip of buff-colored paper.

"I have in my hand a copy of a personal telegram from none other than Major-General Kitchener himself, which I would now like to read aloud."

Adjusting his spectacles, Davenport looks to me with a knowing nod before turning to address the class.

"Dear Lady Finch-Morton, I write to you with a mixture of both pride and sadness to inform that your husband, Colonel 'The Right Honorable' Montague Finch-Morton II, Seventh Earl of Benfleet has distinguished himself most valiantly at the head of his squadron, during the Battle of Omdurman--"

The rest of his words are lost to the annals of time, but they no doubt continued in that same air of stiff upper lip Victorian detachment from human emotion. Equally lacking in emotion is Davenport's use of the term "distinguished himself."

When used in the same sentence as, "I write to you with a mixture of both pride and sadness," it is all too easy to interpret its meaning in one of two possible ways.

In the first, my paternal namesake has been wounded while performing some gallant act of derring-do on the field of battle and is now to be honored by the queen on his return to these shores.

In the second scenario, my father has been cut to ribbons whilst leading his men into battle, and his remains will now be buried with full military honors on their return to these shores.

The mindset of upper class Victorian society perceives both scenarios as equally quite glorious, and something for a young man of breeding to strive for.

With hindsight, and now knowing the circumstances of my father's untimely death, I'm sure, he would not now be so inclined.

Anecdotally, at my father's funeral, I was informed by a fellow officer that my father had charged from the line to assist an injured comrade. His horse shot from under him, and his ammunition exhausted, he had valiantly fought on with sword and lance.

Steadfastly refusing to abandon the badly wounded man, he was personally able to dispatch more than a dozen savages before he himself finally succumbed to a flurry of blows from the cruel Dervish scimitars. After the battle, little was left of him to recover and send home.

Even now, I shudder at the thought of this butchery – but of course, I digress.

I'm still trying to digest the news of father's death when Davenport passes me the second envelope. "This is a note from the headmaster. Your mother, Lady Finch-Morton, wishes you to return home immediately."

It's not the done thing for a young man to publicly blub, or display one's emotions, but I'm struggling to hold back my tears, and the handwriting on the note is little more than a blur.

Sensing my discomfort, but mostly to mask his own, Davenport pats me on the back in an overly manly sort of way. "Chin up, old man. Your father was a bally hero."

One of my classmates nods his concurrence and gets to his feet. "Yes. Bloody good show, Finchy. Your old man has done the country proud."

He then encourages the rest of the class to stand up. "On your feet, lads. Let's have three cheers for Colonel Finch-Morton. Hip hip hooray. Hip hip hooray. Hip hip hoo—"

The last hooray fades away, and Davenport lightly touches my arm. "Hurry away to your dorm now, lad, and pack your things. A carriage is waiting to take you to the station. I'll send along a couple of fags to help load your trunk."

And that was it. That was how I found out about my father's death. Sterile, cold, and typically Victorian. But at least my "father was a bally hero, and did his country proud." What more could a young man ask for?

Davenport nonchalantly waves me away and resumes his recitation. I'm almost out of the door when he remembers something and looks up from his book. "Best of luck, Finch-Morton. Oh and *Dulce et Decorum est pro patria mori.*"

With the benefit of more than ten years of hideously expensive Latin tuition under my belt, I should know the meaning of this phrase, but my mind is an embarrassingly blank page.

Hopeful that at least something of his teaching might have sunk in, Davenport helpfully offers, "It's a quote from the Roman poet, Horace? It was on last terms end-of-year paper?"

Losing patience, he turns towards my classmates. "Somebody? Anybody? Please tell me at least one of you has a brain larger than a pea, and I haven't been wasting my time for the last five years?"

The housemaster scans the room and selects from amongst the flurry of raised hands. "Yes, you, Bretherington. Stand up, and enlighten us, please."

Tobias Bretherington is the class swot, and a notorious sneak. He also has a particular dislike for me that dates back to our time as freshers. The reason for this dislike is long since forgotten, but whatever it was, the dislike is mutual.

Looking particularly smug, he straightens his starched collar before turning toward me to demonstrate his educational superiority. "*Dulce et Decorum est pro patria mori.* It is sweet and fitting to die for one's country."

"Indeed." Davenport nods enthusiastically. It is indeed sweet and fitting to die for one's country."

Without another word, or a single spark of compassion, he turns to continue where he left off, while I leave to pack my possessions.

All the while I'm quietly seething and wishing for one or two others to die a horrible but fitting death for one's country.

Chapter Two

Morton Hall – 23 October 1898

Father's funeral is as grand a fair as one might well imagine. His fellow officers recently returned from the Sudan traveling en masse from their barracks in London to pay their respects in the family chapel. Kitted out in their finest dress regalia, their arrival on horseback is quite the sight to behold. It will also become a talking point in the village for many years to come.

After a somewhat emotionless service delivered by the elderly, and pre-senile Reverend Franklin, it is most refreshing to hear the stirring words of my father's former commanding officer, and the regiment's current Colonel in Chief, retired Lieutenant General Sykes-Carruthers.

A giant of a man, with a fine set of mutton-chop whiskers, and a rack of medals almost as wide as his barrel of a chest, his booming voice resonates through the tiny chapel like only that of a career military man might.

More importantly, I feel very much that the words of his eulogy are straight from the heart, and borne of his own personal experience of leading men in battle. His glowing appraisal of my father, as a fine officer and a gentleman, is made all the more heartfelt by his personal connection. The mention of a posthumous decoration, possibly even a Victoria Cross, is particularly emotive.

Masking my own growing emotion, I turn to Mother, and gently squeeze her hand. For such a moving and touching appraisal of her recently departed husband, she seems unusually calm, and almost detached from the moment.

Noting my concern, she forces a smile, and whispers, "I'm quite fine, Monty. Your father would have wanted me to remain strong."

Not thinking anything untoward in her words, I squeeze her hand again and turn back to the service.

After final hymn's and the Lord's Prayer, Fathers scant remains are interred in the family mausoleum to rest amongst our illustrious ancestors.

We should, I suppose, be grateful for small mercies. Had he been a rank-and-file soldier, or an officer of limited means, his mortal remains would have been interred in the place of his demise.

I silently give thanks then for our privileged position in society. And to his fellow officers, who most diligently kept his butchered remains packed in ice during the long voyage home from Africa.

* * * * * * * *

The venue for the wake is the great hall. Cook has prepared a fine spread of, amongst other things, potted meat sandwiches, kedgeree, Savoy biscuits, and a plump stuffed goose.

A four-piece string quartet is perched on a raised velvet covered podium playing Beethoven's movement number fourteen in C minor, while mother and Aunt Caroline effortlessly sashay around the room attending to the needs of our guests.

The initially somber mood gradually raises in tempo as the young soldiers feast and gorge themselves on ale, claret, and whisky. Although overly boisterous, mother tactfully stands back and allows them to celebrate Father's life and death in the way he would likely have celebrated the demise of another.

Nevertheless, we are all relieved to finally escort the last of the young officers to the door. Thoroughly exhausted, and emotionally drained, I turn to Mother to wish her good night.

The smile she had for the departing young men has long since gone. Now serious, she gently takes me by the arm, "Actually darling, there is something your aunt and I need to discuss with you that won't wait until the morning. Come with me to the drawing room, please."

* * * * * * * * *

A stout log is burning fiercely in the hearth, and Aunt Caroline fills two cut crystal glasses from a decanter of Father's finest claret.

A fine-looking woman in her late-thirties, she was married to the Marquess of Rutland for less than a year, before she too was widowed at just nineteen years of age.

In this case, her husband met his glorious and heroic end on the point of a Zulu assegai at the Battle of Isandlwana in 1879. Despite this, and despite inheriting the responsibility of his estates at such a tender age, she remains a strikingly beautiful woman.

Her lustrous golden locks and ample bosom are a family trait she shares with her sister. Traits that were more often than once the subject of a boyhood fantasy. And not just of mine, I can tell you.

As a fresher at Eton, I was always astounded by the level of attention heaped on Aunt Caroline during her monthly visits. The older boys were always particularly keen to see her. It only really started to bother me, however, as I got older, and the whispers and innuendo became ever more apparent.

Particularly irksome was a rumor circulating that Aunt Caroline was a notorious man-eater with a taste for unusual *sexual proclivities*. At the time, I had no real understanding of the word proclivities. It did, however, sound altogether distasteful.

Finding the source of the rumor and bloodying his nose quickly and effectively put an end to it. The rumor was never spoken of again. Well, not to my face, or within earshot anyway.

Thinking back to my aunts *"sexual proclivities"* now has me blushing. Thankfully, it goes unnoticed, and mother suggests that Aunt Caroline pour a third glass of claret, before she tells me to take a seat.

"No, not there," she says. "Sit in your father's seat. It's yours now. You are the new Earl of Benfleet, after all."

"That's right," Caroline concurs, handing me a glass of the claret. "You are now the head of this house and are responsible for all that entails."

I have an odd feeling that something more is hidden within her words, but I don't know what exactly, and Aunt Caroline raises her glass to propose a toast. "To Montague, the Eighth Earl of Benfleet. May he be everything we need him to be, and more."

Another cryptic message, and I ponder again if I'm supposed to know its meaning. Both women watch intently as I raise my glass to my lips and gulp down the fine claret.

My glass empty, I place it down, and Aunt Caroline takes her seat.

Mother now appears pensive and reluctant to speak. The atmosphere has also changed to something altogether more foreboding. Uncomfortable with the silence, I lean forward to take her hand. "What is it, Mother? You said there was something you would like to discuss with me?"

"Not *like*," Aunt Caroline says softly. "There is something we *need* to discuss with you, Montague."

Turning toward her sister, my mother nods for her to continue. Taking her cue, Aunt Caroline gently dabs a spot of claret from the corner of her mouth, and asks, "Did you enjoy the generals eulogy, Monty?"

I nod enthusiastically. "Yes, Aunt Caroline, very much so."

"And I suppose you particularly enjoyed the part when he was enthusing your father's finer points as an officer and a gentleman?"

I'm not entirely sure where this is leading, but I smile and reply, "That was my favorite part. What young man wouldn't want to hear such fine words spoken of his fath—"

"Well, it was all a pack of ruddy balderdash," Mother suddenly interrupts angrily. "Your father was a rogue, and a no good cad. He was a good-for-nothing wastrel and has left us in dire—"

Stunned by her outburst, and lost for words, I'm thankful for Aunt Caroline's timely intervention. "Now, Charlotte, we agreed to keep calm during this discussion. It is important to maintain our composure, so that our Monty may fully understand the depth of your predicament."

"What predicament?" I blurt. Then turning to my mother, confused and upset, "Why are you saying these horrid lies about Father? Take them back right now. I demand it!"

Mother is now weeping quietly, and I suddenly feel quite guilty for snapping at her. While Caroline consoles her, I nervously reach for the decanter.

Brushing aside my mother's halfhearted protest, her younger sister instead calmly suggests, "Another glass won't hurt the boy, and given the circumstances, it might help somewhat?"

Without waiting for permission, I fill my glass, and Caroline retakes her seat. Noticeably struggling to maintain my composure, I slowly sip at the warming liquid to calm my nerves, before asking rather too sternly, "Well, is somebody going to tell me what the hell is going on?"

A firm scowl from mother swiftly puts me back in my place, and I apologize for my tone, before timidly asking, "I do, however, think I deserve an explanation?"

"Yes, you do." Caroline nods. "May I, sister?"

Yes, dear. Do go on." Mother nods politely.

While Caroline speaks, my mother's eyes barely leave mine for a second.

"Your mother is quite correct, Montague. Your father was very much a man of two personalities. His public persona was one of respectability and duty to his family and the crown. Unfortunately, however, and unbeknown to you, there was also a darker side to the man you called Father. He was also a—"

Unable to contain myself any longer, I angrily slam down my glass. "This is nothing less than slander. Slander of a man unable to speak for himself. Slander of a man who has given his all for queen and country. Slander made all the worse in that it comes from his own wife and sister-in-law. And on the day of his funeral. I demand to know the meaning of this?"

Both women wait patiently for my rant to end. When I've done, mother takes another sip from her glass before placing it back down. "That was a fine speech, Montague. Now be a darling, sit back down and allow your aunt to continue without further interruption, please."

I'm flushed with anger, but yet again, Mother has made me feel like a petulant child in the way that only a mother can. Suitably chastised, I retake my seat and resolve to hold my tongue.

While I'm quietly seething, Aunt Caroline uses her handkerchief to stifle a barely concealed grin before she takes a breath and continues.

"So, as I was saying, Monty, there was also a darker side to your father."

Pausing to gauge my reaction, she then adds, "Like it or not, your father had a taste for some of the more unsavory proclivities of London life."

There it is again. That word, "*proclivities.*" Although I should be concentrating on the subject at hand, my mind wanders to exactly what kind of proclivities it is that Aunt Caroline enjoys.

At the same time, my eyes absentmindedly settle on the fullness of the bosom straining to be free of the white lacing tightly crisscrossing her chest.

I fancy I've been staring for rather too long when mother tactfully coughs to draw my attention. When I look up, I'm blushing again, and I'm sure I detect the faintest of smiles in the corner of Caroline's mouth. She continues, however, without adding to my embarrassment.

"Proclivities such as the gentleman's clubs, where he would regularly indulge in whoring, drinking to excess, and *gambling beyond his means.*"

Her words are a bitter pill to swallow, and not something I would ever have imagined hearing in the context of my father.

All such mentioned proclivities would be considered entirely unbecoming of a family man, gentleman, and an earl, but of all three, Aunt Caroline appears to have deliberately over enunciated the words "*gambling beyond his means.*"

Or am I reading too much into it? I'm still pondering a suitable response when Mother asks, "Do you understand what we're trying to tell you, Monty?"

"Um, well, not entirely," I mutter quietly.

Then with a renewed vigor to defend my father's honor, "But I'd bloody well like to know who it is responsible for spreading such libelous falsehoods. My father was a decent, and honorable ma—"

"Oh, grow up," Aunt Caroline snaps. "Your father *was* indeed a kind and loving father and husband, but he was also a notorious man about town. That itself was bad enough, but he was also an inveterate gambler, and has left your poor mother quite destitute."

She pauses to allow her words to sink in before adding, "Now do you understand?"

Ignoring the question, I turn hopefully to my mother. "Please, tell me this isn't true? None of this makes any sense. What of the family fortune, and esta—"

"All frittered away," Mother interrupts sadly. "And our land and estates are heavily indebted."

Unable to comprehend, and disbelieving, I turn back to my aunt. Her face is sullen and forlorn. "I'm sorry, Monty. But your mother speaks the truth. While your father was alive, there was still a chance of keeping the wolf from the door. But now, well, let's just say—"

Her words trail off as Mother starts to sob again. Caroline does her best to comfort her, while I stare helplessly into the fire. Desperately searching for the right words, my first thought is not for my mother, but for myself. "But what will become of me? Am I to be an earl without means or estates?"

Aunt Caroline's disdain is made instantly clear, and I splutter a hasty correction, "Well, um, what I meant to say is, what will become of us? Surely, there is something we can do to address this predicament?"

Dabbing the corner of her eyes with an embroidered silk handkerchief, Mother straightens up, and takes a deep breath. "Yes, there is something that can be done."

She then takes another breath before adding, "But it falls to you, Montague. As the head of the household, and the Eighth Earl of Benfleet, the responsibility for restoring the family fortune now rests firmly on your shoulders. Are you ready to shoulder that burden of responsibility?"

Until now my succession to earl has meant very little, but Mother's words have hit all the right chords. I'm suddenly flushed with pride and sit ramrod straight in Father's chair. "Yes, Mother, I am, and I assure you, you have nothing more to fear. I'm in my final year at Eton, and will then take up my place at Sandhurst with a handsome stipend sufficient to extend our line of credit until such time—"

Aunt Caroline shakes her head, and laughs dismissively. "Oh, Monty, you really do have your head in the clouds, don't you? Your annual allowance as a subaltern would barely be sufficient to settle your father's outstanding line of credit at the Ritz. And besides, your mother has twelve months at the most before the banks foreclose. And you still have almost a full year left at Eton."

Her words precede an extended and uncomfortable silence, before I nervously ask, "Could you help, Aunt Caroline? Your own estate is—"

"Is barely maintaining itself." She laughs again. "Why only last week, I had to let a number of my domestic staff go. And mark my words, Monty, running an estate of that size with a staff of less than fifty is no easy undertaking."

While she's speaking, my eyes casually appraise her diamond necklace and it's fabulous ruby centerpiece the size of a quails egg. And then to her weighty pear-shaped diamond earrings. Both were gifts from the marquess, and would no doubt fetch a pretty penny.

Wisely keeping my thoughts to myself, and now more confused than ever, I turn toward Mother. "Then I don't understand. You said there was something I can do to help? Please, Mother, pray tell what it is?"

Hesitant, she quietly clears her throat, before leaning forward to take my hand. "Now you must understand, Monty. I wouldn't ask this of you if there were any other way."

Clearly embarrassed, she looks down. Gently squeezing her hand, I softly reassure. "Please go ahead, Mother. Say what you need to say. I'm sure it will be for the best."

Still looking unsure, she raises her head and leans closer still. Then looking me directly in the eye, she quietly says, "You need to marry."

Slightly shocked, but almost sure I've misheard, I nervously ask, "Excuse me, I need to what?"

"You need to marry," Aunt Caroline snaps. "You need to marry, and you need to marry well, if you are to save your mother from the humiliation of a debtor's prison."

My mind is suddenly all a blur. Words that ought not be mentioned in the context of a young man of my age, culture, and breeding weigh heavily on my mind. *Destitute – prison – marry.* What are they talking about? And that question again – "What is to become of me?"

Mother asks if I'm okay, before she suggests to her sister, "Another glass of claret, I think. The boy is suddenly quite pale."

I hungrily swallow the entirety of the glass, before composing myself just enough to stammer, "Have you both gone quite mad? I'm only seventeen years old."

"But eighteen this coming December," Aunt Caroline chirps helpfully. "Your coming of age, Monty"

Now I know for sure. They have both completely lost their marbles.

Try as I might to protest, my feeble arguments are deftly brushed aside one by one. Finally losing patience, Mother raises a hand and firmly asserts, "That's enough, Monty! It's been decided. You are to marry well, and you are to marry soon. Is that clearly understood?"

My stunned silence is seized upon and swiftly punished. "Really, Montague, you would prefer to see your poor mother cast into the street, and her possessions sold for pennies on the pound? Would that be preferable to doing the honorable thing, and saving her from such a public humiliation?"

Still unable to speak, my aunt angrily tuts, "You disgust me, Montague. Your poor father must be turning in his grave."

Turning to my mother she angrily snipes, "I knew this was a mistake, Charlotte. The boy has no spine."

Throughout this rant, Mother has remained quietly composed. With Caroline now quiet again, she calmly nods, and thanks her sister for her support. "But now let us hear what the boy has to say for himself."

Smiling sweetly, she asks, "You have what it takes to save this family, don't you, Montague? And if necessary, you will marry into a family of considerable means to save us from the poor house?"

Backed into a corner, but desperate not to appear weak, I slowly nod. "Yes, Mother. If that's what it takes to restore our fortune, I'll do it."

Then, once more nervous and hesitant, "But how would that be possible? I'm still in school, and my appointment to Sandhurst is yet to be officially confirmed. What family or woman of standing would even consider me a worthy suitor?"

"None." Aunt Caroline sneers sarcastically. "You, my boy, are far from the polished article of eligibility. Before then, we have much work to do, and precious little time in which to do it."

Then to my mother, "We should proceed without further delay, sister."

Perplexed, I ask, "Proceed with what?"

"Proceed with your education," my mother replies, as if to state the obvious.

"Back to Eton?" I ask, again unsure of myself.

Noisily tutting her frustration, Aunt Caroline shakes her head. "You can forget Eton, and you can forget Sandhurst. Your mother is talking about a far more practical form of education."

Before I can respond, or ask what she means, Mother steers the conversation in another new and unexpected direction. "Your aunt is correct. You are to take a trip, Monty."

She then quickly adds, "Have you heard of the Grand European Tour?"

I have, of course, heard of it, but for most young chaps of my generation, the concept is now considered quite outdated. Journeying through the major cities of Europe, an upper-class young man, or young lady, might better themselves through immersion in fine language, culture, and the arts. One might also widen one's sphere of opportunity and influence amongst the eligible young nobles of Europe.

Failing to grasp the relevance to my own situation, I nervously mutter, "But to what end?"

The response from Aunt Caroline is as blunt and as forthright as ever, "Don't be such a dullard, Montague. This tour will be your rite of passage to manhood. During your travels, you will be exposed to the cream of fine European society. Amongst many other things, you will hone your knowledge of etiquette, the arts, and the romance languages.

"You will, of course, also need to work – well, what I mean to say is – you will also need to work on certain other attributes necessary to marrying well."

Despite some obvious hesitation with the last sentence, my mind is already two steps ahead, and I fail to notice the delay. I also fail to notice the knowing look passed between my mother and aunt.

"But when, and for how long?" I ask.

"You leave tomorrow," Mother replies firmly. "A berth is booked for you and your aunt on the overnight steamer to Calais."

My mind now whirring with yet another revelation, I nervously ask, "I'm sorry, are you saying I'm to be chaperoned by my aunt?"

Mother nods, "Yes, Montague. Unfortunately, like you, your father was an only child, and all other men of travelling age on my side of the family are quite unsuitable. And besides, your Aunt Caroline has previously undertaken the Grand European Tour herself. She has an extensive network of influential acquaintances throughout Europe, and quite frankly, I can think of no one better to accompany and make the introductions for you."

Aunt Caroline smiles her concurrence before adding, "We will also be accompanied by my lady's maid, and one of my stable hands, who will act as your personal valet. I trust that meets your approval, Monty?"

With a forced smile and a nod, I sarcastically ask, "And how long might we be away for?"

"That entirely depends on you," Caroline replies. "But for as long as it takes."

She doesn't elaborate, and I turn toward Mother, still hopeful of an escape from this madness. "But am I not expected back at school?"

"No, no. It's all taken care of," she replies. "I've already sent word to your housemaster that you won't be returning. I have also spoken with the general earlier today. He's agreed to speak to the trustees at Sandhurst to defer your appointment for up to three years."

With my immediate future clearly already decided, and nothing left to say that might sway that decision, I petulantly get to my feet. "Well, you both seem to have everything under control, so if there's nothing else to discuss, I'm tired and should like to retire now."

Before I can excuse myself, Aunt Caroline emits a barely audible cough, and signals Mother with a raised eyebrow.

"Oh, yes," my mother stammers, looking slightly flushed. "There was one other thing. Aunt Caroline's lady's maid has drawn you a hot bath. Be sure to scrub yourself thoroughly. You have a long trip ahead of you tomorrow."

Still failing to read between the lines, I thank my aunt and bid both women a goodnight.

* * * * * * * *

The bed linen has been turned back, and a freshly laundered cotton nightshirt has been laid out on the end of the bed. A large tin bath, freshly filled with piping hot water, sits center stage on the floor.

Aunt Caroline's maid is a pretty young thing, barely a few years older than me. Her long raven hair, and barely concealed curves give rise in more ways than one to ideas that a young man ought not to be thinking.

It's still relatively early, but oddly, she is dressed in just her night things, and I assume she's been woken from an early slumber to attend to my bath.

Smiling sweetly, she places a fluffy white cotton towel and a large bar of carbolic soap on the nightstand. "If that will be all, sir, I'll take my leave. I'll be right outside if you need anything."

Finding myself blushing once again, I quickly turn away and mutter, "Thank you, Betsy. That will be all."

I wait for the telltale click of the closing door before daring to remove my clothes. Although exhausted, the bath is a welcome indulgence. I slowly lower myself in, and allow the warmth of the water to do its work on my aching muscles. Thoroughly relaxed, my eyes close and my mind drifts once again to thoughts of *sexual proclivities*.

I picture Aunt Caroline standing beside the fireplace. Her heaving bosoms are calling for release. Calling to me. Calling for Monty to set them free.

And I picture Betsy. Sweet young Betsy. Sweet, succulent, and ripe for the picking.

I'm so far gone in my head, I've no idea I have company until mother politely coughs and giggles. "The boy appears to be dreaming, sister."

Suddenly wide awake, I bolt upright, scrambling to conceal my modesty. Aunt Caroline cranes her neck and nods her appreciation. "And quite a dream it must be. That's quite a root you have there, Monty."

Mortified, and embarrassed like never before, I struggle to find the word's. "Mother, wh – what, I mean – what are you both doing here?"

I'm completely ignored, and both women take a seat on the edge of my bed. My mother is the first to speak. "We're here because your aunt has only agreed to act as your chaperone on the basis of your potential."

"My, um, potential?" I nervously mumble.

"Yes, your potential," Caroline asserts. She gets to her feet and orders firmly, "And now, I'd like to see it. On your feet, boy."

My eyes plead for my mother's intervention. Instead, she smiles and nods politely, "Do as your aunt says, Monty. There's really nothing for you to worry about."

While Aunt Caroline moves closer, I gingerly get to my feet. Thankfully, my previously engorged appendage has receded sufficient enough to allow my hands full coverage and spare me from further blushes. Naked as the day I was born, Caroline slowly circles me like some magnificent bird of prey on the hunt.

"The boy has a fine pert posterior," she comments to nobody in particular. "But he could do with a bit more meat on his bones."

Then to me, "How tall are you now? My guess is a little over six feet. Am I right?"

I nod, and Caroline stares quite unashamedly at my groin area. She then nods knowingly, "And still further room for growth, I wager."

Smiling, she turns to my mother. "He certainly takes after his father. The boy definitely has potential, and those suits we picked out should fit him well enough after some minor alterations."

Thinking my ordeal over, and now shivering, I ask for mother to pass the towel. Aunt Caroline, however, has other ideas. "Not so fast, Montague. You just stay where you are for now."

Firmly believing the day can't possibly get any more bizarre, I'm stunned when she points to the hand covering my genitals. "Have you ever used that?"

I'm so shocked, I can barely string two words together in response. "Have I – um, ha – um, what–"

"Are you a virgin?" she asks in a quite matter-of-fact kind of way. "It's okay if you are, of course. It's just important for me to know where to start."

I'm still babbling like a fool when she places a hand across mine. Looking me in the eye, she smiles, and gently pulls my hand away. Nodding slowly she looks back down before turning to her sister. "Yes, Charlotte. I do believe he's still a virgin."

My attempts at covering myself with my other hand are easily brushed aside, and Aunt Caroline slowly shakes her head. "Just relax and enjoy. You're in safe hands with me, darling."

Her hands are warm and soft like a new pair of silk gloves. Unable to control myself, my manhood swells and throbs under her expert and gentle caress.

Standing tall and proud, I've never felt more exposed. Nor more ready to pop. My breathing noticeably quickens, and I tremble quite involuntarily.

When Mother interjects with a suggestion, I'm quite torn between relief and disappointment. "He looks somewhat flushed, Caroline. Perhaps we ought to let him finish his ablutions now."

Now desperate for release, I hopefully place my hand back across my aunt's, while my eyes silently plead for her to continue. Smiling, she gently pulls away and shouts, "Betsy, join us please."

I'm surprised to see the young woman step from behind my changing screen. Even more surprising, she is now naked from the waist up. Suddenly shy again I turn away, and cover myself with my hands.

Aunt Caroline beckons her maid closer. She then passes her the soap. "Please attend to the master's ablutions, Betsy. And be sure not to miss anything important."

Smiling, the young maid curtsy's politely before stepping into the bath behind me. Moments later, I feel warm water cascading down my back, and the petite young woman goes to work vigorously lathering me up. A good eight inches shorter than myself, she is forced to stretch to reach my neck and shoulders. We are so close, her firm breasts squish tantalizingly into my back, causing my loins to ache with desire.

Working diligently, Betsy expertly massages the foamy lather into the entirety of my back, my bottom, and my legs. My mother, and aunt look on with barely concealed and somewhat salacious approval.

Satisfied with her efforts thus far, Betsy rinses me down, before nimbly edging past and moving to my front. Close up, she is quite the prettiest young filly I have ever seen. Her pert but full breasts are utterly magnificent. Her nipples stand hard, and proud.

Her undergarments are also now soaked through from the bathwater, and the outline of her perfectly rounded peach of a bottom is beautifully silhouetted by the light of the lamp.

Abandoning all semblance of modesty my eyes lower and settle on that most secret of places between her legs. I've never seen one outside of a medical textbook, but I imagine it to be a place of magic, mystery, and beauty.

My own nipples quickly harden under Betsy's divine touch, and I unashamedly groan my pleasure. A smiling Aunt Caroline turns knowingly to her sister, "I think not much longer now, my dear."

She nods to Betsy, and understanding the signal perfectly, the young woman drops to her knees. Her hands slippery with lather, she goes to work on my pole like an artisan. Gently squeezing my plums with one hand, the other expertly massages my swollen tool. Barely able to remain standing, I grunt, and groan, "Oh God, Oh God, Oh Go—"

Flushed with her own excitement, mother quietly gasps, while Aunt Caroline sniggers and jokes, "It's a little too late for that, Monty. Religion is not going to get you out of this little mess."

She's right, of course. She has barely finished speaking when I can hold back no longer. The dam bursts, and great ropes of my seed spurt across Betsy's beautifully milky breasts and neck. One glistening sticky dollop hangs from her chin like a glorious creamy stalactite.

Legs all aquiver, I'm only able to remain standing with the aid of one of Betsy's strong arms wrapped tightly around my thighs.

The performance over, Aunt Caroline gets to her feet and passes a towel to the young woman. "Thank you. That will be all for this evening."

Looking slightly embarrassed, Betsy releases her hold on my legs, and quickly disappears behind the partition. Mother passes me my own towel, and a moment later we hear the door close.

The two women quietly confer, before Mother asks the blindingly obvious, "Did you enjoy that, Monty?"

It almost goes without saying, but however bizarre the question, I know I'm expected to answer. "Um, yes. It was very nice. Very nice, indeed."

"I'm sure it was," Mother smirks. "And so it should be. That was your first lesson."

"First lesson?" I ask. "What do you mean?"

Aunt Caroline shakes her head, before nodding. "Yes, Monty. If I'm to accompany you on this trip, I need you to understand there is more to snagging a well-to-do spouse than simply an appreciation of the arts, culture, and etiquette. Do you understand what I'm trying to say?"

I'm still not entirely sure, but not wishing to stoke her displeasure, I nod anyway. "Yes, I think so, Aunt Caroline."

"Good," she says. "Because as I said earlier, we have much work to do, and precious little time in which to do it. That was your first practical lesson in being a man. There will be many more to come."

Clearly done for the day, she turns to my mother. "Come now, Charlotte. The boy needs his rest. It will be a long day tomorrow."

Both women tenderly kiss me on the cheek, before taking their leave. I wait for the door to close fully, before I discard my towel, and sink back down into the now tepid soapy bathwater.

Racking my brain in the hope of making sense of this evenings unexpected turn of events, I eventually harken back to an earlier thought, and quietly say, "They really have both gone quite mad."

Then with a sly smile to myself, "But didn't Aunt Caroline say she would be bringing her maid along on this little jaunt? I think perhaps then it might be quite enjoyable after all."

Chapter Three

The Overnight Steamer
to Calais – 24 October 1898

The following morning, I'm feeling slightly less sure of myself, but Mother and Aunt Caroline eat breakfast without the slightest hint of embarrassment, or mention of the previous evenings events.

Afterwards, they spend the next few hours fussing over my appearance and preparation. Mother in particular is unusually maternal in the run up to our departure. I don't recall the last time she helped me dress, but today she insists on helping me into one of my father's freshly altered suits.

She also insists on accompanying us to the train station to see us off. In the waiting room her preening is so incessant and over the top, it's a welcome relief to hear a bell sound the arrival of the Dover bound express.

Mother, though, is far from done. On the platform she turns me around before taking an admiring step backward. "Oh, Monty, darling. You are so handsome, and I'm so proud of you."

Then to Aunt Caroline, "Doesn't he look like his father when he was younger? So handsome, and so dashing."

I'm sure she's right. I'm wearing one of Father's Savile Row three-piece suits, his best walking out shoes, and his finest top hat. Mother has also given me a pair of his black leather gloves and a fine silver-topped cane. Why then wouldn't I look like him?

My aunt smiles, and nods her approval. "Yes, sister, very much like his father. And very much the aspiring fine young gentleman. He will certainly do you proud."

Further along the platform, the station master blows his whistle, and calls, "All aboard for Dover, please. All aboard for Dover."

Blushing slightly from the praise, I thank my mother and start to say, "But I think we ought to get going now. I think the train is about to lea—"

Cutting me off mid-sentence, she says, "Now remember, Monty, I've entrusted your aunt with your allowance. Spend it wisely, it's almost all we have left."

Her eyes tear up, and I suddenly feel ashamed of my haste to leave and for thinking ill of her earlier maternal attentions. I pull her close, and tenderly kiss her on the cheek. Aunt Caroline tactfully suggests that she board to allow us a moment of privacy.

Smiling, I kiss mother's cheek a second time. "I promise I will find a way out of this muddle and make you proud of me. You have nothing more to fear. You have my word on it."

Seemingly reassured, she forces a smile and nods. "I'm certain of it, Monty." Then suddenly pushing me away, "Now go, before I get emotional again and change my mind."

A second whistle blows, and the station master hollers, "Final call, all aboard now." Mother waves toward the open door of the first-class carriage, "Go now, Monty, or you really will miss the train."

While she looks on, I board before turning to lower the window in the door. Mother moves closer to the edge of the platform, and I reach through to take her gloved hand in mine. "Take care, Mother. I love you very much."

My words are almost lost in a loud hiss of steam as the train slowly rolls forward, and Mother blows me a kiss. "I love you too, Monty."

Then forced to shout over the noise of the engine, "Just please stay safe, and follow Aunt Caroline's lead. She's a safe and steady pair of hands."

With that, the woman who gave me life is enveloped in a thick cloud of white smoke billowing from the locomotive's stack. By the time it clears, we are far from the station, and Mother has gone.

Staring through the window toward home, I allow myself a knowing smile at the thought of her last words. "Yes, Mother, I think you're right. In fact I'm certain of it. I think I'll be very safe in Aunt Caroline's soft and capable hands."

* * * * * * * *

Still pondering the erotic possibilities, I find the object of my lust gracefully sipping on a glass of champagne in the dining car. Yesterday she was simply my attractive but unobtainable aunt. Now however, I unintentionally find myself standing and gazing upon her in a quite un-nephew like way.

I'm only snapped back to reality when she looks up and frowns. "Do close your mouth, Monty dear. It's not fitting for a gentleman to dribble at the table. And do please take a seat, we have much to discuss."

Brushing aside my flustered apology, she beckons the steward to join us. Immaculately attired with a crisp white linen towel draped over his arm, he asks, "Would the gentleman like to join the lady in a glass of champagne, or would he prefer to peruse the menu for something stronger?"

To be completely honest, it's an unusually warm day for October, and I would prefer an icy glass of lemonade, but I know that's not what is expected of me. I'm about to ask for champagne when the decision is taken out of my hands. "The gentleman would like a large whisky, and a cigar if you have one."

Perfectly understanding the dynamic, the steward politely nods to me before turning back to my aunt. "Very good, Lady Winstanley. I shall attend to it and return shortly."

He leaves, and Aunt Caroline giggles. "Oh, don't look so worried, Monty. In order to be a man, one must act like a man. Champagne is for toasts and ladies. From this point on, you are only to drink claret, whisky, and other spirits, unless the situation dictates otherwise. Understood?"

Heeding mothers instruction, I smile and nod politely. "Thank you, Aunt Caroline, I'm sure you are right. I am though also partial to an occasional mug of stout or beer. Is that acceptab–?"

"Nonsense," she snaps. "Those beverages are for drunkards and the working class only. You sir are an earl, and a gentleman. You will have nothing more to do with them."

"And that's another thing," she adds. "You are no longer to call me Aunt Caroline. You are an adult and may refer to me as Lady Caroline, or simply Caroline when we are alone."

I nod, but am prevented from responding by the return of the steward. He places a large cut-glass tumbler of whisky in front of me and asks, "May I prepare and light the cigar, sir?"

I wouldn't have the faintest idea how to do it myself, so I'm happy for him to continue. While he carefully clips the end with a polished silver cutter, Aunt Caroline raises her glass and nods toward mine.

Raising the tumbler to my lips, I rather naively take a large gulp of the smooth peaty liquor in the same way I've seen my father do many times before.

The strong fiery spirit burns its way down my throat, and it is all I can do to stop myself from choking it back up. A knowing glance, and a barely concealed smirk passes between my aunt and the steward.

I've barely had time to regain my composure when he carefully places the now lit cigar onto the lip of a heavy crystal ashtray. "Please enjoy, sir. It's the finest Cuban."

Left alone, Caroline asks, "Is this your first time smoking?"

"And don't say you've smoked a pipe," she adds perfectly anticipating my response. "Pipes are for schoolboys, old men, and sailors. And you are none of those."

Incredulous, I laugh and shake my head. "Well in that case, it's my first time, Aunt — I mean, yes, this is my first time."

"Well, take it slowly," she says smiling. "It's an experience to be savored." Then unable to suppress a grin, "The same can be said for a fine whisky. Now sit back a while, and enjoy both while we talk."

Doing exactly as instructed, I relax and puff slowly on the cigar. I'm no expert of course, but my first experience is as smooth as intimated by the steward. Whisky in one hand, and cigar in the other, Aunt Caroline looks quietly on with something bordering on admiration.

"My my, Monty, how very grown up you suddenly look. Why with a few whiskers on your chin, and a little more meat on your bones you could quite easily pass for a fine gentleman."

I'm still enjoying the moment when she looks down and reaches into her purse. "I almost forgot something, and a gentleman is not a gentleman without a calling card."

She looks up and hands me a slim sterling silver card holder. "Your mother and I had this made for you. I hope you like it?"

Engraved on the front of the holder in beautiful script are the words,

The Right Honorable,
Montague Finch-Morton I.I.I
Eighth Earl of Benfleet.

The cards inside are similarly printed, but also include the address of Morton Hall, and Father's London residence.

In the space of less than twenty-four hours, I have left behind the childish things of my youth and become a man.

These cards confirm it, and somewhat overcome with emotion, I take my aunts hand. "It's quite wonderful. Thank you so very much. Aunt Caroline."

"That's quite alright," she replies. "But that is the last time you are to call me aunt."

She frowns her disapproval, before suddenly serious she pulls her hand away. "Now, down to business. I'm sure you must have many questions about our travel plans and itinerary?"

Caught off guard, I'm momentarily lost for words, and faced with my vacant expression, her eyes widen with disappointment. "Surely, there is something you would like to ask of me, Monty?"

The only question that immediately comes to mind, is clumsy and has little to do with our travel plans. "Is Betsy somewhere else on the train? You mentioned she was accompanying us on this journey."

Stunned to disbelief, Aunt Caroline shakes her head. "You really do take after your father don't you? He was also prone to allowing his root to do the thinking for him. And look where that has left your poor mother. You disappoint me, Montague."

Shaking her head again she says, "But if you really must know, Betsy has gone ahead with my stable hand, Johnathan, and our luggage. She will meet us on board the steamer in Dover."

Noting my unintentional smirk and the glint in my eye, she then angrily snaps, "But you can forget any wicked ideas you might have about a repeat performance with Betsy. I'll be deciding when, where, what, and how. Is that clear?"

Somewhat blushing and conscious her raised voice has garnered the unwanted attention of some of our fellow diners, I timidly lower my head. "Yes, that's very clear. And I apologize for giving the impression I might have thought otherwise."

Gracefully accepting my apology she nods. "Good, I'm glad that's cleared up. Now, do you have any *non-sexual* questions related to our travel arrangements?"

My mind still in the gutter, I force myself to concentrate and ask, "Actually, yes, I would very much like to know what the plan is after our arrival in Calais?"

Appearing pleased that I've asked a relevant question, Aunt Caroline smiles before taking a moment to consider her response. "It's probably best if we don't get too far ahead of ourselves, but as you know the next leg of our journey is aboard the Paddle Steamer *Castalia* from Dover.

"Dependent on the weather, the channel crossing itself should take no more than three to four hours. Regardless, we will overnight on the *Castalia* before traveling on to our accommodations in Paris. There we will—"

Ah, Paris the city of love and romance. My mind drifts to its legendary *Montmartre* I have heard so much about. The place where great artists, writers and bohemians gather in its cafes and bars. A place of great debauchery and—"

A subtle cough wakes me from my daydream, and Aunt Caroline looks on with wonder, "Tell me. Was it the thought of gazing upon the great works of art in the Louvre, or was it perhaps another fine shape and form that distracted you from my words?"

Raising her eyebrows, she then smirks, "The fine shape and form of Betsy, perhaps?"

It wasn't Betsy, but I blush anyway. "Um, no. I'm sorry. Please do go on."

"Actually, I think our travel plans can wait for another time." Caroline giggles. "It's clear your mind is on other things."

Then nodding knowingly, "And, I suppose after last night who could blame you."

This is the first direct mention of last night's shenanigans, and taken by surprise again, I flush like a beetroot. Now sympathetic, Aunt Caroline takes my hand. "Oh, Monty, I'm so sorry for embarrassing you, but you really need to cure yourself of all this blushing. It's cute in a young boy, but not in a young man."

If her words were meant to soothe and calm, they in fact do the exact opposite. Now blushing even more fiercely, Caroline pushes my glass toward me. "Go on, it will help."

I drain the scotch, and the steward silently appears by my side to refill the glass. By the time he returns to the bar, I'm once again calm and composed. Sizing me up, my beautiful companion leans in. "Okay, Montague Finch-Morton the Third, enough of the games. Ask what you really want to ask of me?"

Worried I may have misread the intent, I'm hesitant, forcing her to repeat herself, "It really is okay. Please go ahead and ask whatever you like?"

The question I really want to ask has been preying on my mind almost constantly since last night. It relates to something mentioned in the context of my continued, but more *practical,* education.

Still unsure of her reaction, I nervously clear my throat. "Um, well actually, I was wondering about something you said last night."

"Go on?" Aunt Caroline prompts.

"Well, it was when you were talking about the Grand European Tour. You spoke of etiquette, the arts, and the romance languages—"

My throat suddenly dry, I cough and reach for my glass before adding, "Um, yes, well you also spoke of needing to work on certain other attributes necessary to marrying well."

"That's quite correct," Caroline comments. "And what of it?"

"Well, I was um, I was wondering—"

"You were wondering if it might have anything to do with what Betsy did to you last night?" Aunt Caroline interrupts with a snigger.

Once more deeply embarrassed and squirming in my chair, she leans in again and whispers, "Oh come now, Monty. Don't tell me you've never tickled your pickle yourself whilst thinking wicked thoughts about a beautiful young woman?"

While she's speaking she looks me directly in the eye. Certain she's guessed my dirty little secret, I pray for the ground to open and swallow me whole. Laughing again she straightens up and calls for a refill of her own drink.

Her glass full, the steward returns to his station, and once more serious, Aunt Caroline quietly says, "I'll be blunt with you, Monty. There is more to marrying well than simply fine breeding and formal education. The real purpose of this trip is to tutor you in attributes that — shall we say, are somehow more appealing to a woman."

Sensing my confusion, she lowers her head. "In simple terms, by the time we return home, there won't be a woman in England able to resist your charms. With my guidance, and if all goes to plan, you will be an expert in the art of seduction, and lovemaking. Women everywhere will fall at your feet."

She pauses, before adding proudly, "Yes, my dear, if all goes to plan, you will quite literally be beating them off with a shitty stick."

"And Mother is fully aware of this plan?" I ask innocently.

"Of course. It was my suggestion, but Lady Charlotte was fully supportive. It makes perfect sense, and neither of us are foolish enough to believe you capable of marrying well under the current conditions."

Aunt Caroline tuts and shakes her head. "Don't look so offended, Monty. This is the reality of your predicament. You are a penniless earl, barely out of short trousers, and poised to blow at the slightest touch. You are hardly the pinnacle of a fine young woman's aspirations."

Sensing my growing embarrassment, she softens her tone and smiles. "Well, not yet anyway. But by the time I've finished, you will have the smooth tongue of a great orator, the stamina of a racehorse, and the touch of a classically trained pianist."

She takes my hand and squeezes it tenderly. "When I told my sister you have potential, I really meant it."

Then with a grin, "Thankfully, your potential is in all the right places. That you can thank your father for. Now drink up, the train will shortly be arriving in Dover."

* * * * * * * *

The docks are just a short carriage ride from the station, and the afternoon is bright and clear. When the PS Castalia comes into view, my pulse noticeably quickens. She is a fine twin hulled paddle steamer, and ascending the gangplank, my heart races at the thought of what lies ahead. And to the other young men of adventure who have gone before me.

At the top of the plank, the ships purser is stationed to greet passenger's and inspect their tickets. There is, however, no such nonsense for Lady Caroline Winstanley. Instantly recognized, the preceding passengers are moved aside to allow her to pass, unhindered by such banal formalities. A steward politely steps forward to welcome us aboard, before escorting us below deck.

Our suite is spacious and tastefully decorated, with two luxurious bedrooms partially separated by an intricately carved mahogany partition. The shared bathroom is bright, modern, and furnished with the most pristine of porcelain conveniences.

Betsy is waiting in the lounge and politely curtsies in acknowledgement of our arrival. In contrast to the last time I saw her, she is now fully dressed in the formal attire of a lady's maid. Her long dark hair is pinned up in a bun, and she is wearing wire-rimmed spectacles. She looks older, and more dignified, but still quite deliciously ravishing.

The young man in his early twenties standing beside her is unknown to me. A few inches shorter than I, but as broad as an oak tree, his new suit does little to disguise his unease at his new surroundings.

I can see why my aunt would choose to bring him along though. His piercing blue eyes, rugged jawline, and the scar on his right cheek give a masculine appeal that I can currently only aspire to. Bowing politely, he says, "I trust you had a good trip, Lady Winstanley."

Then to myself, "It's my very great pleasure to meet you, sir. I'm Johnathan Wade. I'll be acting as your—"

"As my valet," I interrupt. "Yes my aunt, I mean, Lady Caroline informed me you would be joining us from your usual place in the stables."

Although no intentional malice in my words, I can see how they might be perceived by others, and I quickly try to correct myself, "What I meant to say is, it's also my pleasure to meet you, Johnathan. I've never had a valet before, but I'm sure between us we'll work it out."

Looking slightly embarrassed, the young man bows again. "I've laid out your things for dinner, sir. And if you'll be so kind as to leave your current suit and shoes out for me, I'll have them pressed and polished ready for your onward travel in the morning."

"Very good." I nod.

The young man takes his leave and returns to his own quarters, while Betsy follows her mistress into the master bedroom. I'm left alone in my room to ponder how quickly my life has changed in such a short space of time. An hour later, I'm still not entirely sure if it is for the better.

When Aunt Caroline eventually emerges from her room, I have never seen her looking more breathtaking. Her crimson silk gown flows beautifully, and highlights her figure to perfection. Her carefully applied makeup cleverly accentuates her already impressive jawline and the fullness of her lips.

Quite forgetting she's my aunt, I couldn't be prouder, when she asks me to escort her to dinner. "Take my arm, Monty. Your education is about to begin in earnest."

* * * * * * * *

The dining room is compact, but every bit as sumptuous as our suite. Unbeknown to me, Aunt Caroline has deliberately planned for our late arrival, and as hoped all eyes are on her as we make our entrance.

The other guests politely get to their feet, but it is the ship's captain that leaves the greatest impression on me. A bull of a man in his early fifties, with a fine brush of lustrous hair adorning his top lip, it is patently clear that he is a man of refinement. The effortless and elegant way in which he plants a kiss on my aunt's outstretched hand, is nothing less than poetry in motion.

"Lady Winstanley, it's my pleasure to welcome you aboard again."

He escorts us to our seats and asks, "And who may I enquire is this fine young man by your side?"

My clumsy attempt at retrieving a business card from the pocket of my waistcoat, is tactfully concealed by a barely discernible shake of Aunt Caroline's head and a light touch on my leg. Smiling sweetly she addresses the table, "My fellow guests, please let me introduce my nephew, Montague Finch-Morton the Third, the Eighth Earl of Benfleet."

The captain offers a shovel of a hand, and shakes my own quite vigorously, while the rest of the guests nod in quiet appreciation. "Hugo Murray. I'm the captain of this tub, although you've probably figured that out for yourself. It's good to meet you, Montague. I knew your father. He was a decent bloke, and a half decent sailor for a cavalry man."

A number of the other guests are also known to my aunt, or knew my father. Because of this, the conversation flows as freely as the alcohol.

Part way through a quite delicious loin of venison, the captain turns to me and asks, "What do you think of your suite? Comfortable enough, lad?"

"Yes, sir," I reply. "Very comfortable, in fact. I should imagine it's one of the finest aboard."

"Not one of the finest," the captain roars. "It is the finest, young Montague. So fine, in fact, it was occupied by none other than the Prince of Wales himself at the start of his journey from London to India in 1875."

Our fellow passengers look to the captain with renewed admiration. "That's right," he affirms. "I wasn't around at that time myself, but none other than the Prince of Wales himself. That suite has royal patronage, don't you know."

Suddenly turning to the steward, he bellows, "Bring a bottle of my finest brandy. This deserves a toast."

Glasses filled, the captain gets to his feet and asks his guests to join him. Puffing his chest out, he unexpectedly raises an arm toward me to offer the toast. "God save the Queen, God save the Prince of Wales, and God save this fine young man who will be sleeping in his bed tonight."

Roaring with laughter, he swallows the brandy in a flash. His guests politely follow suit before retaking their seats. The steward's clumsy attempt to remove the bottle from the table is brusquely dismissed. "Leave it, and bring another. My guests are thirsty."

By midnight, most around the table are fairly well oiled, myself included. My aunt, however, still looks the picture of dignity and decorum, and the captain looks like he could go on drinking all night.

Thankfully, our fellow passengers soon start to excuse themselves, and shortly afterwards Aunt Caroline follows suit. Turning toward the head of the table, she smiles. "Thank you so much for your wonderful hospitality, Captain Murray. I do hope we have the opportunity to meet again soon."

Murray raises his glass in response. "The pleasure was all mine, and I'm quite sure we shall. Sleep well, Lady Caroline."

Then to me, "Pleasant dreams, young man."

* * * * * * * *

On deck the temperature has dropped below freezing, so it's a relief to reach our quarters and find a log burning in the hearth. We both stand for a moment savoring its warmth, before Aunt Caroline removes her gloves, and places them on the mantle.

I'm about to bid her goodnight when she says, "Change into your nightclothes, then join me in my bedchamber for a nightcap."

"Yes, of course," I reply.

I'm also wondering if she will be in her own nightclothes. Hoping I'm right, I leave her, and find a pair of white linen pajamas, and a silk dressing gown laid out on my bed. Both carry the exquisitely embroidered monogram, *MFM,* and I recognize them as previously belonging to my father.

I quickly change before quietly tapping on the room partition, "May I join you, Caroline?"

"Yes, yes, come in and sit down," she replies.

What I discover behind the partition is vastly beyond expectation. Aunt Caroline is sitting in a chair beside her bed. She has a glass of brandy in one hand, and has stripped down to her expensive and shockingly revealing French underwear.

Better still, Betsy is laid across the bed wearing nothing more than a flimsy, and quite transparent, silk nightdress. Her tousled locks hang loose across the silk pillow supporting her head.

Thankful for the dressing gown to shield my arousal, I'm told for the second time today to stop dribbling.

"I've told you already. It's most unbecoming of a gentleman. And unless you are waiting for an invitation, do come in please."

Aunt Caroline hands me a glass of brandy and points to a chair facing the end of the bed. "Sit awhile. We have much to discuss before your lesson begins."

Both women watch as I take my seat, and I'm sure I catch the tail end of a smile from Betsy. I'm barely able to concentrate, or avert my eyes from her womanly curves, until Caroline asks, "How did it feel when I touched you, Monty?"

"It was, um, it was very nice," I mumble. "Very nice, indeed."

"Just nice? Nothing more?"

Still struggling with shyness, I briefly look away before replying, "It was quite wonderful, Caroline. I didn't want you to stop."

"I'm sure." She smirks. "I rather grant you were enjoying it very much."

Then pointing to the bed. "And when you were with Betsy, how did she make you feel?"

I'm conscious that the young maid is now staring in anticipation of my response. Gaining confidence, I turn and direct my reply toward her. "Like I was in heaven, Lady Caroline. Like I've never felt before."

My words are met with a look of obvious approval from both women, and Aunt Caroline nods. "And I assume, you would you like to feel like that again?"

"Oh God, very much so," I reply rather too eagerly.

My obvious desperation elicits a giggle from Betsy, and a smirk from my aunt. "That's good, but all in good time. Before we get to that, let me ask you another question. When you were in heaven, how do you think poor Betsy felt?"

This question has taken me by surprise, and quite stumped I stutter, "How do I think Betsy felt — um, well I'm not quite sure what—?"

"It's an easy enough question, Monty. When you were in heaven, how was Betsy feeling? Or were you too engrossed in your own pleasure to give any thought to her feelings?"

Before I can offer a response, Caroline turns to the young woman on the bed. "Let's ask Betsy, shall we? Betsy, how were you feeling when Master Finch-Morton gifted his load across your breasts?"

Raising herself onto an elbow, Betsy shakes her head and frowns. "Quite frisky, ma'am."

"Quite frisky?" Caroline repeats.

"Oh yes, ma'am. I was ever so moist below. And not just from the bathwater." She giggles.

While I listen and wonder where this conversation is heading, Aunt Caroline asks, "And how did you feel after you left the room?"

This time, Betsy directs her response toward me, and I find myself burning up. "Most unsatisfied and frustrated, ma'am. It's no fun having to bring yourself off with—"

"Thank you Betsy," Caroline cuts in.

"Did you hear that, Monty? While you were in heaven, this poor young girl was left unsatisfied and frustrated. What have you to say for yourself?"

"I um, well. I wasn't—"

"Exactly! In that moment you weren't thinking of anyone but yourself," Caroline scolds.

"And that is not the behavior of a gentleman. A real gentleman, while skilled in the art of lovemaking, is above all a gentle and considerate lover. Considerate to the needs and desires of his partner. Considerate even to the detriment of his own needs if required. Do you understand what I'm saying, Monty?"

"Yes." I nod. "I think I do. Thank you, Lady Caroline."

Smiling she leans back in her seat. "Good, then I think we are ready for your next lesson. Are you ready, Monty?"

In truth, I've been ready since long before the suggestion of a nightcap. I'd like to say as much, but I don't wish to over presume. Instead, I stand and loosen the cord on my dressing gown.

"No, no, no." Caroline chuckles. "What have I just told you about consideration for others?"

Sensing my confusion, she shakes her head. "Lovemaking is a balance of give and take. And tonight is less about taking, and more about giving. Tonight is not for your pleasure. Tonight you will receive your first instruction in pleasuring your lover."

Smiling, she adds, "Do you know what cunnilingus is?"

The word is unfamiliar, and I shake my head. "I'm sorry, I don't."

Laughing, Caroline tuts, "Of course you don't. You're a man, why would you? I would, however, wager you know perfectly well what fellatio is?"

Suddenly flushed and excited by the prospect, I nervously bluster, "It's when a woman uses her mouth and tongue to—"

I'm cut off again by a raised hand. "That's right. But now turn that on it's head, and imagine when a man does that to a woman."

Caroline then gestures to the bed. "I think Betsy has earned the right to feel like she is in heaven. Don't you?"

"Yes, she does." I nod, barely able to contain my excitement.

"Good." Aunt Caroline smiles and points to the floor. "On your knees."

She then signals to the delicious creature draped across her bed to move closer. Grinning in wicked expectation, the young woman deliberately teases me by slowly hitching the nightdress above her waist to reveal the lush thick bush shielding the wondrous "V" between her thighs.

When Aunt Caroline reaches for a leg to pull them apart, I'm quite unable to stifle a gasp at the sight of the juicy ripe peach comfortably nestled below Betsy's silken fuzz.

Now just inches from my face, my nostrils fill with the delicious aroma of vanilla and chamomile from Betsy's recent bathing.

They also fill with an aroma quite unfamiliar to me. This aroma is altogether more musky and intoxicating, but also somehow more arousing.

Moving closer, Caroline gently pushes down on the top of my head. "Start by her inner thighs. And remember, Monty. Slow and gentle is the way to go."

I shuffle closer and purse my lips. My first tentative kiss causes Betsy to shudder slightly. Emboldened by her reaction, I slowly savor the taste of her inner thighs, before turning my attention toward her valley of the forbidden fruit. Encouraged by my tutor, I gently brush aside Betsy's downy pile, and tremble at my first sight of the glistening jewel concealed below.

Extending my tongue, I carefully probe and tease, until I find that most delicious of nectar within. Inspired by her quiet moaning, and the gentle movements of her body, I increase my momentum, and hungrily devour Betsy's sweet juices.

Quite forgetting the earlier instruction, and now ignorant to Betsy's silence, my feasting comes to a sudden and abrupt end when Aunt Caroline loudly tuts, and pulls me away.

"No, no, no, Monty, that won't do at all."

Then pointing between Betsy's thighs. "It's not a cheap meat pie from the tuck shop, and you are not trying to chomp your way through its crust."

Dragging me to my feet, she orders, "Move aside. I think a practical demonstration is what's required."

Caroline takes my place on the floor and beckons me closer. "Get on the bed where you can see what I'm doing."

Then, impatient with my hesitation, "Come now, this is no time to be shy."

Waiting for me to get comfortable, she repeats, "Try to think of this as less of devouring a meat pie, and more of savoring a delicious oyster."

She leans forward to slowly drag her tongue across Betsy's pubic mound, before looking back up, "This work is not to be rushed, Monty."

Smiling, she softly purrs, "Think back to the oysters you had at dinner this evening, and the way you relished their plump salty flesh."

I watch for five or six minutes, completely fascinated as her tongue flicks back and forth like a hungry lizard searching for a fly. And at how her fingers gently part the soft puffy flesh of her lady's maids quim.

"Savor the moment. Suck deeply on the oysters flesh, and probe with your tongue for the pearl."

Betsy groans, and the lower half of her body pushes back against the wave of ecstasy coursing through her body. Below her, the silk bedspread is already noticeably moist and glimmering in the lamp light. Lost in her pleasure, the young woman unconsciously pulls down on her mistresses head, "Yes, yes, yes. Oh God, yes m'lady."

I'm now leaning so close, I can smell her pleasure. It's only the fear of displeasing my aunt that stops me from trying to taste it.

Caroline continues the lesson, expertly alternating between pushing her tongue deep into Betsy's slit, and nibbling on her hard sparkly button. The young woman is clearly on the edge of the abyss, when a finger disappears knuckle deep inside her. Slowly plunging in and out, Caroline gently introduces a second, and then a third finger before gathering speed.

Betsy is now thrashing and bucking like a woman possessed. Her breathing comes in short labored bursts and her face is brightly flushed. So loud are her screams of pleasure, we must surely be overheard.

The time for taking things slowly is well and truly over. Aunt Caroline bites down hard on Betsy's jewel, while finger fucking her sopping wet cunny like a runaway steam train. Unable to hold herself any longer, Betsy's body stiffens and shudders with the heavenly relief of orgasm.

We both silently look on while the waves of pleasure gradually subside. With the young woman now calm and still, Aunt Caroline raises a slippery finger toward her mouth. Turning to face me, she smiles before slowly licking it clean. Satisfied she has savored every last delicious drop, she smiles again. "And there ends tonight's lesson, Monty."

Nodding toward the exhausted young woman on the bed, she adds, "And I'm sure you will agree when I say that young Betsy won't be going to bed frustrated or unsatisfied tonight?"

I can hardly find the words to respond, but am firmly in awe of my aunt's talent for cunnilingus. And I suspect I'm not the only one.

Betsy has lowered her nightgown and is now standing at the foot of the bed grinning like the cat that got the cream. "Thank you, ma'am. Will there be anything else required of me this evening?"

"No, no. That's all." Caroline waves. "Thank you, Betsy, you can leave us now."

Hopeful my own needs will now be attended to, I'm sadly disappointed when I'm also brusquely dismissed. "We have a long day tomorrow, and I need you on your best form. So, straight to sleep please."

Before I leave, Aunt Caroline takes my hand, and tenderly kisses me on the cheek. "Think about what you have seen tonight, Monty, and put what you have learnt into practice during your next lesson. Believe me when I say, it won't go unrewarded."

I'm almost past the partition when she calls out, "Oh, and Monty, whatever else you may see or hear tonight, you are forbidden from touching yourself. Have I made myself clear?"

After what I've just witnessed, I had every intention of pulling the pud tonight, but after this warning, it is now clearly out of the question.

Pondering what she might mean about seeing or hearing tonight, I mask my disappointment and nod my acknowledgment. "Perfectly clear, Caroline. Sleep well."

* * * * * * * * *

It hardly feels like I've been asleep for more than a few minutes, when I'm disturbed by a faint click. A moment later, a chink of light briefly cuts through the darkness before I hear a second faint click as the door closes. Squinting through the gloom, my heart skips a beat when a silent figure passes my bed, and disappears behind the mahogany room divider.

I hadn't noticed until now, but the shadows thrown out by the lamp in Aunt Caroline's bedroom dance and flicker on the wall beside the partition. She must still be awake, and it is clear she is no longer alone. Brushing aside any thoughts of who it might be, and what they are doing so late, I turn away from the light, and tightly close my eyes.

Ultimately it is to no avail. Whoever her late night visitor is, neither of them are particularly discrete, and the whispered voices are quickly replaced by something much more deserving of investigation.

Pushing back the bedspread, I carefully press my ear against the dividing wall. The voice, though faint, is manly and unmistakable, "Oh yes, Caroline, that's good. Very good, very good."

Unable to resist, I cautiously peer around the edge of the partition.

The captain is standing side on to me. His breeches are around his ankles, and a stark naked Aunt Caroline is vigorously slurping on his enormous maypole.

For a moment, I'm quite torn between staring at Caroline's wonderfully pendulous breasts, and the huge balls swinging below her lovers appendage.

When Caroline suddenly winks and raises a finger to her lips for me to stay quiet, I'm mightily relieved to see the captain has his head turned up, and is groaning toward the ceiling.

Watching this show, it takes all my willpower not to abuse myself. Close to release, the bull pulls away, and easily lifts Aunt Caroline onto the bed with one of his huge muscular arms.

"Yes, Hugo." She groans. "I want to feel you deep inside me."

Flipping her around like a ragdoll, Caroline is now on all fours, and completely at the mercy of this beast of a man. For my part, I have the best seat in the house. My mouth salivates at the sight of her creamy bottom, and deliciously moist conch. Conscious of the rapid increase in my own breathing, I slowly inhale to calm myself.

Exposed and ready, the captain aligns his weighty meat with the entrance to paradise. Unlike the earlier advice given to me, this man has no intention of taking things slow and gentle. Roughly pulling her legs further apart, he plunges himself balls deep, and goes at her like a battering ram."

"Oh, God yes," Caroline screams. "Fuck me hard and deep, Hugo."

He ploughs her without mercy, and seemingly with limitless reserves of energy. The lamplight flickers off his rutting arse cheeks, and the giant loudly grunts his pleasure.

Close to home, he snatches a great clump of his ride's hair, and roughly spanks her behind. This clearly meet's with her satisfaction. "Oh, Hugo, I'm also close. Spank me again, but harder this time."

The huge man strikes hard and Caroline almost buckles. "Oh, fuck, yes, oh fuck." Her orgasm is enough to send the big man over the top. His explosion is accompanied by a massive grunt, and his overflowing seed spills over to soak the bedspread.

Slumping forward across Caroline's back, he breathlessly sighs, "Oh my oh my, that was quite the ride, and you are still quite the nymphomaniac, Lady Caroline."

Laughing she responds, "Maybe so, but you wouldn't have it any other way, Hugo Murray, and I must say, you still have quite the ability to split a woman in two."

Climbing from under the big man, she quietly urges, "You should go now. It will be morning soon."

"Yes." He nods. "And I was due on watch thirty minutes ago."

When he stands to hitch up his breeches, I take this as my cue to leave.

I creep back into bed, and pull the bedspread over my head. A few moments later, the telltale click of the door signals the departure of the late-night visitor. Looking up, I can see the lamp in the next room has been extinguished, and all is quiet again.

Before closing my eyes, I make a note to locate a dictionary at the first opportunity. I feel certain that nymphomaniac won't be the last new word I hear during my travels.

Chapter Four

Paris — 25 October 1898

The following morning, we enjoy a light breakfast in our suite before departing to catch the midday train to Paris. Expecting to arrive by mid-afternoon, we are forced to think again partway through our journey, when a minor landslide on the tracks delays us by nearly three hours.

When we finally arrive in Paris, the sun has already started to set, and the Gare du Nord is bustling with activity. Thankfully, a carriage is waiting for us at the entrance to the station. Now, tired, and hungry, it is a welcome relief when we come to a halt outside our not immodest accommodation on the Boulevard Saint-Germain.

I'm not entirely sure what I was expecting, but with Aunt Caroline in charge it was always sure to be something grand. In a street of fine three-story townhouses, this one is probably the finest. Tucked behind a private gate, the detail of the picturesque marble façade is quite stunning.

While Johnathan unloads the luggage, the carriage driver guides us along a short winding path through tastefully manicured lawns, toward the front of the house. At the top of the stairs, we are met by an exceptionally tall African gentleman. Aunt Caroline is completely unfazed, but my surprise at encountering my first black man is matched only by my surprise at his attire.

Most elegantly dressed, he is wearing a long-sleeved shirt of elaborate white silk, bouffant breeches, white silk stockings and light-colored shoes with a large buckle and a red heel, as was fashionable at the court of King Louis XVI.

A long curled periwig sits atop his head, and heavy white make up adorns his face. Bowing respectfully, I'm surprised again when he speaks. For a man of such impressive stature, his heavily accented words are soft, and somewhat feminine.

"It is my very great pleasure to welcome you back to Paris, Lady Winstanley. Monsieur Lavigne has asked me to pass on his apologies. He was unfortunately called away on business, but will join you for dinner this evening. Please allow me to escort you to your rooms."

We follow him into a large and elegant reception room, before ascending a sweeping wood-paneled staircase to the second floor. The master suite comprises three bedrooms, with a spacious dressing area, and a balcony overlooking the gardens below.

With the tour of our rooms complete, the manservant respectfully lowers his head. "I trust this is to your satisfaction, Lady Caroline?"

"It's most satisfactory," she replies. "Your master has outdone himself, as always. Thank you, Jean-Claude."

He bows again, and Caroline asks, "May I ask the plan for dinner this evening?"

"But, of course," the big man replies softly. "My master will be meeting you at eight this evening at Maxim's."

"Wonderful." Caroline nods. "We look forward to it."

Our escort leaves, and I nod my approval. "This is a grand house. What does Monsieur Lavigne do?"

"Do you mean, how does he make his money?" Caroline laughs. "He's a banker and a businessman. More importantly, he's a highly influential figure in Paris. It's important you make a good first impression on him this evening."

Not quite sure of her meaning, I innocently ask, "And will his wife be joining us for dinner?"

My comment elicits another giggle from my aunt. "Maxim's is one of the social and culinary centers of Paris. It is also a place to take ladies, but never one's wife. Eric will undoubtedly have company this evening, but it won't be his wife. Nor possibly any woman. You will find our host to be a man of eclectic tastes."

"Like his choice in manservants?" I smirk knowingly.

My aunt grins and tuts teasingly, "My my Monty, how very bold of you to make such a presumption."

"But I'm right, aren't I?" I assert confidently. "His manservant is a homosexual?"

"He is." Caroline nods. "Eric picked him up during his service in France's African colonies. Upper Volta, I believe it was."

"And does that mean, Monsieur Picard is also homo—"

"Oh no," Caroline interrupts. "As I've said, Eric Lavigne is a man of varied and eclectic tastes."

She then repeats, "It's important for you to keep an open mind in order to make a good first impression. There may come a time when Eric may be of considerable assistance to you."

"Meaning what exactly?" I ask.

"Meaning, there is no such thing as a free lunch," my aunt replies.

"Or a free dinner for that matter. Every moment of this trip is an opportunity for you to open doors, in order to better yourself. And the most effective way of doing this is to keep your mind fully open to new possibilities."

Slightly unnerved, I ask, "Does that mean what I think it means?"

"There is no need to look quite so frightened," my aunt replies lightly touching my arm. This is Paris, and tonight your education will continue with your first taste of the Bohemian lifestyle. You must take every moment as an opportunity for betterment. I'm quite sure you won't be disappointed."

"Maybe not," I mumble. "I'm quite sure I'll be shocked, however?"

"Without a doubt." Caroline laughs. "Without a doubt."

* * * * * * * * *

Monsieur Lavigne has arranged for his personal hansom cab to collect us, and we are ferried in style to No. Three rue Royale, in the eighth arrondissement of Paris. Open just five years, Maxim's is already one of the most famous restaurants in the world. In keeping with this, its clientele are representative of the finest of Paris society, and I marvel at its stunning art nouveau décor, as the maître di escorts us to our table.

Like Captain Murray before him, Monsieur Lavigne rises to plant a tasteful kiss on my aunts outstretched hand. "My beautiful, Lady Caroline. You look simply enchanting this evening. I trust you had a good journey, and my home is to your liking?"

Lavigne is a short, stout man with a neatly trimmed greying goatee. In his late fifties, or early sixties, his dark pinstripe tailcoat and spectacles neatly fit the profile of a city banker. Smiling, my aunt replies, "Thank you, Eric, our journey was pleasant enough, and your new home is quite exquisite."

I'm introduced and seated next to our host. Aunt Caroline takes a seat on the opposite side of the table beside an attractive buxom redhead. In her early to mid-forties, I find out later that Mademoiselle Cecille Moreau is the favored mistress of our host. The other guests at our table are a mixed bag of Monsieur Lavigne's European friends and acquaintances.

Aunt Caroline is of course, quite correct. None of the gentleman in attendance are accompanied by their wives. I'm informed by Monsieur Lavigne that his own wife is spending the autumn and winter in Lourdes. "The waters there give great relief to her arthritis."

He then playfully squeezes my leg and chuckles. "They also give great relief to me, Montague. I love her very much, but the woman can be quite the dragon."

The last guest takes his seat, and the waiter arrives with dinner menus printed on cotton handkerchiefs. I'm struggling to translate when Eric unintentionally saves my blushes. Nodding across the table he suggests, "Cecille, my love, why don't you order for the table?"

She is poised to speak, when Aunt Caroline interrupts, "Actually Eric, might I suggest that Monty order for us? It is important he takes the opportunity to improve his French while we are here."

"A most splendid suggestion." Eric nods. The waiter moves beside me in obvious anticipation, and I nervously look down to the menu before clearing my throat. "Um, yes – I mean – Ah oui, je pense, on va commencer par la bisque de homard."

"The lobster bisque, an excellent choice." Lavigne nods. "And for the entrée, Montague?"

Still nervous, I bluster, "Um, thank you. Um' Merci Monsieur Lavigne. I, um, well–"

"Go on," my aunt encourages. You are doing well."

Putting the audience to the back of my mind, I nervously continue, "Je pensais à un plat de poisson de filet de sole, suivi côtes de bœuf aux pommes Macaire, et une salade de haricots verts."

The waiter politely smiles his appreciation, while Eric nods and claps enthusiastically. "Bravo, my boy. Not perfect by a long stretch, but a fine effort nonetheless."

Then turning to the waiter, "And two bottles of the eighty-seven Château Lafite."

The rest of the table applaud my efforts, while Aunt Caroline silently smiles her approval.

Throughout dinner, Eric is the perfect host. He effortlessly divides his time and attention between each of his guests, and I'm awestruck at the seamless manner in which he navigates all manner of conversation, across multiple languages. His vast knowledge and insight into such a diverse range of subjects leaves me feeling quite inadequate. It does, however, give me a greater understanding as to why I've been brought to meet him.

If I am to meet other men of such culture, refinement, and charm during our travels, I will surely return home vastly more eligible than when I left. From this moment on, I resolve to study and learn as much as I can from each of our hosts.

With half a dozen bottles of Lafite and two carafes of Cognac already demolished, I'm decidedly lightheaded when Eric turns his attention towards me. Topping me up from the dregs of a third carafe, he leans in and whispers, "I hope you don't mind, but your aunt has informed me of your recent family difficulties, and the reason for your travels."

He then squeezes my leg again. This time it's at the top of my leg, and his hand lingers in place a moment longer than might be considered proper.

My guard lowered by the alcohol, and sure it was unintentional, I think nothing of it. On the other side of the table, I find Caroline engaged in animated conversation with Cecille.

They are chatting in fast and fluent French, and quite unable to follow them, I turn back to our host. "Yes, sir. My father has left us in quite a precarious position. The reason for our travel is to prepare me for—"

"I'm fully aware of the reason for your travel," Eric interrupts. "And your aunt was quite right in bringing you to me first. I'm a man of the world, and so will you be, by the time you leave Paris. Rest assured, Montague. You are among friends here."

Pointing to my glass he encourages, "Drink up, and I'll order us a real drink."

Already three sheets to the wind, I can't imagine we haven't had a real drink already. Turning to my aunt, my confused expression is acknowledged with a raised eyebrow, and a knowing smirk. Moments later, our waiter arrives back to our table, and a raucous reception from our fellow guests.

Perched precariously on a silver tray, he is balancing a tall bottle of bright green liquor, and a dozen glasses. When the tray is placed on the table, I also see a dozen spoons, a jug of water, and a silver bowl filled with sugar cubes.

Getting to his feet, Eric says, "Montague, it is my very great pleasure to introduce you to La *fée* verte. The green fairy. That wonderful creation they call Absinthe."

Pointing proudly to the bottle, he asks, "Have you ever seen anything quite so magnificent?"

In pondering the question, my mind aimlessly wanders to the previous evening, and to that wonderful creation they call Betsy. I'm still mentally exploring her delicious curves when a subtle cough breaks the spell, "Monty, dear, Eric asked you a question?"

"Yes, of course," I stutter. "My apologies, Monsieur Lavigne. No, I don't think I have ever seen anything quite so magnificent."

"No need to apologize, lad. And no need for the formality either. My friends call me Eric."

Smiling he adds, "If this is your first time drinking Absinthe, you are in for a real treat. But we don't simply pour and drink. First, we must perform the Absinthe ritual."

He hands me one of the glasses. "You can see this is no ordinary glass. The stem is hollow. It is a reservoir for measuring the correct amount of Absinthe."

Eric places the glass with the others before instructing the waiter to proceed. Once each of the stems are full, the waiter balances a spoon across the lip of each glass. He then places a sugar cube in the bowl of each of the spoons.

"Watch what he does now," Eric says excitedly. "This is where the magic happens."

The waiter carefully pours cold water from the jug over each of the sugar cubes. As each of the glasses fill with the water and dissolved sugar, the holy green spirit is magically louched to a milky opalescent white.

His face beaming, Eric exclaims, "Et voilà, Montague. And that is the magic of the beautiful green fairy."

He passes a glass to each of his guests. "Drink up, my friends. The night is still young, and so are we."

My first sip of this mythical liquor is enough to answer my earlier question. At almost twice the alcohol content of most other spirits, it might easily be said that this is my first real drink. The bitter anise liquid almost scalds the back of my throat, and I struggle to manage more than a small sip at a time.

I'm still laboring over my first glass long after my more experienced companions have moved onto something else, and Eric loudly declares, "Okay, my friends. There are three cabs waiting outside to take us to La Chat Noir. Please join me for cabaret, a late supper, and drinks."

Eric helps me into my overcoat, and leads me toward the door. Outside, the early morning air is crisp, fresh, and intoxicating. It rushes to my head, and I'm only prevented from falling by the steadying arms of Aunt Caroline, and her enigmatic banker friend. Helped into the cab, they position themselves on either side of me like a pair of human bookends.

Squeezing my leg for a third time this evening, Eric says, "Don't you worry yourself, Monty. You are in safe hands."

When I wake, it is still dark and my head is thumping harder than the Corps of Drums, of the Grenadier Guards. I have vague recollections of watching a show, of dancing, and of conversing with any number of beautiful women. But what I don't recall, is how and when I returned home. If indeed, I am home?

I screw my eyes tightly closed and take a deep breath. When I open them again, my eyes slowly adjust to the gloom, and I begin to pick out small details of the room in Monsieur Lavigne's home. I'm also alerted to the fact I am not alone. To the side of the bed, I hear whispered voices.

Startled, I fumble for the valve on the side of the lamp, and bluster, "Is somebody there?"

Flickering brightly, the lamplight casts an ethereal glow over the faces of the two women sitting beside my bed. Smiling reassuringly, Aunt Caroline touches my hand. "Quiet dear, we were just watching over you. You had us quite worried."

"Worried," I croak. "Worried about what?"

Aunt Caroline chuckles quietly to herself. "You really don't remember?"

"I'm sorry. I don't remember very much after leaving Maxim's."

Frowning, she says, "Well, you were quite the life and soul of the party, Monty. Quite the dancer, and quite the ladies' man in fact."

She sniggers again and then adds, "Until you passed out, and cracked your head on the pavement getting out of the cab."

Groaning, I carefully brush my hand across the quails-egg size swelling on my forehead. "I suppose that would explain the brass band playing in my head."

"Yes, it would." Caroline nods sympathetically. Then lasciviously raising an eyebrow, she stuns me by standing up and allowing her nightdress to fall to the floor.

The young woman beside her quickly sheds her own, and while they position themselves either side of me, her mistress softly purrs, "Thankfully, we know a thing or two to ease your suffering."

Pulling back the bedsheets, these magnificent creatures of the night waste no time in suckling hungrily on my engorged nipples. Whether this is a dream, or I'm in heaven is of no real consequence. I eagerly imbibe the essence of their womanhood, and tremble at the soft hands that explore and caress.

While Caroline nibbles tenderly at my neck and earlobes, sweet Betsy journey's south. Her hands lightly brush over my balls, and her tongue flickers teasingly close to my aching shaft. Groaning my approval, I impatiently reach down to pull her head closer.

Easily pulling away, a smiling Betsy laughs and shakes her head. "All in good time, sir. All in good time."

Slowly massaging with one hand, she gently squeezes my jewels with the other, before raising her head to allow a trickle of drool to drip from her mouth onto the tip of my rod. Diligently working her lubricant into my entire length, she suddenly stops still.

Then, poised like a Cobra about to strike, the talented young woman winks her intent, before launching her heavenly assault. Like bolts of lightning through my heart, each subsequent pass of her moist tongue across my shaft is more exhilarating than the last.

When her lips finally part, and she swallows me whole, I squeeze hard on my aunt's hand, and groan quite unashamedly, while somewhat reminiscent of a woman bobbing for apples, Betsy takes me to a place I could never have imagined.

Fumbling for the top of her head, I pull down and gasp, "Oh my good God, Betsy. That is ama—"

On the very edge of my release, the young woman suddenly breaks away from the task at hand. Looking up, her eyes twinkle with mischief, and her plump lips glisten with a sweet mix of her salivation, and my seminal juice.

Unsure of her intent, I turn hopefully to Aunt Caroline. Nodding slowly, she whispers her assurance, "Don't worry, Monty. This wicked young minx is far from done."

Confirmation is quickly forthcoming when Betsy nimbly climbs aboard to straddle me. She skillfully positions her moist cunny over my pulsating shaft, and her breasts hang invitingly close to my mouth. Pushing me down by my shoulders, she gasps and groans, whilst slowly sliding herself back and forth along her meaty prize.

All the while, a bullet of a nipple slips in and out of my mouth, while Aunt Caroline feasts on the other. Her breathing now fast and irregular, the young woman pauses at the very tip of the lance. Using it to gently probe herself, she inhales deeply, before taking the plunge.

Balls deep, and tightly encased in her velvet dungeon, I have truly died and gone to heaven. But there is only one thing on Betsy's mind tonight. And it has nothing to do with how I'm feeling.

Riding me like a woman possessed, she howls like a banshee and ignoring my growing discomfort, her nails tear deep into my chest.

Grinding her mound against my pelvis, her vaginal muscles clench tightly around my distended phallus, while Aunt Caroline stares at her wide eyed with admiration, and more than a small hint of jealousy.

Regardless, her words of encouragement are more than enough to spur her charge on toward the finish line. "That's it, Betsy. Yes, Betsy, go on, you are almost there."

Then positioning her mouth closer to my ear, "Don't you dare cum yet. There is much more to come for you this evening, my darling."

Rather ironically, I think to myself, "I couldn't right now, even if I had wanted to."

Perspiration glistening on her forehead, the magical nymph sitting astride my chariot suddenly cry's out. Shuddering with pleasure, an enormous and unstoppable tidal wave of orgasm breaks across her body.

Thoroughly exhausted, and quite forgetting herself, she slumps forward and wraps her arms tightly around my chest. Momentarily forgetting my own station, I place an arm around her and tenderly kiss the top of her head.

We are both quickly put back in our place, by an all too familiar and subtle cough. "If the young lovers are quite finished, I think Master Finch-Morton would rather enjoy a second round of fellatio."

While Betsy breaks her embrace, her mistress smiles, and adds, "Perhaps he might enjoy it even more if it was from both of us?"

Delirious with excitement, it is all I can do to stop myself from boiling over right there and then. Laughing, Caroline says to Betsy, "Go fetch the bindings, and the blindfold."

"Don't look so worried, Monty," she softly assures. "When your hands are bound, and your sight is taken away, the brain forces your remaining senses into overdrive. The pleasure you have felt already tonight, is nothing compared to what you are about to feel."

Taking my head in her hands, she kisses me full on the lips causing me to tremble in anticipation. "Trust me, darling. You are in safe and capable hands."

Trusting her completely, I allow Betsy to bind my wrists with soft silken ropes before she lashes them tightly to the headboard. Sliding the thick blindfold over my head, she adjusts it before securing it at the back, and gently pushing my head down onto the pillow.

The smell of Caroline's cologne invades my nostrils, as she leans in to kiss me again. This time, the kiss is longer and more insistent. Her tongue parts my lips and hungrily searches for my own. Pulling away, she whispers, "Enjoy, be quiet, and let yourself go."

On either side of me, the bed creaks as my companions settle in and get comfortable. Unable to see or use my hands, I inhale the air, and allow my imagination to run wild. Unseen hands explore every inch of my body. Sweet lips kiss my own, while a salivating tongue slowly circles my aching rocks.

Leaking copiously, a finger from one hand swirls the sticky juices across my bell-end, while the other hand firmly works me over.

Now, two sweet mouths at once. On either side of my pole, they slowly work upward until they meet with a kiss. Helpless, and blind, I can only guess whose tongue is now probing deep into my single eye.

Head to head, and mouth to mouth, the unseen diners hungrily compete for my glistening sap. Bobbing ever deeper, my meat soon finds the back of a throat.

I'm so far gone in my ecstasy, it's almost halfway home before I notice the slippery index finger working its way ever so slowly into my bottom. Stiffening up, my halfhearted protest is quickly stifled by a hand across my mouth, and the sweet voice of Aunt Caroline. "Quiet now, Monty. I don't want to have to gag you. Just relax. I think you will find it most agreeable."

She removes her hand, and the finger gently resumes its journey. Although unusual, it's also strangely pleasant. While one hungry mouth slobbers around my shaft, the unseen finger gently fucks my virgin asshole. It's so pleasant, it's not long before I find myself pushing back for more.

In response, a second finger quickly joins the first, and my tormentor fucks me with renewed and enthusiastic vigor. Desperately praying to prolong the pleasure, I'm just moments from eruption when the blindfold is abruptly pulled from over my eyes.

Squinting against the sudden burst of light, Aunt Caroline looks down on me smiling. Behind her on a chair, I see Betsy sitting across the lap of a half-naked Cecille Moreau. The young maid is quietly suckling on a milky white breast, while the lover of Monsieur Lavigne enjoys the show.

Nervously glancing down to the source of my pleasure, I momentarily freeze when I see the top of a greying head of hair and Eric's mouth stretched around my member. His man servant's long slim fingers are still buried deep in my ass.

Torn between my desire for release, and an overriding sense of shame, I look to my aunt for guidance. Reading me perfectly she leans in, "It's only wrong if you say it is. Otherwise you should open your mind and enjoy." She allows a moment, and then asks, "Would you like them to continue, Monty?"

On this occasion my carnal desires are considerably stronger than my misgivings, and I breathlessly whisper my consent, "Yes, I would like that very much, Caroline."

Smiling, she gently touches her friend on the shoulder.

Now able to see, I look on with fascination. The banker sucks me as expertly as any woman might, and his huge African moves further up beside me. This allows him to work both my nipples and ass at the same time to great effect.

On his knees, his own engorged meat is as thick and as long as my forearm. As dark as coal, I'm imagining what it might feel like when my pulse quickens. Unable to hold back, I let loose into the mouth of our host.

Quite expecting him to disengage, I'm mildly taken aback when he doesn't. His cheeks swelling under the weight of my load, he smiles then swallows it down like the fine Lafite from earlier in the night.

From the chair, Mademoiselle Moreau squeals her delight, "Bravo, Eric. Bravo, Monty. Bravo Jean-Claude."

I'm still out of breath, when the three women get up to join us. Gently nudging my side, Aunt Caroline orders, "Move over. This is a big bed, and it is not just Eric and Jean-Claude that still need to be pleasured tonight. You have much work to do, Montague."

* * * * * * * *

By the time our little soiree breaks up, the first chinks of daylight are already peeking through the bedroom curtains. Thoroughly exhausted, and thoroughly sated, I have seen and experienced more in just a few hours than most young men might experience in a lifetime.

Gazing upon the beautiful woman sleeping beside me, I marvel at the rise and fall of her magnificent breasts, and ponder the fates that have brought me here. I then consider the events of the last few days, and ask what more could possibly be in store for me. Surely this is as crazy as it's going to get. I'm still contemplating the answer to that when fatigue overtakes me, and I sleep like I've never slept before.

* * * * * * * *

When I wake, my aunt has gone, it is fully light, the curtains are open, and Johnathan is standing beside the bed holding a glass of water. My mouth is as dry as a bone, and I hungrily drain the glass.

"What time is it?" I croak.

"Just after midday," the young man responds. "Lady Caroline has requested your company in the dining room, sir."

My head is thumping harder than ever, and I wearily slump back in the bed.

Unperturbed, Johnathan fills a porcelain basin with warm water, and places a towel on the bed. "I'll tell her you will be along shortly, will I, sir?"

"Um, yes." I groan. "I'll be there in ten minutes."

By the time I reach the dining room, my ten minutes have become closer to forty, and Aunt Caroline is quick to express her displeasure.

"It's not becoming to keep a lady waiting, Montague. It's also not becoming for a gentleman to idle his life away in bed."

I consider reminding her of the time we slept, but wisely think better of it. I'm in no condition for a sparring match with Lady Caroline, and would most likely lose even if I was. And besides, she only slept herself just a few minutes before me. Instead, I apologize, and take my seat.

In stark contrast to my own disheveled appearance, Caroline looks as radiant as ever. While one of Monsieur Lavigne's housemaids pours coffee, I ask, "How is it that you look as fresh as a daisy today, and I feel like I have been run over by a steam train?"

Smiling sweetly, she delicately sips from a glass of freshly squeezed orange juice before saying, "Experience, stamina, and pacing oneself."

The first two I understand. The last I'm unsure of.

"Pacing?" I ask.

"Of course," she responds. "It's neither fitting, nor expected of a lady to match the gentlemen drink for drink."

"But you seemed to be drinking as—"

"An elaborate fantasy, Montague. An illusion. An act perfected over many years." Caroline chuckles.

"And after your own performance last night, you might want to work on an act of your own," she playfully teases. "That might be overlooked as high jinks on your first night in Paris, but it will quickly become tiresome."

Feeling slightly offended, I foolishly retort, "Maybe so, but there was no doubting my stamina last night, was there?"

"Stamina." Caroline chuckles. "Is that what you call it? Three hours between the sheets can hardly be described as stamina. Particularly when you spent most of it on your back." She chuckles again.

"But I – I mean, that's not fair," I stammer.

"Oh, Monty, I'm just teasing you." Caroline giggles. "You performed admirably last night, and you most certainly left a good first impression on Eric."

The thought of the mutual pleasure bestowed upon each other makes me blush, and keen to change the subject, I ask, "Will Monsieur Lavigne be joining us for breakfast?"

Aunt Caroline frowns and shakes her head. "It's nearly one in the afternoon, so no, he will not be joining us for lunch. And if I know Eric as well as I think I do, he will have been in his office since bright and early this morning."

Noting my amazement, Caroline quietly mouths, "Experience, stamina, and pacing, Montague. Eric is the master of all three, and you will do well to follow his lead."

"Thank you, Aunt Caroline." I nod. "I will."

Hungry but somewhat nauseous, I force down a small piece from a buttery croissant, and ask, "May I ask how long we will remain in Paris?"

"Up to four weeks," Caroline replies. "Between myself and Eric we have put together quite a detailed itinerary for you. It's challenging, and will require your full commitment, but we are confident we have allowed sufficient time for our plan to achieve its aims."

"Which are what exactly?" I ask.

"Which, I will explain to you now." Caroline nods.

Turning to the maid she says, "Fresh coffee, please. I will be needing my nephews full and undivided attention for the next couple of hours."

Chapter Five

The Folies Bergère
& The Moulin Rouge – 26 November 1898

The following month is a relentless onslaught of both formal and informal education. Of socializing, dining, and opening of doors. And of course, of oh so much pleasure. The sexual appetites of Monsieur Lavigne, his associates, and it seems Parisian's in general are nothing if not staggering. Naturally then, there is little chance for boredom in the evenings.

My first week is spent at the Sorbonne in the Latin quarter of the city. Here I brush up my French, and am introduced to the wonders of philosophy through the works of Jean-Jacques Rousseau. At the weekend, I visit the great cathedral of Notre Dame, and the Palace of Versailles.

Next, I spend a week touring the museums and cultural centers of the French capital. At the Louvre, I marvel over the art works of DaVinci, and great sculptures attributed to Michelangelo. In private, and courtesy of my Parisian benefactor, I am granted exclusive viewings of previously unseen works by Pierre Auguste Renoir, Paul Gauguin, Paul Cezanne, Edgar Degas, and of course the master of impressionism, Claude Monet. I find his work simply breathtaking, and it opens the door to a part of my mind previously unopened.

The third week is spent almost exclusively in the company of Monsieur Lavigne himself. We converse almost entirely in his native tongue, and he introduces me to the intricacies of banking, and business. Over lunch in his club, we discuss politics, science, and philosophy with other men of great standing and influence. This week is by far the most enlightening yet.

The final week is a flurry of crisscrossing the city in cabs, for tuition in gentleman's fashion, dance, fines wines, and etiquette.

I find it all most enjoyable, so when I wake on the morning of our last full day in Paris, my feelings around our imminent departure are decidedly mixed.

I am however comforted by the knowledge we shall be returning to Paris toward the end of the return leg of our travels. With this in mind, I finish my morning ablutions and excitedly dress for breakfast.

* * * * * * * *

Since my first experience of breakfast in this fine city, and the reprimand from Aunt Caroline, I have made a point of arriving at the table well before her. Today is no exception. I have however been beaten by our host, as has been the case on almost all other occasions we have taken breakfast together.

He looks up from his newspaper, and smiles, "Ah, good morning, Montague. I trust you slept well?"

"Good morning, Eric." I nod. "I slept very well, thank you."

"Was that before or after that saucy young thing left your bed?" Eric chuckles. "The way you've been going at her recently, it's a wonder she has energy left to tend to the needs of Lady Caroline."

A month ago, a comment like this would have had me blushing quite uncontrollably. Today, it takes something a little extra. From the doorway, Aunt Caroline says, "You would think so, wouldn't you, Eric? But like my nephew, it would appear Betsy has also recently developed quite some stamina."

Wishing us both a good morning, she elegantly glides into the room as effortlessly as if she was on castors. She takes her seat, and without needing to be asked, the maid brings her coffee, and her freshly squeezed orange juice. A second maid places a large plate of ham, eggs, and buttered bread in front of me, before pouring my own coffee.

Smiling, Aunt Caroline says, "You've developed quite an appetite since we've been here, Monty." Then looking me up and down seemingly pleased with what she's seeing, "You're filling out, and your whiskers are coming along quite nicely."

Turning to Eric, she asks, "What do you think? He's quite different to the young man you met for the first time, just one month ago."

"Vastly different." Eric nods. "The shy young man, is almost a gentleman." His words suddenly falter, and his eyes moisten. "It has been a most wonderful month, and I shall be quite sad to bid you both farewell."

Caroline tenderly reaches for his hand. "The pleasure has been all ours, Eric. You have been as charming and hospitable a host as one might possibly wish for."

"Thank you, Caroline." He nods whilst wiping his eyes. "You are very kind to say so."

Taking a breath to compose himself, he straightens up and smiles. "But enough of this emotion. Today is not for sadness. Today is for laughter and merriment."

Turning to me he says, "This is your final night in this great city of Paris, and to mark the occasion I have lined up something very special for you."

Wide eyed, he excitedly continues, "Tonight my young friend, we will venture deep into the ninth Arrondissement to the Folies Bergère. From there, my driver will then take us on to Montmartre, and the famed Moulin Rouge."

Allowing a pause for me to digest the news, he then asks, "What do you have to say about that, Monty?"

Not very much it would appear. I was starting to think we would be moving on without experiencing either of these icons of Paris nightlife. The revelation that our host has deliberately left the best for last has quite literally left me speechless. All I can offer, is a nod, and a mumbled, "Thank you so much, Eric."

Thankfully, my understated gratitude goes unnoticed. At least by our host, anyway.

Smiling, he gets to his feet. "Good, that's settled then. But if you will excuse me, I need to leave you now to attend to some business."

Gallantly bending at the waist, he kisses Aunt Caroline's hand. "Au revoir, my child. Enjoy the rest of your day, and I shall see you both this evening."

Once he is gone, I casually pass comment, "That's unusual for Eric to be conducting business on a Saturday. And particularly on our last day, don't you think?"

"And you don't think perhaps it might be business of a personal nature?" Caroline frowns.

"After a month in his company, surely you must realise there is more to Eric than just banking. Eric is a man of deep emotion with many strings to his bow."

Slightly embarrassed, I mutter, "Um, yes, sorry, I didn't think of that."

"Yes, well, sometimes it's better not to think at all," Caroline chides. "A man's private affairs should never be the subject of another man's speculation."

Suitably admonished, I lower my head to continue my breakfast in silence. The maid removes my plate, and judging my penance complete, Aunt Caroline pours fresh coffee before chirping, "I'm very glad to see you finish that, Monty. Tonight will be your first real test. It's important you keep your strength up."

She doesn't elaborate on her statement, and I don't venture to ask. I finish my coffee and join her an hour later for lawn tennis in the grounds of our hosts beautifully manicured gardens.

Evenly matched after two hours of frenetic play, I breathlessly call a halt to the proceedings. "Thank you, Caroline. That was most exhilarating, but I really should excuse myself and rest before this evening."

"And by rest, you mean sleep?" Caroline smirks.

"What else?" I laugh.

"What else indeed?" She frowns.

Then smirking again. "It's no matter. Betsy is running an errand for me, and she shan't return for at least another two hours. Sweet dreams, Montague."

We arrive at the Folies Bergère a little after eight in the evening. The small queue of revellers waiting patiently in line look on with a mixture of wonderment and awe as the concierge lifts the silk rope barrier, and moves them aside to allow the newcomers through. As always, all eyes, both male and female are almost exclusively on Caroline.

While I've been busy furthering my education, she has been busy in the salons and great fashion houses of the Champs Elysée, courtesy of a generous expense account, funded of course by Eric.

A beautiful woman under any circumstance, this evening she is simply breathtaking. Her gown is from The House of Worth and has been tailored from the finest of silks. It epitomizes the height of fashion, sophistication and Parisienne haute couture.

Around her neck, a stunning sapphire is the centrepiece of an equally stunning pearl and diamond studded choker. The matching earrings hang serenely from her tear drop earlobes.

My first time seeing this jewellery, I surmise they must certainly be a recent gift from Eric. Irrelevant of where they came from, they complement her attire perfectly.

It is little wonder so many are left speechless in her presence.

* * * * * * * *

Given the month we've had, it is of no great surprise to find our table is close to the stage and is one of the best in the house. It is also slightly elevated and allows for an unobstructed view of the rest of the comings and goings.

As expected, the theatre is already at capacity. A lively stage show is in full swing, and our fellow patrons appear to be an eclectic mix of businessmen with their wives or mistresses, military officers, civil servants, and minor European nobility.

All are in high spirits, and the volume of chatter is almost as loud as the show itself, which none of them appear to be watching with any great interest.

While Eric peruses the wine list, I peruse the artworks adorning the walls. One particularly intriguing canvas catches my eye, and slightly unsure of myself, I ask, "Is that an original Manet?"

Aunt Caroline smiles her approval. "Why Eric, it would appear that Montague's time in Paris has not been wasted after all."

Our host nods. "You are quite correct, my dear young friend. It is Manet's, *A Bar at the Folies-Bergère*. It was a gift from Manet himself to his good friend, and long-time patron of the Folies, the composer Emmanuel Chabrier. Monsieur Chabrier has been kind enough to loan it to this fine establishment."

Placing the wine list on the table, he then says, "I was going to order a bottle of Lafite, but I've changed my mind. This is our last night together, and it calls for something special."

Turning to the waitress he suddenly barks, "A magnum of the Château Pétrus 1889, if you please. And an assortment of savoury petit fours."

The startled young woman scribbles on her pad, before scampering away with the sound of our giggles ringing in her ears.

"Eric, you are so naughty," Caroline teases. "You quite scared the girl out of her wits."

"Maybe." Eric nods. "But I'm sure her tip will help in steadying her nerves."

He is still grinning when the waitress returns with a tray of light bites in one hand, and the hefty bottle of wine in the other. Conscious of her audience, the young woman is noticeably relieved to uncork the wine without incident.

Offering the first taste to Eric, he politely declines and points toward me. "My young friend will do the honours. If you please, Montague?"

Now my turn in the spotlight, I nervously try to recall my recent tuition in the intricacies of wine tasting. Carefully swirling my glass by the stem, I lift it to the light, to check the wines colour, its opacity, and its legs.

When I lift it to my nose, Eric says, "Describe what you are smelling please?"

"Um, yes," I say. "I can smell earthy notes, and ripe fruit. I think possibly blackberries, and cherries?"

"Very good." Eric smiles. "Now go ahead and taste it."

I gently swirl the wine across my tongue before slowly allowing it to slide to the back of my throat. The fine Pétrus is deep, and intense. My smile oozes my satisfaction. Deftly palming a large banknote into the waitresses' hand, Eric encourages, "Please go ahead and pour my dear."

She leaves us, and our host proposes a toast. "To my very good friends, Caroline and Montague. I wish them well on their travels. And I wish they may both return to Paris happy, healthy, and prosperous."

I thank Eric, and Aunt Caroline affectionately touches his hand. "You can be assured of it, my friend."

Just then the music dramatically rises in tempo. Suddenly interested, Eric straightens up and excitedly points to the stage. "Turn around, Monty. You won't want to miss this, my boy."

The curtain's rise, and a chorus line of beautiful young women troupe onto the stage.

Apart from lace-up, white-leather ankle boots, and bright feather headpieces, all are completely naked. Unsurprisingly, the hubbub in the room quickly fades to a low murmur.

Behind me, Eric chuckles loudly. "I don't expect you would ever see something like this in any city in England, eh Monty?"

I nod my concurrence, but my eyes remain focused on the stage, and to the rather exotically garbed creature now emerging from the wings. Tall, elegant, and beautiful, her commanding presence on the stage is enough to silence even the most raucous of men in the audience.

"Who is she?" I ask.

"That is Madame Liane De Pougy," Eric replies. "She is one of the Folies most celebrated attractions. She is a fine vedette and dancer."

Unfamiliar with the term vedette, I ask Eric to explain.

"Yes, yes, of course. A vedette is the main female artist in a show. A vedette is an accomplished singer, dancer, and actress."

"They also specialize in the art of burlesque." Aunt Caroline smirks. "They specialize in striptease, and nude performance."

Turning to me she raises her eyebrows before smirking again. "Unfortunately this evening you are out of luck. But I'm sure you will enjoy her singing."

The performance begins, and Eric leans in. "Lady Caroline is quite correct. Most notably though, Madame De Pougy is also a highly sought-after courtesan."

Caroline loudly tuts to herself. "Well, that's an interesting euphemism, if ever I've heard one. What Eric means to say, is Madame

De Pougy is also a highly sought-after prostitute. Unfortunately, her taste is for men of wealth, power, and influence."

Smiling sympathetically, she gently touches my hand and teases, "For now, she is a little out of your price range, Monty. Perhaps when we return."

Laughing it off, I joke, "And why not? Finch-Morton men have never been shy of taking on a challenge."

"And that is just as well," Eric says. "Did Lady Caroline inform you of the plan for tonight?"

"Not entirely," I respond. "She did mention something about tonight being my first real test, but she didn't go into any further detail. Perhaps one of you would be so kind as to enlighten me now?"

"Yes, yes, all in good time," Eric blusters. "But before then we should enjoy the show with this fine bottle of wine. Eighteen-eighty-nine was a landmark year, Monty. Not only did it mark the completion and inauguration of our famed Eiffel Tower, it was also the finest of years for Château Pétrus. Not a single drop may be wasted. Drink up, my boy."

* * * * * * * *

By the time the last of the Pétrus is drained, it is also time to be moving on. We depart the Folies for the district of Montmartre, and still none the wiser, I impress upon my companions to share the details of this evening's test. They finally do, just as the iconic red windmill on the roof of the Moulin Rouge comes into view.

Aunt Caroline finishes explaining, and Eric asks, "So, Monty, are you up for the challenge?"

Already emboldened by my share of the Pétrus, I smile, and nod. "Yes, of course. And like I said earlier, I'm a Finch-Morton man. We like nothing more than a challenge."

Then slightly less cocksure, "It does of course depend on who exactly I'm supposed to be seducing?"

"All in good time." Eric chuckles for the second time this evening. "All in good time."

* * * * * * * *

In stark contrast to the mostly upmarket clientele in the Folies, the patrons in the Moulin Rouge are as diverse and eclectic as the city itself. They are, however, just as raucous. The volume of chatter and volume from the stage makes it hard to be heard as we follow our waitress to our table.

Tapping Eric lightly on the shoulder, I raise my voice and ask again, "I said, am I to know who it is anytime soon?"

"Yes, of course." He nods. "But first, I would like you to meet a friend of mine."

The gentleman waiting at our table, gets to his feet and smiles. Diminutive in stature, with a dark goatee, and wire-rimmed spectacles, he is dressed in an ill-fitting dark suit, and is leaning heavily on a cane.

His shoes are also badly scuffed, and the bowler hat on the table has clearly seen better days. Pondering his connection to Eric, I can't help silently comparing him to a most unflattering caricature of himself.

The gentleman in question has, of course, now sadly passed away, but at the time of our meeting, he was one of the most talented, and colourful characters in all of Paris. A gifted painter, printmaker, draftsman, illustrator, and rather ironically a caricaturist, I am stunned when Eric proudly announces, "Monty, please meet my very good friend, Monsieur Henri de Toulouse-Lautrec."

Almost lost for words, I enthusiastically shake his hand. "Monsieur Lautrec, I have heard so much about you."

"And I about you, Montague." He nods politely. "I have been looking forward to meeting you and am sure it will be a most enjoyable evening."

Before I can ask his meaning, he turns away, and plants a kiss on Aunt Caroline's hand. "A pleasure to see you as always, Lady Caroline. But a very great pity that we must now part ways. Perhaps when you return to our fair city you will allow me the pleasure of your company one evening?"

"But of course." Caroline smiles. "Nothing would make me happier, Henri."

Kissing her hand again, the pocket-sized genius reaches down to retrieve his battered headwear from the table. Completely misreading the intent for the evening, I'm about to sit when Lautrec loudly bawls, "No, no, Montague. Tonight, there is a place for you at my table. Come with me."

Unsure, I look to Eric and my aunt. Both nod, whilst Eric calmly assures, "Go on, Monty. You are in safe hands. Toulouse will guide you through the next steps of the plan."

That phrase again. "You are in safe hands."

Every time I hear it, things invariably become quite bizarre, and now following a man with an adult torso, and child sized legs limping back to his table, I don't suppose tonight will be any different.

Lautrec's table is front and centre to the stage. It is so close in fact, one can almost smell the cologne of the dancers as they perform an energetic rendition of the can-can. A man might also enjoy a most impressive view of their silky undergarments when they swirl their skirts and high kick their legs if he were so disposed.

I, however, have my mind on other things, including my task for the evening and my fellow guests who comprise an oddball mix of my host's artist friends and acquaintances.

While introductions are made, one of them pours me a glass of absinthe from an almost empty bottle. The other guests are also exclusively drinking absinthe. On the table there are already three empty bottles, alongside two full ones.

I find out later that Monsieur Henri Toulouse-Lautrec is a notorious alcoholic. Indeed, his abuse of alcohol is a later contributing factor to his premature demise at just thirty-six years of age.

That, and the complications from syphilis contracted from one of his favourite prostitutes, the aptly named, Rosa La Rouge. At the time, of course, I know nothing of this, and smiling, I gratefully accept the glass.

"You've previously partaken of La *fée*–"

"La *fée* verte," I confidently interrupt. "Yes, Monsieur Lautrec. Monsieur Lavigne was kind enough to introduce me to the wonders of The Green Fairy."

"Very good." Lautrec nods. "I must compliment you on your French, Montague, and please, call me either Henri, or Toulouse."

I nod, and he adds, "Perhaps later, you will allow me to introduce you to an absinthe creation of my own, Tremblement de Terre?"

Unsure if I've translated correctly, I hesitate before mumbling, "The earthquake–"

"Bravo." Lautrec laughs. "Yes, yes, Montague. The earthquake cocktail. It is most delicious."

I shudder to think what else the drink might contain, but smile my agreement anyway. "Thank you, I look forward to it, Toulouse."

"Maybe so," he says. "But for now, I think you are distracted. I think perhaps you are wondering who is to be the object of your attentions this evening. Am I correct?"

"Yes, sir. You are," I reply. "Might you give me some clue?"

Turning his head toward the stage, this legend of the Montmartre nods knowingly. "Tonight, you are to seduce one of these young ladies into returning with you to the home of Monsieur Lavigne where you will make love to her."

Slightly taken aback with the apparent ease of the task, I ask, "But aren't most of these young ladies also courtesans? This is hardly a test worthy of–"

Chuckling to himself, Toulouse interrupts to say, "I shouldn't get too far ahead of myself, my eager young friend. This evening you are tasked with seducing the young woman third from left in the chorus line. She is the longtime mistress of a dashing young major of dragoons and is fiercely loyal to him."

Turning to his friends, he asks, "Isn't that right?"

"Fiercely loyal," one repeats.

"Fiercely loyal, and notoriously frigid." Another laughs.

"And he should know." Toulouse smirks. "Mademoiselle Béatrice Aguillard has turned Bruno down on more than one occasion. Isn't that correct, Bruno?"

Shrugging his shoulders, Lautrec's friend laughs. "The woman is either frigid or a lesbian. There is no other possible reason for her snubbing me so frequently."

Then turning to me, he says, "She will be a fine test, Montague. But you should prepare yourself for disappointment."

While my new companions loudly debate my odds of success, I focus my attention on the young woman third from left on the stage. In a line up of beautiful women, she is a striking and obvious standout.

Pondering my own chances of success, I turn and ask, "Why her, Toulouse? Why was she chosen to test me?"

"Because so many have tried and failed before you." He smiles.

Then slightly more serious, "And Lady Caroline felt it important to challenge you early on in your travels. She has told me how much is dependent on you, Montague."

Suddenly aware of what is at stake, a lump comes to the back of my throat, and I nervously ask, "But how am I to even get an introduction to such a woman?"

My question is answered by Bruno. "I'm quite right when I say Béatrice Aguillard is as frigid as the day is long. She is however a very good friend of none other than Monsieur Henri Toulouse-Lautrec and myself. She will be joining us after her set finishes."

Smirking, Bruno then adds, "Which will be in just a few moments."

Catching my panicked expression, Toulouse tuts. "Ignore him. By the time she changes and joins us, it will be at least thirty minutes. You still have time to finalize your plan of attack."

Finalise my plan? How might that be possible when I don't yet have the faintest idea how I might begin my seduction of this apparently loyal beauty? Suddenly less confident of myself, and feeling the odds are stacked against me, I reach for my glass and a much-needed shot of liquid courage.

* * * * * * * *

By the time Mademoiselle Aguillard finally makes her appearance, I'm another two glasses in, and am once more feeling good about myself. Obviously familiar to the rest of my companions, the young woman greets her friends first, while I stand and wait patiently for an introduction.

When she finally turns toward me, I waste no time in making what I hope is a good first impression. Taking inspiration from my tutoring in etiquette, I lower my head, but maintain eye contact while kissing her hand. "Enchanté, Mademoiselle."

Beside her, Toulouse smiles knowingly, and says, "Béatrice, please let me introduce another good friend of mine, Montague Finch-Morton the Third, *the Eighth Earl of Benfleet.*"

The shameless enunciation of my title elicits a smile from the young woman, and she softly purrs, "My, my, an earl. And one so young and handsome."

Pleased with this apparent early success, I politely pull back the chair next to my own. "Mademoiselle, if you please?"

I'm quickly brought back to reality, when she completely ignores me, and instead seats herself next to a grinning Bruno. Not one to give up so easily, it's thankfully just moments before another chance to ingratiate myself presents itself.

Turning down the offer of a glass of absinthe, Béatrice sighs. "I may be the only woman at the table, but surely it's not too much to ask for a drink more befitting of a—"

"More befitting of a lady," I interrupt. "You are quite right, Mademoiselle. And I was just about to suggest champagne, or perhaps even a bottle of Pétrus?"

The men around the table all have a look that says, "You sly dog."

Thankfully Béatrice doesn't notice. Smiling, she asks, "And which of those would you suggest is most fitting for a lady such as myself, Montague, Eighth Earl of Benfleet?"

"Why of course, the Château Pétrus," I reply confidently before turning toward the waiter. "A bottle of the eighty-nine my good man."

The young man nods politely. "Might I suggest a magnum for the table, sir?"

He can suggest all he wants, but I doubt the allowance in my purse this evening would stretch to a magnum of Pétrus. Knowing full well I can't very well go cap in hand to Eric if I come up short, I point to the bottles on the table in hope of salvation. "I think, actually, my companions are happy to continue as they are?"

Mercifully, all are in on my scheme, and none seek to embarrass me in front of the lady. To a man they nod their concurrence.

"Very good." Toulouse nods. "A bottle of Pétrus and two glasses, please."

While we wait for it to arrive, I'm encouraged further when Béatrice moves into the seat next to mine. She justifies the move by saying, "It can get awfully loud when the music is playing, and I do hate it when I can't clearly hear what is being said to me."

Her words are accompanied by a hand lightly touching my leg. Badly misreading the signal, I lean in and whisper, "You are a very beautiful woman, Béatrice, and I—"

"Yes, I am," she firmly interrupts. "I am also engaged to be married, and you have only just met me," she playfully scolds.

"I am however impressed with your audacity. Most men usually wait at least until I've had a drink before they show their hand."

"Nothing ventured, nothing gained." I shrug.

"Agreed." She nods. "But your efforts are wasted on me. I am saving myself for another."

"Yes, so you said." I smile. "So, you are engaged to be married?"

"Well, not exactly," she replies. "But as soon as my love Bernard returns from his manoeuvres on the Prussian border, I'm quite sure of it."

"And will that be anytime soon?" I ask hopefully.

"In perhaps two to three weeks," Béatrice replies. "So, any ideas you might have for—"

"But there is nothing to stop us from enjoying a drink as friends?" I cut in.

"Nothing at all." Béatrice smiles. "As long as that is as far as it goes?"

Deliberately ignoring the question, I gesture toward the approaching waiter. "Our Pétrus is here. I think you will find the eighty-nine a most agreeable vintage."

* * * * * * * *

With more than half the bottle gone, and no obvious indication my target is wavering, or is at least a little receptive to my attempts at flattery, I decide on an altogether more risky change of tactics.

Leaning in, I take her hand and slowly shake my head, but deliberately don't speak and look away.

Her interest piqued, Béatrice asks, "What? What is it?"

I pretend to shrug it off. "Oh, it was nothing. I was just – no forget it. It was nothing really."

Knowing perfectly well my prey is on the hook, I ignore her again and turn toward the stage.

As hoped, she places a hand on my shoulder. "Please, Montague. If there is something on your mind, I would like to hear it?"

My face serious, I retake her hand and slowly nod. "I was just thinking – well what I mean to say is. Well, it must be very hard on you and your Bernard spending so much time apart from each other?"

"Yes, yes, it is." Béatrice nods. "But our love keeps us strong."

Nodding sympathetically, but somewhat insincere, and deliberately provocative, I then add, "Yes, I'm sure it does. But it must be particularly hard on Bernard. After all, a man like that has his needs."

"What does that mean?" Béatrice suddenly snaps pulling her hand away. "Bernard loves me, and would never–"

"No, no of course not," I seek to reassure her. "I'm sure he loves you very much. But separation can be very hard on a man and a woman."

Waiting a moment for her anger to subside, I casually reach for her hand again. "But for a military man, months of hard campaigning far from home can take its toll. It's only natural that–"

This time, I resist her attempts to remove her hand from mine. Pulling her closer, I quietly say, "I'm only saying this because I understand, and speak from experience. My father was also a cavalry officer. He too spent long periods away from home. And it was only natural then for him to seek comfort in the arms of another."

"Noo," Béatrice quietly wails. "Bernard would never betray me like that."

Seizing my moment, I tenderly wrap my arms around her, and whisper, "Yes, yes, I'm sure you are right. And it must be hard on you too. A woman also has her needs. Particularly a beautiful woman like you."

Her resolve weakening, her head slowly lowers and comes to rest on my shoulder. "Yes, yes I do," Béatrice quietly purrs. "I get so very lonely sometimes."

On the opposite side of the table, a grinning Toulouse shakes his head and quietly mouths what his friends were thinking earlier. "You sly dirty dog."

The comical bodily movements of his companions are silently vulgar, and wildly amusing to them, but mercifully go unseen by the woman nestled in my arms.

I'm far from the home straight, however. Before I can say or do anything else, Béatrice suddenly pulls away, straightens up, and composes herself. "But like my Bernard, I too will remain strong."

Silently cursing myself for not immediately pressing home my advantage, I'm pleasantly surprised when she stands up and extends her arm. "I would however, very much like to dance. Would you do me the honour, Montague?"

The timing could not be better. The stage show has reached its interval, and the house orchestra has just transitioned from a lively Viennese waltz to something slower and far better suited to my intentions.

In fact, this really couldn't be more perfect. My recent tuition has made a marked improvement on my skills as a dancer, and a slow waltz presents the perfect opportunity to move in close and whisper sweet nothings.

Taking Béatrice's hand, I smile and lower my head. "I can assure you, the honour is all mine, Mademoiselle."

We find a space on the dancefloor, and I place an arm around her waist to lead off. As light as air, and as beautiful and poised as a ballerina, this is a woman I could easily fall in love with – if there wasn't so much more at stake of course.

My mind firmly in the game, we execute a perfect turn, and I confidently pull her towards me. With our hips pressed tightly together, my early arousal is patently obvious as I whisper, "Why would you deny yourself, sweet Béatrice? I'm sure Bernard would not deny you a moment of pleasure."

A fleeting moment of hesitation to break away is another clear indicator of a weakening resolve. She eventually moves slightly away but doesn't release her grip on my hand. Frowning, she quietly says, "I think you are something of a rogue, Montague. But you are also a very good dancer, so I will forgive your—"

Looking below my waistline she frowns again before lifting an eyebrow. "So I will forgive your little indiscretion."

"That is most gracious," I reply with a grin. "But I can assure you, my indiscretion is not so little."

My joke is rewarded with a smile and a sweet girlish giggle from my dance partner. She also moves slightly closer, and whispers again, "Are all English royalty as roguish as you?"

I'm about to correct her when I think better of it. "Oh, yes. And most are far worse than me. Why the Prince of Wales is a notorious rogue."

Suddenly stopping dead, Béatrice excitedly squeals. "You know the Prince of Wales?"

"Oh, yes," I lie shamefully. "Prince Edward and I are extremely good friends."

"But isn't he so much older than you?" Béatrice asks looking puzzled.

"Um, yes, well that's quite right," I stammer. "But he was good friends with my father, and we were guests at the palace many times."

Now wide eyed, Béatrice nervously asks, "You have stayed at Buckingham Palace?"

Almost kicking myself for not mentioning my "*royal*" connections sooner, I lie again, "Yes, of course. My family and I are regular guests of the royal family."

Her face now flushed with excitement, I can now dare to imagine what deliciousness she is hiding beneath her undergarments. For her part, the poor thing is so in awe of my connections she is quite lost for words and hasn't even noticed the music has stopped.

Bowing politely, I thank her for the dance. "And perhaps you would like to hear more about the royal family back at our table."

"Yes, I would like that very much," she replies breathlessly. "I would like that very much."

* * * * * * * * *

I empty the last drop of Pétrus into Béatrice's glass feeling mildly confident I almost have her. My tales of hobnobbing with royalty have her enthralled, and when I casually suggest she visit me in London and stay at the palace, it is all she can do to stop herself from drooling over the table.

But still, a tiny nagging doubt remains. Although the interest is clearly there from her, I'm not completely sure I've done enough to bed this feisty young vixen tonight. With time rapidly running away from me, I think fast and discretely signal my new friend, Toulouse.

Perfectly understanding my intent, and dilemma, Toulouse gets to his feet and loudly declares, "My friends, the time to part ways is almost upon us. But not until—"

The great man allows a deliberate pause to build the anticipation, before theatrically raising a finger. "But not until we have all partaken of — Tremblement de Terre!"

The waiter hustles away to prepare the drinks, while Toulouse's friends thank him, and boisterously assure me I'm in for a treat.

I'm sure I am, but the real treat I'm hoping for is sitting beside me looking rather ravishing. She is also looking rather tipsy all of a sudden. My confidence renewed, I lean in and whisper, "I'm going to have you tonight, Béatrice Aguillard."

"What was that?" she asks somewhat glassy eyed.

"I said, the waiter is here with our drinks, Mademoiselle."

The waiter places two large wine glasses in front of us, and Béatrice mumbles, "This stuff, this earthquake cocktail of his, is quite vile."

Then raising her glass to her lips, she adds, "But Toulouse will get offended if we don't drink it."

The glasses are filled with a potent mixture of half and half, cognac, and absinthe. I take a small sip of my own, then watch stunned as Béatrice completely drains her own glass.

For a moment she sits in quiet contemplation of her achievement. Then ever so slowly, her eyes close, and she slumps sideways with her head resting on my lap.

Around the table, the friends of my host silently clap.

Toulouse himself smiles and whispers, "I think it is time to take your prize home before she fully regains her senses, my young friend."

* * * * * * * *

Feeling somewhat like a kidnapper, I hustle my sleeping beauty into one of the cabs waiting outside. Brushing aside her slurred protests about where I'm taking her, I direct the driver to take us to the home of my Parisienne benefactor.

Thankfully, Béatrice sleeps most of the way, and only begins to stir when we are approaching the Boulevard Saint-Germain.

"Where – where are we?" she slurs

"I've brought you to the home of, Monsieur Lavigne," I reply.

Suddenly alert, she jumps up and blurts, "Why? Why are we here?"

Feigning innocence, I slowly nod and do my best to offer some assurance. "You really don't remember? We discussed and agreed it was for the best."

Obviously still disoriented she stares at me wide eyed. "Agreed what? I don't remember. What did we agree?"

Moving closer, I place an arm around her shoulder. "Calm now, Béatrice," I say softly. "You were feeling a little under the weather. We both felt it better for you to freshen up before you returned to your own accommodations."

Nodding again, I smile and add, "We will be there shortly. You can use my bathroom to freshen up. Afterwards I will arrange for a cab to take you home."

Seemingly reassured, she smiles and lightly squeezes my hand. "Yes that is probably for the best. You are very kind, Montague. Very kind."

I'm still wondering if she will be thinking so kindly of me in the morning when the cab arrives at our destination. The driver dismounts to open the door, and we both assist Béatrice onto the pavement.

Although she is now relatively lucid, she is still decidedly unsteady on her feet. I'm therefore extremely grateful to be met at the door by Monsieur Lavigne's faithful manservant.

The gentle leviathan aids me in taking Béatrice into the drawing room, where he gently sits her down on a blue silk covered chaise longue beside a roaring fire crackling in the hearth.

Before leaving us alone, Jean-Claude lowers the lamplight, and turns to me with an assured and knowing nod, "You won't be disturbed in here, sir. Do call if you need anything."

Smiling he hand's Béatrice a glass of water. "Goodnight, mademoiselle. I do hope you feel better soon."

The door closes, and wasting no time, I move behind the chaise longue, and carefully place a hand across the young woman's forehead, "How are you feeling? You feel a little warm."

"No, no. I think I'm feeling a little better," she replies.

A barely noticeable effort to turn toward me is easily stopped by a firm hand on her shoulder. "No, no. Just relax and stay where you are. You feel tense, Béatrice. And if you will allow me to assist you, I have recently received tuition in massage and manipulation of the pressure points to relieve one's anxiety and stress."

"Oh, but I'm not anxious or stressed—" she starts to say.

Whether she is or isn't is of no real consequence. Without waiting for an invitation to proceed, I gently work my fingers into her shoulders, and the young woman moans softly. A soft kiss on the side of her neck causes the fine hairs to rise, and she shudders involuntarily.

"But that is so nice." She gasps. "Perhaps you might continue just a little longer. A little longer wouldn't hurt, would it?"

"Not at all," I whisper in her ear.

My firm manipulation of her neck and shoulders, is soon rewarded by gentle movements of her body, and a soft feminine purr. Inspired, I lean in, and plant another kiss on the lower part of her neck, before slowly working my way up to nibble on the sweetness of her earlobe.

She is so taken by my nibbling, she fails to notice the wandering of my hands. No longer on her shoulders, they skilfully move to loosen and uncouple her garments.

Emboldened by her lack of complaint, I move in front and unbutton my shirt. Deliberately teasing her, I slowly lift it over my head before tossing it aside. Although still fighting her womanly desires, the young woman's eyes glint an easy betrayal.

They are filled with an obvious and burning hunger, and her words of protest are lacking in vigour, or emphasis. "What — what are you doing, Montague? This is so wrong. I'm promised to another man."

"And where is this man?" I sneer arrogantly. "He is far far away, but I am here, and you want this as much as I do."

Turning her head away, her embarrassment is at odds with her words, and is a clear admission of what she really wants. "No, this is not right. This is not what I wa—"

"Yes, it is," I snarl, dropping to my knees. "You are a beautiful woman, Béatrice. A beautiful woman with needs, and desires. Is that so wrong?"

Suddenly aware of her unbuttoned blouse, her hands move quickly to protect her modesty. My own hands easily move hers aside, and she makes very little effort to replace them.

Mouthing the words, "You want this," I tear open the blouse to reveal the wondrous heaving globes below. Firm, and ripe, both are topped with a sweet dark nub.

Standing proud and inviting in the lamplight, I slowly roll my tongue across each of them in turn, before teasing, "Tell me you don't want this, Béatrice? Tell me you don't want this, and I will stop right now."

The hand pulling on the back of my head is an instant and unequivocal response. The accompanying insult I'm sure is quite unintentional. "You're a bastard, Montague — but — but but. Oh, you — you — bastard—oh God, it's been so long."

Overwhelmed by wave after wave of pleasure, the young woman abandons all semblance of resistance, and breathlessly sighs. "Bite me — yes, harder, bite me harder."

Her passion now unbridled she loudly moans, and suddenly orders, "Down. I want you to go down."

The firmness in her words is an incredible turn on, and who am I to disobey such an order? Purposely maintaining eye contact, I wink and slowly lick my lips, before hitching her skirts up to her waist.

Now at this stage of the game, you might be forgiven for thinking me unshockable. But you would be wrong. Not only is Béatrice completely naked below her skirts, but she is also as hairless as the day she was born. Slowly shaking my head, I think to myself, "Not so innocent or frigid after all."

As smooth and inviting as a Carolina peach, I stare upon her lips so beautifully formed and inviting. And at the perfectly formed fleshy pearl proudly perched atop her vulva.

Inching closer, I softly inhale. Like the finest Pétrus, her aroma is deep, rich, and intensely satisfying. What then must she taste like?

Suddenly impatient, the voracious young woman pulls on my head and urges, "Tongue me, Montague. Tongue me now."

Obedient to the last, I tease and probe in response to the grinding of her hips, and her womanly groans which are now hungry and demanding, "Oh yes, that's right. Go deeper. Yes, yes, yes."

Her hands tear at the back of my head. At times I can barely breathe, but this woman is wild and intoxicating. She is also saturated with her womanly nectar, and it is all I can do to keep up.

Noisily gulping her sweet juices, I'm nearing cunnilingus exhaustion, when she abruptly pushes me away.

My new orders are delivered not by a woman of grace and refinement, but by a woman overtaken by her carnal and animalistic desires. And they are very obviously not open for debate.

"Fuck me, Montague. Fuck me long and hard."

In a month of firsts, this is another. I've never seen such a dramatic change in a woman. This angel from heaven is really a devil in disguise. But who am I to complain? I'm as hard as granite and have work to do.

It's also now my turn to take charge. Sparing the niceties, I drag her skirts over her ankles, before roughly flipping her over, and ordering, "On your knees then, bitch."

Now subservient to me, I wrench back hard on her golden plaits, before roughly forcing her back down. Her ass jutting toward the sky, her face squidges against the soft fabric of the chaise longue. Her splendidly perky breasts hang loose from her open blouse, and her quim glistens like moonlight on a duck pond.

Lost in my own desire for release, I have no intention of taking things slow. I do, however, have every intention of ploughing her long and hard, as was her request. Taking inspiration from Captain Murray, I spread my prize apart, and unceremoniously sink my meaty dagger to the hilt.

My ungentlemanly efforts are rewarded with a shocked gasp, and something distinctly religious panted in French, "Oh merde. Oh, mon Dieu."

"He can't save you." I grunt, as I noisily pound into her.

Pulling on her hair again, I drag her upward and snarl in her ear before pushing her back down, "You're mine now. Say it, you're mine."

"Oh yes, yes." She squeals. "I'm yours, Montague. I'm all yours."

"Louder," I bark, before slapping her creamy ass cheeks and demanding, "Scream it. Tell me you're my slut."

The poor girl can barely catch a breath, but I know my words are driving her crazy with desire. I slap her again, but this time with real venom. Her cheeks glow brightly and radiate heat. Her whimpers are soft and catlike, "Oh God, yes. I'm your slut, Montague. I'm yours, and yours alone."

"Yes, you are." I smugly nod to myself. "And I'm going to ride you harder than a runner in the Epsom Derby."

Going at her like a steam hammer, my mount is everything I imagined her to be and more. Perspiration glistens on her flawless skin, and close to her climax she grunts and pants like a woman in labour.

My own climax is just moments away, and I remember the words of my Parisienne mentor. "To cum together, is the ultimate pleasure, Monty. It is the holy grail of lovemaking."

I'm not sure I could describe this as lovemaking, but I'm yet to achieve this holy grail, and will myself to hold on just a little longer. Thankfully, a little longer is all it takes.

Just moments later, Béatrice's body stiffens and shudders. Her vaginal muscles contract and she howls, "Oh, God. Oh, God. I'm cumming. I'm — oh merde!"

Oh, merde indeed. I couldn't have said it better myself. The intensity of my lover's climax sends me over the top, and just half a second behind her, I grunt and unload myself deep inside her. Drained and exhausted, but still buried to the hilt, I fall forward across her back.

Both panting heavily, a good few seconds pass before either of us have strength enough to talk or move to uncouple ourselves. When we do, we slump down and Béatrice pulls one of my arms around her.

Her face is flushed and radiant. Her look is one of deep satisfaction. Smiling sweetly, she looks up and says, "That was incredible. I mean — you are incredible."

I nod, and return her smile, but am still too breathless to speak.

Smiling again, I'm shocked to hear her say, "I think, I might be in love with you."

Love was not my intention for this evening, nor for any evening with this young lady for that matter. Not unless she is in line for a large inheritance I don't know about.

Trying not to choke, I mask my shock and calmly ask, "Is that so, Béatrice?"

"Yes." She responds sweetly. "And do you think you might also be in love with me?"

Again, not something I was expecting to hear or be asked this evening. But what the hell, I think to myself. One has already lied to her many times this evening, and if it will shut her up, another little fib won't make a difference, will it?"

Pulling her closer, I tenderly kiss the side of her head and softly coo, "Yes, my darling. I think I could be in love with you."

Delighted with my response, she smiles and nestles her head upon my chest. Quiet for a moment, I'm hoping with my task complete, she will soon leave, or at least sleep a while.

Unfortunately, with neither seemingly forthcoming anytime soon, Béatrice suddenly sits up and takes a deep breath, "And was it true what you said about Buckingham Palace. Will you really take me there? And will you really introduce me to the queen, and the Prince of Wales?"

Deliberately avoiding eye contact, I lightly stroke her hair, and tell her what she wants to hear, "Yes, of course, my love. But you should rest awhile now to gather your strength."

"Go on," I assure her. "Close your eyes and rest. I promise to wake you shortly, and escort you home."

* * * * * * * *

I'm woken the following morning by a strong hand on my shoulder, and a soft familiar voice. "Good morning, sir. You should go to your own room now to rest. You have a long day ahead of you."

Groggy and hungover, I force myself to open my eyes. It's clearly still early, but the fire in the hearth has long since burned itself out, and I'm suddenly aware of the clatter of Eric's household staff going about their business in the kitchen below stairs.

Still not fully awake, Jean-Claude repeats more forcefully, "Come now, sir. You really should rest and freshen up. Monsieur Lavigne would like you to join him for breakfast before you leave today."

"Before I leave?" I mumble. Suddenly remembering and panic stricken, I sit bolt upright and turn to my side, "Where – where is–?"

"The young lady left more than two hours ago sir. She asked me not to wake you."

"You were here when she left?" I ask.

"Yes, of course." Jean-Claude nods. "It is my responsibility to take care of any guests in this house."

Unsure of what to expect in response, I nervously ask, "And was the young lady okay when she left? I mean, how did she seem?"

The flamboyant manservant is no fool. He knows exactly what I mean. He wouldn't however be so indiscrete, or improper to discuss such personal things with his betters. Completely stoic, he replies, "She was quite well, sir."

"Quite well, Jean-Claude?"

"Oh yes, sir. Quite well, indeed. In fact, when I escorted her to her cab, she was, how you say, in high spirits."

"Yes, I'm sure she was," I mumble to myself. "The poor deluded girl thinks I'm taking her to Buckingham Palace. It's just as well we're leaving today, and I'll never have to see her again."

* * * * * * * *

Eric and Aunt Caroline both look typically resplendent in their Sunday finery, but aside from the customary morning greetings, breakfast starts out as an unusually subdued affair.

I'm almost beginning to suspect my companions might also be suffering from the effects of the previous evening, when Eric suddenly looks up and smirks, "So then, Monty, my boy, how was your evening?"

Taken by surprise, I splutter, "My evening, sir? Um, thank you for asking, it was most enjoyable."

Across the table, Aunt Caroline struggles to suppress a giggle. "I'm sure she was, Monty." Then turning to Monsieur Lavigne, "Mademoiselle Aguillard must be very excited to be visiting Buckingham Palace."

"I'm sure she must." Eric chuckles loudly.

Burning up, but on the defensive, I angrily bark, "You were bloody well listening in?"

"Not just listening in," Caroline replies, before proudly declaring, "We also had a grandstand view, and I must say, your performance was most impressive."

Barely able to register, the words cloy at my throat, and I stammer, "You what – I mean, how – where, I mean. Where were you?"

"The mirror above the fireplace," Eric replies. "A most remarkable feat of engineering and invention."

Smiling, Caroline adds, "It was a gift from an inventor friend of Eric's. He calls it a two-way mirror."

"And I call it a voyeurs dream." Eric laughs. "Lady Caroline is quite right, however. It's a prototype gifted to me, by a Russian chap named Bloch. And it's quite remarkable. I'd be happy to show it to you before you leave."

Sensing my annoyance, Eric reaches across the table to pat my hand. "Come now, Monty. We've seen it all before, and how else were we to verify the success of your efforts?"

My irritation quickly waning, I slowly shake my head and repeat a thought from the previous evening. "In a month of surprises, I really shouldn't be surprised that you were spying on me, should I?"

"Not spying," Caroline chirps cheerily. "We were viewing and assessing your progress. Eric has made a considerable investment in your education, Monty. It is only fair he be allowed to assess the value of his investment."

"Spoken like a true banker," Eric loudly chortles. "I couldn't have said it better myself."

I patiently wait for the laughter to subside before asking, "And what value do you now place on your investment? Did I pass your test, Eric?"

"With flying colours," the banker booms across the table. "What say you, Lady Caroline?"

My aunt frowns, and is slightly less enthusiastic in her appraisal. "Granted the seduction was achieved. It was however achieved through a mix of flattery, lies and strong drink. Not exactly the behaviour expected of a gentleman, Eric."

"Nonsense," Eric booms again.

Then laughing himself silly, "It's exactly the behaviour expected of a gentleman. And let's give credit where credit is due, the lad discovered the holy grail."

Almost won over, Aunt Caroline is now trying to hide an increasingly obvious smile. "Yes, I suppose I'll give him that."

She then frowns again before adding, "He was however a little rough for my own liking. My personal preference is for a somewhat slower performance."

Tutting loudly, I smirk and ask, "Are you sure about that? Don't forget you're not the only voyeur in this family, Lady Caroline."

Knowing exactly what I'm referring to, but completely unflappable, my aunt casually brushes aside my comment, and instead deftly turns the conversation back to me. "And I wasn't overly impressed with the reference to riding her harder than a runner in the Epsom Derby."

Ignoring Eric's schoolboy sniggers, she turns to me and smiles. "But in answer to your question. Yes, you have passed the test, and we are both extremely pleased with your progress thus far."

"Hear hear!" Eric loudly concurs. "And it's onwards and upwards from here my boy."

My mentors both look on with unabashed admiration, while I find myself blushing and momentarily lost for words. Growing somewhat uncomfortable, it eventually falls to Eric to break the silence.

The banker reaches into his jacket pocket to retrieve a small elaborately decorated wooden box, which he slides across the table. "I was going to give you this at the station, but unfortunately I have been called to an urgent meeting at the ministry of finance, so would like you to have it now."

I lift the box and nervously ask, "What is it?"

"A gift," Eric replies. "An early birthday gift, and a token of my esteem."

Gesturing to my hand, the banker smiles and politely encourages, "Please, go ahead and open it."

The lid of the box is held in place by a brass hinge and is loosely secured by a short length of dark blue ribbon. I pull on one end and the ribbon silently falls onto my breakfast plate.

Carefully lifting the lid, my gasp of astonishment is barely worthy of the treasure I find inside. Quite unable to speak for a second time, Eric reaches across the table to touch my hand. "I hope you like it, Monty. I noticed you didn't have one, and it's only right for a gentleman to have a fine pocket watch."

Like my gasp before it, the word fine is barely sufficient in justifying the magnificence of this gift. Hand crafted in twenty-four karat gold by the watch-making artisans from the House of Breguet, it is quite simply a work of art.

My words of appreciation are sincere but woefully unworthy of its beauty. "Eric, it is magnificent. I'm not sure I will ever be able to thank you for everything you have done for me."

"You've done enough," the banker replies modestly. Then excitedly pointing to the timepiece, "Flip it over my boy. I've had it inscribed."

The beautifully inscribed words are both heartfelt, and succinct.

To my good friend,
Monty,
and the fine gentleman
he has become.
From his very good friend,
Eric Lavigne

Welling up with emotion, I've barely had time to recover from this first surprise when Eric reaches below the table and places a black leather belt with a sturdy brass buckle in front of me.

Obviously confused as to why I might need an additional belt, I politely offer my thanks, much to the amusement of our host, who chuckles. "The watch is just for show, Monty. This gift is something a little more practical for your travels."

Pulling the belt toward him, Eric flips it over to reveal a zipped compartment concealed below an additional flap of leather. "In here, you will find six of your Queen Victoria's gold sovereigns."

"But, why?" I ask, still a little confused.

"For use in an emergency," Eric replies. "One can never be too careful when traveling. But they are only for use in an emergency you understand? Not for whoring, or merriment." He grins.

"Yes, I understand." I nod. "But I really don't know what to say. How can I ever thank or repay you, Eric?"

Suddenly choked with emotion himself, our host gets to his feet. "By looking after Lady Caroline and fulfilling your destiny. And by returning safely to my home at the end of your travels."

Nodding slowly, he adds, "That will be thanks enough, Monty."

Squinting at his own watch, Eric suddenly looks disappointed and shakes his head. "Unfortunately I must leave now for the ministry. We should say our farewells."

Crossing to my side of the table, his embrace is warm, and paternal.

It is also tinged with more than a little sadness. But refusing to show any more emotion than he already has, Eric kisses me on both cheeks and wishes me well. Turning he smiles and tenderly kisses Aunt Caroline's hand. "Stay safe and travel well, my beautiful friend."

Then to both of us, he gives a final elegant Parisienne flourish. "Au revoir, mes amis. When you are ready, Jean-Claude will escort you to the station."

Chapter Six

The Orient Express
& Munich – 27 November 1898

As is his style, Eric has spared no expense with our onward travel arrangements. Not only has he booked us passage on The Orient Express, but he has also arranged for us to stay in four sumptuous adjoining cabins.

Although each of the cabins are unique in their design and architecture, all ooze the same sense of style and panache. From the burnished marquetry panelling on the walls, to the hand decorated porcelain tiles in the washrooms, every detail has been considered and designed to reflect luxury and opulence.

I'm suitably impressed myself, so I can only wonder what Betsy and Johnathan must be making of all this. My aunt allocates the third and fourth cabins to her staff, whilst we take the first two and settle in.

While Betsy fusses around her mistress, and Johnathan unpacks my dinner jacket, I ponder how best to amuse myself.

The distance from Paris to Munich via train is a little over four hundred miles thereabouts, so allowing for scheduled stops, and barring any delays or miscalculation in my arithmetic, we should get into Munich by late afternoon tomorrow. "That's a long time staring out of windows," I think to myself.

"What say we partake of light refreshments in the dining car?" I suggest to my aunt.

"A splendid idea," she replies. "Just the one drink, though. I'm rather weary after last night, and I should like to rest this afternoon. We should then dine and retire early this evening."

* * * * * * * *

True to her word it's not yet nine in the evening when we finish dining. I escort Aunt Caroline back to her cabin and am about to leave for my own when she invites me in, under the pretext of helping her with the clasp on her necklace. "I can never quite manage it myself, and I don't wish to bother Betsy with something so insignificant. Would you mind awfully, dear?"

"Not at all," I reply following her into the room.

I should of course know by now, there is always an ulterior motive when it comes to my mother's younger sister. She turns away and lifts her long blonde tresses to allow me easy access to the back of her neck.

Like everything else she owns, the golden clasp securing the necklace is a quality piece. Its action is smooth and light. It opens easily, and Caroline catches the weighty necklace in her free hand.

Removing the pins in her hair, she shakes it out, then turns and smiles before quickly turning away again. "Would you also be so kind as to unbutton my gown, Monty?"

What a question to ask of a red-blooded male. Aunt or not, I know what wonders lie beneath, and am only too keen to help. Reaching forward, I nervously unbutton her to the waist, before boldly leaning in to kiss the back of her neck.

This was a turning point in my pursuit of Béatrice. Aunt Caroline, however, is a different proposition entirely. She turns with her hands held tightly across her chest to protect her gown from falling.

Frowning, she slowly shakes her head. "That was rather presumptuous of you, Monty."

Then without waiting for a response, "Do you think you are ready for a real woman?"

Before this question, I clearly thought I was. Now however, I'm rather less sure of myself. My throat suddenly dry, I nervously stutter, "Yes — I um, think I am."

To my very great relief, Aunt Caroline smiles and nods her approval. "Good. Because I rather think you have been neglecting me recently, in favour of young Betsy. And that won't do at all Montague."

She's probably correct about me, but she could hardly call herself neglected. Living in such close confines, I am perfectly aware that when I've been with Betsy, she has invariably been getting serviced by either or all of Eric, Jean-Claude, and Johnathan.

I'm also perfectly aware of her own nocturnal assignations with Betsy, and Eric's mistress, Mademoiselle Cecille Moreau. Add to that the considerable rutting delivered by Captain Murray, and the lessons imparted on me in the company of others this past month, she could hardly be described as neglected.

Regardless, I have every intention of ploughing her tonight, and I have no intention of rocking the boat, or upsetting her. Locking away my thoughts, I smile sympathetically and move closer. "You are quite right, and I'm so sorry for my neglect. How might one begin to make it up to you?"

Looking me directly in the eye, Caroline drops her hands to allow her gown to fall forward. Truly the stuff of dreams, her breasts are as creamy and splendid as the first time I laid eyes on them.

Moving with purpose toward me, she firmly places a hand across the front of my breeches, and my rapidly stiffening member.

"You can start by taking these off," she purrs. "I shall guide you from there."

* * * * * * * *

The next three hours are a whirlwind journey through the carnal arts of satisfaction. From slow to fast, from gentle to rough, from considerate to selfish. Nothing is off limits, and nothing is too much, or too little for Lady Caroline Winstanley.

My experiences thus far with Betsy and Béatrice easily pale in comparison to the talents and sexual hungers of my aunt.

And if there was any doubt in my mind before, the meaning of the word nymphomaniac is now perfectly clear. The woman is quite simply insatiable. Ridden to the point of exhaustion, we are two orgasms apiece, before she finally pauses a moment to allow me to draw breath.

Both perspiring heavily, Caroline hands me a glass of water. While I drink, she playfully pokes my old man, and teases, "I do hope there is something still left in the coffers, Monty?"

I'm not entirely sure there is, but I've come this far and don't wish to lose face. Sitting up, I confidently boast, "Oh don't you worry about that. There is plenty more where that last lot came from."

"Very good." Caroline nods before reaching for a small handbell. "Because it is only half time. And much more is expected of you."

She then rings the bell and tells me to pick up my clothes.

"What's going on?" I ask, looking more than a little confused.

A moment later, the adjoining door opens behind me, and Johnathan appears in the doorway. He is barefoot and stripped to the waist. His torso is muscular, taut, and glistening with perspiration.

I'm suspecting what is about to happen but am still a little unsure when Aunt Caroline touches my arm. "You've played rugger at Eton, Monty. So, you must be familiar with the term, half-time?"

"I am," I reply. "But what does that mean exact—?"

"It means it's time to change sides." Caroline giggles. "I'm sure Johnathan has warmed Betsy up nicely for you."

Gesturing toward the door, she gestures for the young valet to come in, and casually says to me, "Off you pop then, Monty. Don't keep the girl waiting. I'll see you bright and early in the morning for breakfast."

As we pass, the slightly sheepish young valet respectfully tips his head. "Have a good evening, sir."

And that was that. Just when I think I'm on top of the world, I'm substituted in favour of a domestic servant, and am sent scurrying away disappointed, with my tail quite literally tucked between my legs.

It isn't all bad though. Sweet young Betsy Cooper is a remarkable tonic for all ills. She is also a quite remarkable distraction. After just five minutes in the sack with her, I've quite forgotten the reason for my disappointment, and I wake the next morning happy and surprisingly well refreshed.

* * * * * * * *

I join my aunt in the dining car, and although it's never been directly or implicitly expressed to me, there is an unwritten rule of sexual etiquette I have learned well enough these past weeks.

It is not appropriate for one to discuss or refer to one's sexual exploits whilst dining. And it is most certainly not appropriate to refer to those exploits over breakfast. Unless, of course, one's host or one's better refers to them first.

Up to now on this trip, this is exactly what has happened. I'm still hopeful however of an opening or some comment on my performance last night but am left sadly disappointed by a conversation bordering on the mundane.

Sure that Lady Caroline is deliberately avoiding the subject to provoke a reaction, I rudely interrupt to steer the chatter away from the practical use and merits of Latin prose.

"Yes, well, that is all well and good, but why don't you tell me again about this duke chap we will be staying with in Munich? How well do you even know him?"

As dignified as ever, Aunt Caroline slowly sips her coffee, and makes me wait for her reply. By deliberately overlooking my tone, and maintaining her poise, I am made to look foolish and immature, and quickly realise there is much more I can learn from this magnificent woman. And not just in the bedroom. Slightly ashamed of myself, I lower my head and apologise for my outburst.

"That's quite alright." Caroline nods. "The mark of a man is partly in his willingness to admit his mistakes and apologize for them in a timely manner."

"Oh, and I know the Grand Duke of Hesse very well." She smirks. "Ernst is a first cousin of my dear departed love, the Marquess of Rutland."

"So, that would make him my—"

"Yes, your uncle." Caroline cut's in. "Well, an uncle of sorts anyhow. But more importantly, Ernst is one of the most powerful men in Germany. He has vast estates and has kindly offered us the use of his hunting lodge on the edge of the Allacher forest for the duration of our stay in Munich."

In my imagination, a hunting lodge on the edge of a German forest is somewhat altogether grim and uninviting in comparison to the recent luxury and delights of Paris.

Failing to learn from my earlier mistake, I innocently but foolishly ask, "Won't that be rather tedious and dull?"

Now losing patience, Aunt Caroline noisily places her porcelain coffee cup into its saucer and shakes her head. "It would do well for you to remember the precarious position you are in, Montague. And to be grateful for the assistance of men like Ernst. Without the likes of him, this journey would invariably be far harder."

Firmly put in my place yet again, I sheepishly lower my head. "I'm sorry, if I've caused any offence, Caroline. That certainly wasn't my intention."

"Maybe not," she snaps, "But you might want to learn a little humility, Monty. Ernst is a proud man. He doesn't suffer fools lightly, and you will do well not to incur his displeasure."

I'm now imagining the image of a terrifying Germanic barbarian familiar to me from the textbooks on the Roman empire. I'm still imagining this monster when my companion says, "And in fact, your time in Munich will be far from tedious and dull. Ernst is a man of action. He will no doubt have devised a full program of physical activities to test you."

Up to now, the physical activities on this tour have primarily revolved around dancing, and those in the bedchamber. Suddenly interested again, I'm about to say something sarcastic when I'm quickly closed down in no uncertain terms, "And you can wipe that idiotic smirk off your face. Paris is far behind us, and the time for foolishness and playtime is over."

As serious as I've ever seen her, Aunt Caroline grasps my hand. "In Munich you will be tested and pushed to your limits."

Then pulling away she slowly nods to herself, "You'll be thankful though when it's done."

Now more than a little perturbed, I nervously ask, "What does that mean? Only you're making it all sound quite ominous?"

Suddenly cheerier, she straightens up and smiles. "No, no. It's nothing like that. Ernst is just a very serious man. You shouldn't take things too lightly when you are around him."

Keen to change the subject, she stands and excuses herself from the table. "Get some rest now, and dress warmly, Monty. Munich can be rather chilly at this time of year."

* * * * * * * *

More than twenty minutes have now passed since our arrival in Munich, and there is still no sign of the duke or his driver to meet us. More annoyingly it is now getting late, and the temperature has started to drop rapidly.

Although I've heeded the earlier advice and worn my thickest overcoat, outside the station entrance there is precious little protection from the icy winds howling down the Bayerstrase.

Conscious however of not wishing to cause offence again by disparaging our host further, I hold my tongue, and stamp my feet to keep them warm.

Thankfully, I'm not the only one cold and frustrated. Caroline shakes her head, and to nobody in particular, she says, "Really, this is not like Ernst at all. He is usually the model of German efficiency and punctuality."

"Really?" I think to myself. Then quite unintentionally, I mutter, "Not today it would seem."

My unintended sarcasm is met with an angry scowl, and I quickly move to correct myself, "What I mean is, perhaps there was a miscommunication around our travel dates, Lady Caro—"

"There is no miscommunication," she barks. "I'm sure there is a perfectly good explanation why there is nobody here to meet us."

Turning away from me, she hands Johnathan a slip of paper. "This is the number for the lodge. The station master will have a telephone in his office. Run along and find out what is happening, please."

The young man has barely had time to acknowledge the request before we are suddenly disturbed by the frenetic tooting of a horn, and the unfamiliar put put of rapidly approaching combustion engines.

Until today I've only ever seen one other Motorwagen up close. Now however, I'm stunned to find myself looking upon two identical, brand new shiny automobiles barrelling down the Bayerstrase.

"Well, this is unexpected," I say to my aunt. "Did you know about this?"

Clearly as surprised as I am, she shakes her head. "No, not at all. But it would appear Ernst has purchased himself some new toys."

The vehicles come to a halt beside us, and I briefly marvel at these wonders of engineering before turning my attention to the drivers. Both are identically dressed in heavy black wool overcoats, breeches, and black leather calf-high boots.

Each man is also wearing a flat cap, and both have thick brown leather gauntlets to protect their hands from the worst of the evening chill. Finally, both men are wearing a thick pair of driving goggles. I assume these are to protect their eyes from the effects of thundering along at such high velocity.

I'm still wondering about this when the lead driver climbs down from his seat. Singling out Aunt Caroline, he smartly clicks his heels together, before briefly speaking to her in German. My own German is sadly lacking, but Caroline smiles, and the driver assists her into the back seat of his vehicle where he carefully covers her legs with a magnificent sable fur blanket.

While the driver assists Johnathan in the loading of the luggage, Aunt Caroline suggests, "Monty dear. You should ride in the other vehicle with Betsy. Johnathan shall ride with me, to help keep me warm."

It's not so much a suggestion, as an instruction, and I'm too damn cold to argue, anyway. I assist Betsy into the second automobile and pull the luxurious blanket tightly across us. All the while the second driver makes no attempt to move or offer any assistance.

"That's damned odd," I say to my companion. "And damned rude if you ask me."

"Sorry, sir. What was that?" Betsy asks.

Full of my own self-importance, I haven't noticed she is shivering. "That fella up there. He hasn't even had the decency to acknowledge us. I shall be having words with his master when we see him. Doesn't he bloody well know who I am?"

Her teeth now chattering, the young woman quietly mumbles, "Yes, sir, you do that. It's important he knows who you are, sir."

Although unintentional, her words leave me feeling like a pompous ass, and my cheeks are suddenly glowing and warm. In comparison Betsy is shaking like a leaf.

Ignoring any social graces, I pull her toward me and wrap an arm around her. "I'm sorry, Betsy, you must think me a real—"

"Yes, sir. I do," the young woman interrupts. Then raising an eyebrow cheekily, she smiles and snuggles into me more tightly. "But I've just heard Lady Caroline tell Johnathan it is a forty-minute drive to the duke's hunting lodge. That is more than enough time for you to think of ways to keep me warm."

"Saucy mare." I chuckle. "But I'm a little chilly myself, and that's not a bad idea at all."

Checking that our driver is still looking ahead, I fumble under the fur for Betsy's hand and place it over my crotch. "Why don't you warm your hands on that while I do some thinking?"

"Oooh." Betsy giggles. "That is ever so warm, sir."

Up front, the engines of both vehicles sputter to life, and I'm almost certain I see our driver shake his head.

"So, you understand English," I mumble to myself. "That makes your insolence even more contemptible."

"Oh, forget him," Betsy says noticing my distraction. Then mirroring my own earlier action, she takes one of my hands and forces it below her skirts onto her already warm and moist cunny.

"But how?" I ask with obvious surprise.

"Maybe the vibrations from the engine." She shrugs. "Who care's though, I've never done it in a motor carriage. Have you, sir?"

"My first time." I smile. "So, let's not waste any time. Hop aboard, Betsy."

* * * * * * * *

In point of fact, it's almost an hour before we finally enter the grounds of the duke's estate, and whilst our earlier exertions have kept us warm, a cold chill is now once again creeping through our bones.

Although thankful for our shared warmth, I reluctantly push Betsy aside and straighten up when the lights from the lodge come into view. Despite my earlier reservations, as a secondary property the lodge is an impressive structure, almost as large as Morton Hall itself.

Although I have yet to meet the chap, I'm thus far impressed with the hospitality shown to us by the Grand Duke of Hesse. I must however remember to inform him of the lack of courtesy shown by our driver.

We come to a halt on the gravel drive and are met by a gaggle of liveried staff who assist us down from the vehicles. Johnathan and Betsy are quickly led away to the servants' quarters, while Aunt Caroline and I are shown into the great hall by an elderly butler who speaks to us in broken English. "If you will be so kind as to make yourself comfortable in here, the duke will be along in just a moment."

He leaves us alone, and we both immediately move toward the fire to warm ourselves. The walls of the room are adorned with an array of heraldic shields, trophy heads, and ancient edged weapons. Sitting in the centre of the room there is an impressive solid mahogany table with seating for thirty diners.

The table is laid out with fine silver and glassware, and if I didn't already know it, our host is clearly a man of wealth and substance. I can't however rid my mind of the total lack of respect shown by one of his drivers.

"That was a rum turn of events don't you think?"

"What was that?" Aunt Caroline asks sounding uninterested.

"That second driver. Did you notice how he didn't offer to help with the luggage, or make any effort to assist us aboard? Why the chap didn't even bother himself with offering a greeting."

Frowning and clearly bored with my whining, Caroline asks derisively, "And you were somehow offended by that were you, Monty?"

"Well not so much offended, but one would expect better of a driver in the employment of royalty. German royalty I'll grant you, but royalty nonetheless. I've a good mind to—"

"A good mind to do what?" Caroline angrily interrupts. "Will you be bold enough to inform our host that one of his staff has offended your delicate sensibilities?"

"Well – um, no," I bluster. "That's not what I meant at all."

The doors to the great hall open, and Aunt Caroline sneers, "This must be the duke now. Good luck."

I turn toward the doors and am surprised to see both drivers enter the room. They join us by the fire, and the lead driver removes his cap and goggles before once again clicking his heels, and gallantly kissing Aunt Caroline's hand. "Lady Caroline, welcome to my humble lodgings."

His English is fluent but slightly guttural and is tinged with his native tongue. My aunt can barely suppress her smile as she makes the introductions. "Montague, please let me introduce you to another of my very good friends, Ernst Ludwig Albrecht, The Grand Duke of Hesse. And to his beautiful wife—"

The second driver removes her own cap and goggles before shaking out her long dark hair, and genteelly offering her own hand to be kissed.

"—and to his beautiful wife, Princess Eleonore of Hesse-Darmstadt."

I estimate the duke to be in his late fifties at least, but the beauty standing before me is in her mid-twenties at best. Despite her current masculine style of dress, I can easily picture the curvaceous body beneath, and as I kiss her outstretched hand, I absent-mindedly imagine myself pumping this beauty sometime soon.

"Monty," My aunt repeats loudly. "The duke was speaking to you."

"Um, yes. Sorry, I um, I was distracted by your fine collection of trophy heads."

"Yes, they are quite magnificent," the duke says quite unaware of my innuendo. "Before the end of your stay in Munich, I will ensure you have the opportunity to hunt with us, and perhaps even add to our trophy collection."

My mind is of course on a hunt of quite a different kind. And of course, on a magnificent trophy to add to my own collection. Pushing those thoughts to the back of my mind for now, I smile and shake the duke's hand. "Thank you, I'm very much looking forward to that, sir."

"Very good." He nods. "Anyhow, I was just apologising for keeping you waiting, and for my lack of formal introduction at the station. It was a little cold, and I felt it best not to hang around. I hope I didn't cause any offence?"

Before I'm able to respond, Aunt Caroline interjects, "Actually, Ernst. My nephew did want to say something about our arrival in Munich. Isn't that right, Monty?"

Blushing slightly, I shake my head. "No, no, it was nothing really — I was just — I mean, I was just going to say what a delightful surprise it was to be picked up in your Motorwagen's, and how much I'm looking forward to learning more about them."

Aunt Caroline is silently revelling in my embarrassment, and I'm sure I feel Princess Eleonore's eyes boring into me. And for good reason. If her English is as fluent as the dukes, she will know exactly what I had been intending to say.

Mercifully, the duke himself seems oblivious to my discomfort, and his attention is swiftly diverted away from me by the entrance of the elderly butler carrying a silver tray laden with a crystal decanter and four short glasses.

"Ah, very good," the duke declares. "Some schnapps to warm us up before dinner."

He hands each of us a glass, before raising his arm for the toast. "To my newfound nephew, Montague Finch-Morton the Third. May his stay with us be both enlightening, and a test of his courage, and endurance."

That same ominous feeling returns to the pit of my stomach, and while I drink, I study my companions for any sign of what might be in store for me in the days ahead. All remain stoic and none give anything away.

The duke finishes his drink and places his glass on the tray, before excusing himself and Princess Eleonore to take their leave. "Manfred will escort you to your quarters when you are ready. Dinner is in here at eight-thirty sharp."

Our hosts leave, and in the absence of the butler, I pour two fresh glasses of schnapps.

"This is jolly good stuff," I say, handing the second glass to my aunt. "I'm feeling warmer already."

"Yes, you must have been quite frozen on that drive in." Caroline smirks. "I'm sure a nice bottle of schnapps would have taken the edge off the chill a little."

"Or perhaps, the company of a strapping stable boy," I sarcastically retort. "Or am I wrong, Caroline?"

"Hmm, touché, Monty," she concedes. "But enough of that, and speaking of such things, you can forget any ideas you might have about rooting Princess Eleonore. That young woman is quite out of–"

"What?" I protest. "That thought never occurred to me. I wouldn't dream of insulting the duke in such a–"

"Monty!" Caroline interrupts with a raised hand. "Please don't take me for a fool. You were positively slathering over the woman just now. If you value your family jewels, you will listen to what I am saying. Princess Eleonore is out of bounds. Am I making myself clear?"

"You are." I nod. "Princess Eleonore is out of bounds."

My aunt is far from convinced, but for now she allows me the benefit of the doubt. "Good, because for the next few weeks your energies will be far better utilized in other more productive ways."

"How very cryptic of you to say so once again." I frown. "Am I to know exactly how I will be utilizing those energies anytime soon?"

Pausing to take a sip of the warming schnapps from her glass, my aunt smiles and softly replies, "I'm sure Ernst will enlighten you over dinner, Monty. Until then, please be patient."

* * * * * * * *

Although we are the only other guests dining tonight, the arrival of the duke and his consort is an oddly formal affair. While a pair of footmen hold open the doors, the head butler sounds a gong before loudly announcing, "His excellency, The Grand Duke of Hesse, and Princess Eleonore."

The duke is formally attired in the uniform of a colonel of hussars. He sports a monocle in one eye, and his whiskers have been elaborately waxed and shaped. My own have grown handsomely in the last few weeks, but these easily put mine to shame. I also notice for the first time that he has a small duelling scar on his left cheek. These little touches all serve to make my host the epitome of an aristocratic German officer.

The princess, however, is something else entirely. Without the benefit of her driving boots, she is suddenly very petite. But oh, so perfectly packaged. Her sparkling blue eyes mirror the shade of her fitted silk gown to perfection. Her complexion is flawless like fine porcelain, and her tight bosom rises and falls ever so slightly as the duke escorts her to the table. Her hair has been arranged in a tight weave, and atop her head she is wearing an exquisite diamond and sapphire encrusted tiara.

Although I'm formally dressed in a bespoke new suit from Monsieur Lavigne's personal tailor, and Aunt Caroline is looking as stunning as ever, we must look rather dull in comparison to our hosts. As they approach, I'm wondering if this little show is entirely for my benefit, or this is how all German nobility normally dine.

We rise to our feet, and I take the young woman's hand to place a kiss. "Princess Eleonore, it is my very great pleasure to see you again."

"And I you," she responds. "And I am very much looking forward to learning about your travel adventures thus far, Montague."

This is the first time I have heard her speak more than a few words, and I'm pleasantly surprised. Her English is perfectly fluent with only the faintest hint of her Bavarian ancestry.

I smile and compliment her language skills. "Your English is quite perfect, Princess."

"Thank you," she replies modestly. "I had an excellent teacher. I was also fortunate to spend several years studying in your capital city."

The duke takes his place at the head of the table, with my aunt seated to his left. I'm pleased to be seated next to Eleonore on the right-hand side of the table.

As expected, the meal is an elaborate performance comprising many courses of exotic dishes, most of which I have never heard of. For their part, the duke and princess are attentive hosts. Throughout the meal, both show a passionate interest in their guests, but particularly in me and my time in Paris.

I'm unsure however if their interest would go as far as my sexual education, so when questioned on what I have learned thus far, I focus purely on the arts, etiquette, dancing, and languages.

Toward the end of the meal, I'm yet to find out what the duke has in store for me, and feeling we have made enough small talk, I turn to the host. "Your Excellency, would you mind very much if I ask about—"

"Oh, that's right," he booms. "You must think me a dreadful bore. You wanted to know more about my automobiles."

"Um, yes," I reply. "But what I actually wanted to—"

I'm interrupted again by Aunt Caroline who playfully scalds, "Don't be rude, Monty. Ernst is going to tell you about his new toys."

"Not toys." He laughs. "They are the wonder of the modern age, and are courtesy of my good friend, Herr Karl Benz."

"And what's more," he says proudly. "I am the only man in the state to own two of the contraptions."

"That is wonderful." I nod. "And was it very difficult to master the art of driving?"

The duke points to his young wife and roars with laughter. "Not difficult at all, Montague. Why with just a few hours of tuition, it's even possible for a woman to get behind the wheel of one of these beauties. Isn't that right my love?"

This is clearly not the first time Princess Eleonore has been subject to this particular witticism. Completely unmoved by the dukes mocking affront to the feminine capacity for learning, she dips her head and smiles sweetly. "Quite right, my dear. Quite right."

"Quite right." The duke roars again. "It's how you English might say a piece of cake. And Herr Benz has excelled himself with this new velocipede of his, and it's first of a kind static internal combustion engine delivering one point five horsepower, and a top speed of—"

While the duke prattles on about his automobiles, my mind wanders between my desire to interrupt and ask about the plan for my time in Munich, and my desire to bed his saucy young wife.

I'm imagining myself hitching her skirts and bending her over the table. The thought of casually ploughing her, whilst discussing the merits of one automobile over another with her husband causes an unintentional smile and a slight nod to myself.

"Good, I'm glad you agree," the duke says breaking the spell.

Unsure of what I might have missed, I nervously ask, "Um, sorry. Agree with what?"

To the side, Aunt Caroline frowns, but unperturbed the duke loudly huffs, "Agree that the work thus far by Benz on the internal combustion engine is far superior to your own Herr Daimler?"

I really wouldn't have the slightest clue, but keen to move on, I nod enthusiastically, "Oh yes, sir. Far far superior. And I must say, I would very much like to have a crack at driving one of your machines sometime?"

Before the duke can respond, Eleonore turns toward me and lightly touches my hand. Smiling sweetly, but hiding something more devilish, she turns back to the duke, "Why husband, I think your nephew is almost as excited to learn about the automobiles, as he was to ride in one."

"Is that so?" the duke booms quite innocently.

"Very much so." Eleonore smiles. "I think both he and his pretty young traveling companion enjoyed the ride in it very much. Isn't that right, Montague?"

I'm struggling to conceal my blushes, but I'm now more determined than ever to have this woman. And if I'm reading the room correctly, the duke himself is more interested in tinkering under the bonnet of his automobiles, then he is in tinkering under the skirts of his filly.

And if I'm right about this, which I think I am, the fragrant Eleonore must surely be in desperate need of a bloody good seeing to.

"And Monty old boy," I mutter to myself. "You are just the man for the job."

Confidently looking her in the eye, I smile and nod. "You are quite correct, Princess. And I'm looking forward to riding with you again soon."

Completely oblivious to the back-and-forth innuendo, the duke enthusiastically slaps a hand on the table. "Wonderful, that's agreed then. I shall have my personal secretary make a revision to your program to allow for some time to master the workings of the velocipede."

Pleased for the opening, I thank the duke before asking, "And while we are on the subject of my program, might I ask the plan for the next few days?"

Seeming to ignore the question, the duke instead tugs on a heavy gold chain to retrieve his pocket watch, before he loudly exclaims, "Good heavens, is that the time already? I have an appointment tomorrow in Berlin and must catch the early train."

Rising to his feet, he respectfully dips his head. "Lady Caroline, Montague, if you will excuse us, we will bid you a good night."

Then just to me, "I would suggest you also retire for the night, Nephew. You have an early start in the morning."

Before I'm able to enquire further, I'm quickly shut down by Aunt Caroline, "Monty, that is enough of your questions for this evening. The duke is weary and has an early start tomorrow."

Our hosts leave us, and I casually pass comment, "If one was the suspicious type, I might suspect you don't want me to know what the duke has in store for me?"

"Really, Monty?" Caroline tuts. "You are so dramatic at times. The duke was tired, nothing more. All will become apparent in the morning, anyway."

She takes a sip from her glass of champagne before adding, "Oh and if anyone ought to be suspicious, it ought to be me."

"Why so?" I ask, trying my best to sound innocent.

"Why so?" Caroline angrily exclaims. "I've told you before, Monty. Don't ever take me for a fool. Ernst may have been blind and deaf to your flirtations, but I most certainly was not."

Stunned by this sudden outburst, my spluttered apology is quickly quashed. "Enough, I don't want to hear it. And this is the last time I will warn you. Princess Eleonore is forbidden fruit. Mark my words, Monty, Ernst is not the kind of man you want as an enemy."

My aunt turns away, and for a moment there is an uneasy silence. Remembering something she said to me on the Orient Express, and feeling decidedly ungrateful for her unbending support, I reach for her hand. "I'm so sorry for upsetting you, Caroline, I really couldn't have made this journey without the benefit of your support and advice. I will be eternally grateful if you could find it in your heart to forgive, or overlook my lack of gratitude?"

"And you'll forget about any foolishness with the princess?" she asks hopefully.

"Yes," I assure her sincerely meaning it. "I will."

I may well be sincere, but I can't help but wonder if the princess will forget about any foolishness with me. Unlikely, I think to myself. But it won't be me that makes the first move.

"Then you are forgiven." Aunt Caroline smiles. Now let us finish our drinks and retire. I'm also now feeling somewhat drowsy."

* * * * * * * *

I'm midway through a rather naughty dream with a hand on my pecker when the curtains are thrown back, and the room floods with the first rays of the morning sun.

"On your feet." A gruff voice snarls in heavily accented English.

Squinting against the sunlight, I can barely make out the form of the figure standing beside the bed. "Who in God's name are you?" I croak. "And what the devil are you doing in my room?"

"I am Feldwebel Heinrich Meyer, and for the next two weeks I am going to be your worst nightmare," the voice sneers. "Now on your bloody feet, man."

Suddenly aware this is not a jape, I sit up and rub my eyes. "Sorry, Feld what?"

My tormentor is a good deal shorter than myself, but what he lacks in height he more than makes up for in bulk and menace. As stocky as a bulldog, his head has recently been shorn, and he has the crooked nose of a prize fighter.

He is however, immaculately attired in a pressed white linen shirt, and thick dark wool breeches with a thin red stripe down the sides that give him the distinct bearing of a lifelong military man.

"Feldwebel," he barks. "The equivalent of sergeant-major in your army."

Losing patience, he hurls a set of clothes onto the end of the bed. "You are to put these on, along with these boots. Your training begins in ten-minutes. I will be waiting for you in the courtyard. Do not keep me waiting any longer."

Still half-asleep and confused, I nervously stammer, "What is this? It can't be more than six in the—"

"You are wasting time." The bulldog impatiently scowls before cautioning again. "You have ten minutes and no longer."

He leaves, and I rub my eyes again, and mumble, "What in God's name was that little charade all about?"

"Well, there is only one way to find out," I think to myself. "I shall go and find out what the duke's lapdog has to say for himself. Whatever it is, he has another thing coming if he thinks a Finch-Morton so easily rattled."

I finish my ablutions, before dressing in the clothes left by the sergeant-major. They are identical to his own, and the ankle-high boots are made from thick black leather. The soles are studded with heavy cast iron rivets.

Decidedly unwieldily, I noisily clump down the polished timber staircase, and out into the courtyard. The bulldog is waiting with a silver stopwatch in his hand. Behind him three ranks of identically dressed young men are standing smartly to attention.

"You are forty-seven seconds late, Herr Finch-Morton. That won't do at all." He scowls. "And now you must be punished."

"What on earth are you talking about?" I bluster. "Don't you know I'm a guest – no, I'm the nephew of–"

"I know exactly who you are!" Meyer roars. "And until the grand duke deems otherwise, you are a cadet of the Baden Schloss military academy. You will therefore be subject to the same discipline and punishment as all other cadets. Now drop and give me thirty good push ups."

"I will not," I protest. "And quite frankly, I've had more than enough of this pantomime."

The burly NCO walks slowly toward me, and leans in. "Are you refusing to obey an order, Cadet Finch-Morton? Are you refusing to do push ups?"

Firmly believing myself untouchable, I look down on the man and arrogantly sneer, "I am, and if you will excuse me, there is a rather saucy dream I'd like to get back to."

I turn away, but am shocked to see Aunt Caroline, and the duke standing in the doorway. Both are dressed for travel, and behind them, one of the household staff is standing beside a trolley heavily laden with luggage.

"What the hell is this?" I ask slightly confused. "And will someone please tell this loathsome little lickspittle who I am?"

Aunt Caroline smiles, before slowly shaking her head. "Just do as the gentleman tells you, Monty darling. Ernst has invited me to join him in Berlin. All going well, we should be back in a week or two."

She has barely finished speaking before I'm grabbed from behind and roughly pushed to the floor. The leering sergeant-major kneels to snarl in my ear, "If thirty is not enough for you, I would be happy to make it forty."

Determined not to appear weak in front of my aunt or the duke, and resigned to my fate, I take a deep breath, and stretch myself out. The count has barely reached five before Aunt Caroline takes her leave. "Chin up, darling. And when things get a little tough, don't think too badly of me. Oh, and above all, don't forget you are a Finch-Morton."

My request to know exactly how long she will be gone goes unheard, and by the time I've completed my punishment, my aunt and the duke have long since departed.

The same pair of junior NCOs who previously pushed me down, now unceremoniously haul me to my feet in front of Sergeant Major Meyer, who looks me up and down before turning slyly to his colleagues. "The lad has hardly even broken a sweat. I think a spell with the tornister might do him good."

One of the NCOs disappears inside the house, before returning a few moments later with a heavy looking steel framed field grey backpack. Moving behind me, he places the straps across my shoulders which immediately sag under the weight of the wet sand filling the pack.

"Now!" Meyer roars. "Get fell in you – you – what was it you said? You snivelling little lick spittle!"

A vicious shove in the small of my back sends me sprawling toward the ranks of cadets. They move to allow me a place in the middle, and I've barely had time to gather my breath before Meyer barks, "Cadets will turn to the left. Left – turn. In columns of three – quick–march!"

One of the cadets at the head of the squad calls the timing, "Links, rechts, links, rechts, left, right, left–"

We have barely covered five hundred yards, and I'm already struggling under the weight of my load. The thin straps of the tornister cut viciously into my shoulders, and the boots on my feet might just as well be a couple of anvils.

If I wasn't sweating enough for Meyers liking before, I am now sweating like a stoker in a boiler room. Struggling to keep time, I once again incur the wrath of the demonic NCO. Forcing a path through the ranks, he screams in my ear, "Bloody well get yourself in step, Englishman!"

"Left, right, left, right., left, right." He continues to bawl until finally satisfied with my coordination, he returns to his place at the side of the column.

My relief at his departure however is sadly short-lived when the bulldog puffs up his chest and orders, "At my order, the column will double – double – march!"

Until now, I've barely managed to keep time, or keep up. With the increased speed, the extra weight on my shoulders, and my unfamiliarity with this routine, it will now be nigh on impossible. Barely two hundred yards further on, I find myself struggling badly and falling back.

The cadets directly behind, prod, and jab at the back of my pack – and not in an encouraging sort of way. The hushed comments are also less than complimentary, "Get a move on, English. You are making us look bad."

Some are downright aggressive. "Typical rich boy, no guts, and no bloody balls. He had better watch himself tonig–"

"Quiet!" Meyer screams. "Or you will all bloody suffer."

Continuing to struggle, I have almost fallen back to the rear of the column when there is another sudden change of tempo. At the blast of a whistle the cadets sprint away like hares in the direction of a nearby forest.

Wincing at the blisters I can feel growing on my heels, it is all I can do to limp after them and hope I can keep them in sight. Meyer orders one of his subordinates to stay with me. "Meet us in the clearing, and don't let him stop, or remove his load."

* * * * * * * *

It is two more excruciating miles before we finally reach the forest clearing. The cadets are arranged in a circle running on the spot, and most are now sweating heavily. All scowl aggressively and I strongly suspect I'm the reason they are being worked so hard. I'm so exhausted, however, the only wellbeing I'm interested in right now, is my own.

Trembling and lightheaded, I can barely stand let alone run on the spot. Mercifully, Meyer calls a halt and orders the cadets to sit. My escort moves behind me, removes my pack and hands me a canteen of cold water.

"Don't gulp it," he cautions. "You will give yourself cramps."

Ignoring him and throwing caution to the wind, I hungrily alternate between gulps of fresh air, and gulps of the cool water. I also wonder how quickly my fortunes have changed. Last night I was imagining myself rogering a princess. Today I would happily settle for a hot bath, and a cold pitcher of ale.

I'm still daydreaming when the canteen is roughly snatched from my hands. "That's enough," Meyer snarls. "And it's a long march back to the academy from here."

"The what?" I ask somewhat incredulous. "Aren't I going back to the lodge afterwar—"

A vicious backhand slap sends me sprawling backward. "You speak only when you are spoken to!" Meyer bawls. "You are not at Eton now, Herr Finch-Morton."

I'm only brought back to my senses when someone upends the remainder of the canteen over my face. When I open my eyes, two of the young cadets are expertly trading blows in the middle of our makeshift ring. After three minutes of relentless pummelling with neither man gaining the upper hand, Meyer blows his whistle. The young men remove their gloves and hand them to the next pair of fighters.

This routine continues until I am the only cadet yet to take a turn in the ring. Ordering me to my feet, Meyer sarcastically sneers, "It would appear we have an odd number of fighters."

Then playing up to his audience, "Do you think Cadet Finch-Morton might have any objection to sparring with an old war horse like me?"

The response is rousing and unanimous. To a man they are openly hostile and eager to see the toffy nosed Englishman take a pasting.

"Well," I think to myself. "If that's what they want, I have no intention of going down without one hell of a fight."

Gathering my reserves of strength, I take a deep breath, and pull on the heavy leather gloves. A grinning Meyer joins me in the ring, and raises his fists in a fighting stance, before suddenly seeming to think better of it.

Smiling he lowers his hands and slowly nods, "As a newcomer to this, I'm going to give you a free shot. That's only fair don't you think?"

Clearly this Germanic upstart doesn't know the first thing about me. Because if he did, he would know I have represented Eton at middleweight and am in fact quite an accomplished pugilist.

Thinking I might perhaps have the upper hand, I feign ignorance. "A free shot?"

"Yes, a free shot," Meyer repeats. "You may strike me, and I will make no attempt to move or defend myse—"

Reliant on the element of surprise, I clumsily lunge for the side of his head whilst the bruiser is still speaking. I have though underestimated the toll taken on my strength by the march in. My punch is weak, and the edge of my right glove barely connects with the bulldogs chiselled jaw.

Brushing it off as nothing more than a mild inconvenience, Meyer sarcastically chuckles. "Come now, is that the best you have, Englishman?"

Then, nimbly switching his weight from foot to foot, he drops his hands and taunts, "Again, Cadet Finch-Morton, another free shot."

Despite his offer, he easily avoids my next three lunges. On my fourth I find myself over reaching and unbalanced. I never see the uppercut to my ribs coming. But I feel it, and it lifts me from the floor. Meyer's second and third shots are to either side of my head. Already knocked senseless, the final blow is merely to make a point. My knees buckle under me, and I fall face first into the dirt.

I have no idea how long I am unconscious for. I only know that when I'm helped to my feet, the column has already reformed with Meyer at its head. Still faint, I'm led toward the rear of the column by the two junior NCO's who assume a position on either side of me.

Presumably, they are there to stop me from falling. Any thoughts I might have however, of a modicum of compassion, or an easing of my suffering are quickly dashed, when one of the NCO'S grins and lifts the tornister across my shoulders. "You don't want to forget this. It's a very long way if you must come back for it."

At the front of the column, I barely register Meyer's order to advance.

We march for I don't know how long, but by the time the Baden Schloss military academy comes into sight it is already getting dark. Located on the side of a hill with sweeping views of the valley below, it is an imposing late eighteenth-century castle, with typically high granite fortifications.

It is also surrounded by a deep moat, and the only way in or out is via a huge medieval timber-style drawbridge. Not that I was aware of any of these details at the time, of course. Without food or water, my final mile up the hill is nothing more than a delirious stumble.

Supported on either side by the junior NCOs, it is all I can do to place one foot in front of the other.

As we get closer, the column is finally called to a halt in front of the drawbridge which slowly lowers. Rather surreally, an officer mounted on a magnificent white stallion slowly clip clops across the bridge and comes to a halt in front of us. Resplendent in the uniform of a colonel of Hussars, and sporting a monocle in one eye, I stare upon my saviour and breathe an immense sigh of relief, "Your Excellency, it is I, Montague."

Although my throat is bone dry and my words are faint, I'm sure he must have heard me. But when there is no response, I painfully croak again, "Ernst, it is I, your nephew. Have you come to take me back to the lodge?"

The officer turns his steed and slowly trots toward me. "Is this him?" he asks dismissively pointing with his riding crop.

Meyer comes to attention and clicks his heels. "Jawohl, Herr Colonel. This is the Grand Duke's nephew."

The aristocratic colonel looks me up and down with barely concealed disgust, before he turns to scowl at the burly sergeant-major. "The man looks half dead, Meyer. You were instructed to train him, not kill him."

Shaking his head, he asks, "How much water did he have on the march back?"

Suddenly uncomfortable, Meyer nervously squirms. "Well, sir, his canteen was – I mean, it was already empty before the start of the march."

"Idiot!" the colonel angrily exclaims. "If this boy dies in your care, it will be you explaining yourself to the Grand Duke. Get him inside and have one of the other cadets assigned to looking after him."

Meyer nervously salutes. "Jawohl, Herr Colonel. Right away, sir."

He turns toward the column and calls us to attention. Behind him, the colonel tugs on the reins and steers his mount across the bridge and out of sight.

All the while, I've been deliriously mumbling to myself about hot baths, icy cold flagons of cider, and warm beds.

When Meyer gives the order to fall out, my escorts let go of my arms. Quite unable to support the weight of the tornister any longer, my legs buckle under me, and for the second time today, I crash to the ground like a sack of rocks.

Chapter Seven

Baden Schloss
Military Academy – 30th November 1898

"Is he still asleep?" someone asks. "You should wake him and make him eat something. He won't survive the day otherwise."

"That won't be any great loss. The man is a weakling," someone else sneers.

"Don't be an asshole, Von Werner. I'd like to see how you would have done hauling that tornister there and back."

"Yes, and with nothing to eat or drink all day," a new voice says.

I'm vaguely aware of a hand on my shoulder. "Hey, English, you must wake up and eat something. Come on, wake up."

I force open my eyes, and immediately close them again to block out the harsh light. "Hey, no more sleeping. Meyer will kick your arse if you are not ready for training today."

Squinting, I look up to the smiling face of a young man I recognise from yesterday's column. Politely nodding his head, he hands me a glass of water. "Good morning, Englishman. I hope you are feeling better?"

Parched, I gulp down the cold liquid, and splutter, "Where am I?"

"You really don't remember?" He frowns.

"No," I reply, shaking my head. "The last thing I remember was seeing the Grand Duke on his horse and—"

"That wasn't the Grand Duke." The young man laughs. "That was Colonel Von Strauss, the commandant of the academy."

Painfully lifting myself up in the bed, I blink again and try to take in my surroundings. Three other young men are standing close to the end of the bed. Others are busy in the dormitory dressing or are busy polishing equipment.

"So, this is—?"

"Yes." The young man nods offering his hand. "Welcome to Baden Schloss military academy. My name is Hofmann, and these fellows are Neumann, Schmitt, and Von Werner."

"Finch-Morton," I offer.

"Yes, yes we know." Hofmann laughs. "And you slept the entire night, so I expect you must be feeling better?"

"Yes, I think so. Thank you."

"Good, good." Hofmann nods before pointing to a tin cup and plate on a small footlocker at the end of my bed. "I've brought you some coffee, and breakfast. Finish that and then take a shower. Your uniform is hanging in the locker, and I have polished your boots."

I'm about to thank him when he stops me. "Save your gratitude, Englishman. This is the first and last time I do your work for you."

"Yes, I understand, but thank you anyway," I offer. "It is very kind."

My words somehow make Hofmann uncomfortable. Blushing slightly, he turns to leave, before he remembers something important and looks back. "Morning parade is as eight sharp. Do not be late. Oh, and eat all your breakfast. It's important you regain your strength."

* * * * * * * *

I push back the heavy grey woollen blanket and am suddenly aware I am wearing nothing more than a long cotton nightshirt. Somebody has also applied ointment and dressings to the blisters on my feet. I'm wondering if I can thank Hofmann for this when my stomach rumbles most horribly.

Remembering I haven't eaten for more than thirty-six hours, I turn hungrily toward the footlocker. The coffee is thick, black, cold, and bitter, but I slurp it down, anyway.

The breakfast is a huge hunk of dark pumpernickel bread, a wedge of cheese, and a good size piece of garlicky German sausage. To the very great amusement of the cadets watching from afar, I gobble down my meal like I've never eaten before. With each bite, I can feel myself getting stronger, and can almost feel the energy seeping into my muscles.

Feeling somewhat revitalised, I hobble toward the shower block, naively confident in the knowledge I can take whatever is thrown at me today.

The shower block itself is almost empty. Just two cadets are standing under the row of shower heads washing themselves. Two others are at the sinks completing their ablutions. None of them turn or acknowledge my presence when I join them.

Wiping condensation from one of the mirrors, I lean in to inspect the swellings on either side of my face. I vaguely recall the backhander and subsequent battering from Meyer, but thankfully the padded boxing gloves have saved me from any real damage. My injuries are superficial at best. In fact, it's my blistered feet that are more of a concern. If there is to be another forced march anytime soon, I will be in real trouble.

Painfully lifting the nightshirt over my head, I then stare into the mirror at the aching red welts on my shoulders. The memory of having to haul the tornister makes me shudder, and I resolve not to give Meyer any excuse or opportunity to punish me in such a way again.

Turning toward the shower heads, I maintain a respectful distance and step under the one furthest away from the other young men. I am hopeful the warm water might help ease my aches and pains; my hopes are woefully naïve.

Almost glacial, the water pricks at my skin like a million tiny icicles, and I lurch backwards and cry out, "What the Dickens!"

To my side the other bathers snigger, while one sarcastically passes comment, "Get used to it, rich boy. This is not your Buckingham Palace."

Determined not to lose face any more than I already have, I force myself back under the water and soap myself down as casually as I'm able.

The other cadets initially look on expecting a show, but with nothing more to see, they quickly lose interest and leave.

As soon as they are gone, I step out and hastily dry myself on my nightshirt, before returning to the barrack room to dress.

The uniform hanging in the locker comprises a lightweight blue woollen tunic and breeches. Both are adorned with fine scarlet piping and the tunic has a long line of polished brass buttons to the front. The black woollen visor cap has a simple red button where one might ordinarily expect to find some sort of insignia.

Most surprising however are the boots. The heavy studded monstrosities of the previous day have been replaced by soft soled leather marching boots. In the next bed space, Cadet Hoffman is quick to pick up on my confusion. "The other boots are Meyer's idea of a joke. But don't take it too personally, all the new boys get to wear them on their first march."

"And I suppose they all get to carry the tornister?" I ask hopefully.

"Oh, no." Hoffman chuckles. "That was a special privilege just for you, English. And unless you want that privilege again, you should get a move on."

I finish dressing, and after a quick once over by my new guardian angel, he deems me fit to join the rest of the cadets on parade. Just moments later, Sergeant-Major Meyer marches smartly into the centre of the square. Resplendent in a dress uniform adorned with a heavy row of medals and other regalia, he clicks his heels and calls the parade to attention.

Behind him a drummer beats a slow rhythm whilst two junior NCOs raise the academy flag. With the ceremony complete, Meyer begins his inspection. When he reaches me, my heart is almost in my mouth. Expecting some disparaging comment or abuse, I'm pleasantly surprised when he merely looks me up and down and nods before moving on.

I wonder if he might have been warned off, or if perhaps he is saving his wrath for the next forced march. Whatever it is, I'm grateful to have this small respite. As it later transpires, my respite from Meyer is to last almost another week.

With the inspection complete, the sergeant-major leaves and the junior NCOs spend the best part of the morning marching us up and down the parade ground. Although my German is still basic at best, by lunchtime I have almost mastered the art of marching in pairs, and as a squad.

Lunch is more of the same from breakfast, but the coffee is hot. The meal itself is eaten in silence on long heavy timber benches in the academy mess hall. The afternoon is then divided between tuition in fencing and military tactics, followed by dinner comprising a hearty stew of pork and potatoes. After that we spend the next three hours cleaning and polishing our kit before lights-out at nine pm.

And so, to my very great despair, this is my routine for the next week. Up at six am every day for ablutions, breakfast, and morning parade at eight, followed by a varying program of drill, musketry, horsemanship, fencing, physical training, and military tactics.

The routine is only broken on Sunday, by a trip to the chapel and an afternoon of light duties, before the week starts again on Monday.

Just after lights out that evening, I'm wondering how much longer I might be here when Hoffman sits up in his bed. "Oh, Finchy, I almost forgot to say, but no parade tomorrow morning. Tuesday is for the march and boxing in the forest. We start at seven."

Although I'm now almost fully recovered, this sudden knowledge leaves me feeling nauseous to the pit of my stomach. My subsequent sleep is fitful at best, and I'm haunted by dreams of lead boots and a tornister three or four times its actual size and weight.

When I wake the next morning, I'm soaked in sweat and exhausted. Forewarned that we won't be eating again until the evening, I dress for the march and force down as much breakfast as I can manage before I head out to join the others.

* * * * * * * * *

Although I'm sure I've arrived at the parade ground in good time, Meyer abruptly stops his stretching exercises, and barks at me to stand still. "Not so fast, Cadet Finch-Morton."

Reaching for his pocket watch, he deliberately takes his time to make me sweat. Even though I know I'm on time, it is still a great relief when he smirks and tells me to fall in. "Not there," he snarls. "Somewhere toward the front, so that you might have a chance to keep up this time."

A few of the cadets quietly snigger at the comment, but not as many as would have done a week ago. Taking this as a minor but important victory, I fall in and steel myself for the march ahead.

Ten minutes in, Meyer gives the order to double, but unlike the last march where I was heavily weighed down by the tornister and studded boots, this time around I feel as light as a feather and give a good account of myself. Well for the first three hours, anyway.

By that time, the constant friction of my boots has done a great job in reopening my previously healing blisters, and through no fault of my own, I slowly start to drop back. Inevitably when Meyer blows his whistle to signal the final sprint, I am once again left behind as my fellow cadet's sprint away toward the forest. This time however, I am left alone to fend for myself.

I finally reach the clearing a full ten minutes after my colleagues and am met by a grinning Sergeant-Major Meyer, "So glad you could join us, Cadet Finch-Morton. Did you enjoy your little stroll in the park?"

Wisely holding my tongue, I take my place amongst the cadets and watch on as the first pair do battle. Equally matched in size and skill, the match ends in a stalemate, and they retake their seats.

Fully expecting to be kept until the end again, I'm surprised when Meyer orders me into the makeshift ring. "Up you come Finch-Morton. And yes–um, Von Werner you to."

Now, if you remember well enough, Cadet Von Werner is the one that called me a weakling while I was still groggy after my first night in the academy. I have though got to know him a little during this last week, and the chap is actually a decent enough sort.

I do however also remember him from last week as a jolly good scrapper, and although I have a height advantage of at least four inches, I know I'm not going to have an easy time of it. He is also carrying at least twenty extra pounds, and none of it is fat.

Feeling fit, but slightly apprehensive, we tap gloves and Meyer blows his whistle. "And – fight."

For a moment we dance around, sizing each other up and looking for an opening. My first blow is as much a surprise to me as it is to my opponent. My right fist springs forward and catches him square on the nose. Although it snaps back his head, it doesn't appear to cause any real damage and Von Werner quickly counters with a left and right to my ribs.

It's here that his weight advantage makes the difference. Both blows knock the stuffing out of me, and my opponent is quick to press home his advantage. While I'm still gasping for air, he launches a flurry of precision jabs at my face and the sides of my head. Somehow though, I manage to stay on my feet. I even manage to get in a few more shots of my own before Meyer finally calls an end to the bout which he quite rightly calls in favour of Von Werner.

Before I sit back down, I'm surprised to hear Meyer offer something almost touching on respect. "Good effort, Finch-Morton. You may not be quite as useless as I thought."

The remainder of the bouts play out exactly as before, and after my blisters are redressed, I'm issued a full canteen of water and take my place in the column for the march back to the castle.

This time, I have the benefit of knowing exactly the distance we need to travel. Gritting my teeth all the way, I somehow manage to maintain my position in the column, and I make it back more or less in one piece.

More importantly, by the time we are ordered to fall out, I not only feel I've achieved something today, but I also feel I've started to earn the grudging respect of my fellow cadets, and perhaps even of Meyer himself.

Which is just as well, because almost another full week passes without word from Aunt Caroline, or any sign of my imminent return to civilization. Naturally by the morning of the next forced march my patience is wearing decidedly thin, and I angrily push my breakfast aside.

"Something on your mind?" Hofmann asks.

"Yes, you could bloody well say that." I scowl. "My damn blisters have only just started to properly heal again – and well, if I don't–"

Conscious of leaving myself open to ridicule, I cut short my words and instead reach for my coffee.

Curious, Hofmann leans in and asks, "What were you going to say, Finchy?"

"It was nothing." I shrug. "Forget I said anything."

Unconvinced, my friend shakes his head, "And is that nothing enough of a reason to put you off your breakfast?"

"Maybe not." Von Werner suddenly chuckles loudly, before playfully offering his clenched fists. "I think it might be the thought of going up against these sledgehammers again that has him quivering in his boots."

"Is that it?" another of the cadets asks mockingly. "Are you worried about getting another pasting from this ignorant little twerp?"

Whilst the cadets jokingly argue amongst themselves, I finish my coffee and wait for them to settle down before saying, "I was actually going to say, if I don't get out of here soon, I'm going to miss my birthday."

The table falls silent, and Hofmann quietly asks, "Really, when is it?"

"I'll be eighteen on the fourteenth," I reply. "And this is not how I imagined spending my eighteenth birthday."

"That is just two days from now," Von Werner mutters to himself.

"The man is a genius," Hofmann tuts. "Well done, Willie, did you work that out all by yourself?"

Noting my growing frustration, the young cadet tries to offer some words of encouragement. "I'm sure they can't keep you here much longer, and didn't your aunt say she would only be gone for a week or two?"

He's right of course, but how am I to know if she was telling the truth. For all I know, I might very well have been abandoned here as a hopeless case. For all I know, I might never see her, my mother, or my home again.

Wallowing in a deep pool of my own putrid self-pity, I fall in for the march, and silently curse the misfortunes that have brought me here.

I am in fact so deeply enthused in cursing Aunt Caroline and the duke for abandoning me to this misery that when the time comes for Meyer to blow his whistle, it takes a moment for me to register I'm still with the column.

I'm also feeling uncharacteristically good. I have however been caught off guard and am determined not to be left behind for a third time. Gritting my teeth, I dig in and hare away in pursuit of the others.

Somehow my steps are light and easy, and I soon find myself in the middle of the pack. Two weeks ago, that would have been a major victory, but today, that's just not good enough, and I'm desperate to give a good account of myself. Thankfully, just up ahead, I see exactly the inspiration I need.

Like the bullseye on a target, the back of the gorilla's shaven head spurs me on. Sucking in huge gulps of air, I lengthen my stride and kick for the forest clearing. I'm almost upon him, when suddenly alerted by my laboured breathing, Meyer casually glances over his shoulder.

Now caught off guard himself, it takes the burly NCO a moment to register what is happening. But when he does, the reaction is swift, unflinching, and typically characteristic.

Distracted by an encouraging smile, I don't see the elbow heading towards my ribs until I'm doubled over and gasping for breath. By the time I look back up, Meyer has long since disappeared and I curse myself for being so easily caught out. "You should have bloody well seen that coming, Monty old boy."

In the end I'm pleased to still be amongst the leading group to arrive in the clearing. And oddly enough when you consider my recent poor form, I'm also looking forward to the boxing today.

Although my last bout was tough, I feel it has given me enough of an insight into Von Werner's fighting style to exploit his weaknesses if we are drawn together again. Hoping for the opportunity to even the score, I'm left disappointed by the wily sergeant-major who has other ideas.

With three bouts already completed he turns and orders, "Hofmann, Finch-Morton, on your feet."

Our faces say it all, and Meyer sarcastically sneers, "What is wrong, ladies? You don't want to fight each other?"

Now, of all the cadets I could have been matched against, Hofmann is the last I would have wished for. Not because he is a gifted fighter.

Quite the opposite in fact, and I don't think he would mind me saying, there are freshers at Eton more skilled and aggressive than Klaus Hofmann. Which is also possibly the reason he was assigned to nursemaid me.

Meyer knows this only too well of course. He also knows we have become firm friends during the last two weeks. The sadistic NCO is no doubt looking forward to watching us beat the living hell out of each other.

Pulling our gloves together, he leans in and snarls, "If I think either of you pansy boys are taking it easy, you will suffer. Do you understand me?"

We both nod, and the slathering bulldog blasts his whistle. "Now fight!"

Hofmann lacks any kind of natural rhythm or balance, and his punches come with an advanced warning which makes it difficult not to dodge them. We do though put on a fair enough show for the first sixty-seconds, until unconvinced by our efforts Meyer screams, "Hit him, Hofmann. Hit the Englander swine!"

Nodding to him, that it's ok, I deliberately drop my guard to allow a couple of shots through to my face and chin. I follow up with a few convincing shots of my own. One of them is a little too convincing, and Hoffman stumbles backwards.

"Good," Meyer bellows. "Now follow up. Quickly, before he recovers."

My reaction is far too slow for the NCO's liking and allows time for my opponent to steady himself. Now incandescent with rage, everyone is taken by surprise with what Meyer does next. Stepping between us he turns toward Hofmann and screams, "If you won't fight each other like men, then you will fight me."

Poor Hofmann barely has time to register what's coming before he is battered unconscious. The snarling Meyer then turns toward me with murder in his eyes. His knuckles are slippery with blood, and from the side of the ring, Von Werner shouts just in time, "Get your guard up, Finchy."

The first blow hammers harmlessly into the side of my gloves. The second is not so harmless. Meyer buries his right knuckle deep into my ribs, and I lurch sidewards. Two more fast and furious blows rain down on the back of my head.

Miraculously, I somehow manage to remain standing, and although I have no intention of letting Meyer have it all his own way, I also resist the urge to jab wildly in the hope of a lucky hit.

Instead, I keep my guard up, and bide my time waiting for an opportunity to present itself. Meyer though, is an old pro, and when I feel myself starting to weaken, I revert to type and lunge for the side of his head.

Unlike my last fight with him, this time around my punches are far more effective. To his very great surprise, I land three fast and accurate punches, before a fourth opens a small cut above his right eye. Blood slowly trickles into the corner of his eyes, and confident the bout has swung in my favour, I batter away at the old bull trying to wear him down.

Meyer however is a veteran of many battles, and with vastly more experience and greater stamina, he easily absorbs my punches without any obvious sign of weakening.

If anything, the taste of his own blood makes him stronger and more aggressive. Dropping his guard, he looks up and sneers, "Is that the best you have, Englishman?"

He answers his own question by launching a renewed and more savage assault. Ungloved his fists power into my body like miniature sledgehammers, and although I know I'm being softened up for an inevitable uppercut, there is precious little I can do to stop it.

Just moments later, a huge fist slams upward into my chin. A hand on the back of my head appears to stop me from falling. It's there however, to steady me for the coup de grâce. I'm now on my knees and the grinning sergeant-major looks down and lifts my chin. "It's been a real pleasure knowing you, Finch-Morton."

Punch after vicious punch pounds into my face, and knocked senseless, I barely comprehend the voice of authority that stops the fight. "I said that's enough, Meyer. Get him cleaned up and the men ready to move."

I'm carried to the side of the ring and laid next to Hofmann who has thankfully regained consciousness. Although still groggy, he forces a smile and croaks, "Cheer up, Monty. It's over for—"

"It's what?" I gasp. "What do you mean?"

Before Hofmann can answer, Meyer blows on his whistle and angrily barks, "Get fell in you filthy animals!"

Behind him, Colonel Von Strauss looks on with obvious displeasure. "Really Feldwebel, is that kind of language absolutely necessary?"

Von Strauss and Meyer are clearly very different kind of men, but it's a source of comfort to know the academy commandant will be joining us on the return march.

"There is no way he will allow Meyer to finish me off," I console myself. "Or am I wrong?"

I help my companion to his feet, and we both shuffle painfully toward the column. Hofmann is ordered to the front, but I'm suddenly stopped by Meyer. "Not so fast, Cadet. Haven't you forgotten something?"

The sadistic bastard is no doubt referring to the tornister, but with very little else left to lose, I defiantly snipe, "No, Sergeant-Major, I don't believe I have."

Suddenly looking beaten, Meyer slowly shakes his head and with obvious regret, he orders, "Fall out, Herr Finch-Morton. You are dismissed."

Evidently confused, I stand for a moment unsure what to do next. In response, Meyer impatiently points a finger toward the woods. "Well, what are you waiting for? Go, before I change my mind."

It's only now I hear the gentle purr of the velocipedes internal combustion engine idling at the edge of the forest. Hardly able to comprehend, I slowly turn and see the duke dressed in his full driving ensemble.

Aunt Caroline is wrapped in a luxurious mink overcoat to protect against the winter chill. Her bonnet is securely fastened under her chin by a wide buttercup yellow silk ribbon, and her smile is as warm and inviting as a summer's day.

She gestures me over, and completely ignoring my glaringly obvious injuries, the duke helps me into the back seat. "Very good to see you again, Monty. It is good to see you have a healthy glow to your cheeks."

He affectionately pats me on the leg before adding, "Now just relax, and we will have you back to the lodge in no time."

My eyes burn into the back of Aunt Caroline's head, and although relieved to be rescued, I'm also seething at my abandonment. Seeming to read my mind, she turns and smiles. "I'm sure you must have a million questions about the last two weeks, Monty, but—"

"Yes, you could say that," I interrupt with a scowl.

"Yes, yes, I'm sure." She nods. "But you must be exhausted, and there will be time for questions after you have bathed and rested."

She turns away, and the duke steers his Motorwagen toward the lodge. A few minutes later we slow down to pass the column on the road ahead.

Spotting the duke, Meyer snaps his heels and smartly salutes. Behind him in the first rank, Hofmann also salutes. He also smiles, waves, and silently mouths the words, "Good luck, Finchy."

* * * * * * * *

As expected, back at the lodge a steaming hot bath and a saucy young ladies' maid are waiting for me in my room. Mindful of my injuries, Betsy carefully helps me out of my uniform and boots before assisting me into the bath.

Smiling sweetly, she starts to undress herself, before completely exhausted and out of character, I ask her, "Actually, would you mind awfully if we didn't just now? I'm really not up to it. I just need to rest."

My eyes close for a moment, and she nods sympathetically. "Yes, of course, sir. You should rest. You have a big day tomorrow and the day afterward."

"Oh really?" I ask straightening up. "What have you heard?"

Suddenly aware of her indiscretion, Betsy turns away slightly embarrassed and mumbles, "It's probably not my place to say, sir.

Reaching for her hand, I force a smile, "But you should say it, anyway. I promise not to tell."

Noticeably relieved, she pulls a chair close to the bath and takes a seat. "Well, sir," she says excitedly. "Tomorrow morning, you shall be having a driving lesson with the duke, and in the evening, there will be a hunt. All the duke's friends will be coming, and I heard it will be ever so exciting."

"Yes, I'm sure it will." I nod. "And what of the next day?"

Looking slightly incredulous, Betsy hesitates a moment before saying, "The next day is your eighteenth birthday, sir. I'm sure Lady Caroline and the duke will have something quite marvellous planned for you."

"Hmmm, I'm sure they will," I mutter under my breath. "A spell of hard labour in a diamond mine, perhaps. Or sold into slavery on a sugar cane plantation in the West Indies."

Deliberately overlooking my sarcasm, Betsy tenderly touches my hand. "I'm sure whatever it is, it will be for the best, sir. Your aunt is a very good woman and only has your best interests at heart."

"Yes, I'm sure you are right." I sleepily nod. My eyes close, and a moment later, I hear the bedroom door shut. I lay in the bath for another ten minutes, pondering Betsy's words, and what I'm intending to say to my aunt when I see her next. "What kind of woman abandons her nephew to the care of a sadist? Is that really the action of someone who has my best interests at heart?"

With my anger building, but too many questions whirring in my head to allow for rational thinking, I dry myself off and slump exhausted onto the bed. Face down in the pillow, I've barely taken a breath before I descend into a deep but fitful sleep.

* * * * * * * *

When I wake, it is already dark, and a lamp is burning at the side of the bed. Soft hands gently glide across the fading welts on my shoulders, and the faint odour of lavender oil invades my nostrils.

Unsure if I'm dreaming, I reach behind myself and mumble, "That is so nice, Betsy, but please let me sleep a little longer."

Firm full breasts squish into my back, and Caroline tenderly kisses the back of my neck and giggles. "Is that what you really want? Or would you like your aunt to help ease your suffering?"

Suddenly remembering the cause of that suffering, I angrily try to turn but am pushed back down, "I'm sure you think you have every right to be angry with me, Monty, but everything I do is to make you a better man."

"And that includes torturing me?" I moan. "Do you know I nearly died on that first march? That bloody madman Meyer—"

Firmly pushing me down again and working her oiled breasts into my aching shoulders, Caroline cuts me off with a soft purr in my ear. "That madman Meyer did a fine job toughening you up, is what he did. You may not think it now, but sometime soon you will thank me for that."

Her hands roll across my biceps, and she purrs again. "And these muscles have grown quite nicely while you've been gone."

My resolve weakens as quickly as my anger dissipates under her magical touch. Still tired, I give up the fight, relax and petulantly mumble, "Yes, well, only time will tell, won't it?"

Knowing I'm already beaten, Caroline smiles knowingly to herself. "Yes, I'm sure it will Monty. Now turn over, lay still, and save your strength."

I slowly turn, and her eyes sparkle like diamonds, as the glistening oil covered beauty looks hungrily upon my throbbing appendage. "My my." She drools. "And It isn't just your biceps that have grown."

Reaching for my orbs she gently squeezes and weighs them up, before grinning. "Oooh, and I think my nephew has a fine load saved up for me. Or am I wrong?"

Without waiting for an answer, she reaches for the bottle of lavender oil and works a generous splash into my shaft. Her hands are somehow soft, gentle, and firm all at the same time.

Sensing my impending climax, Caroline lays down and orders me onto my knees. "On my breasts and in my mouth. Come on, quickly before it is wasted."

With one hand expertly squeezing my sack, the other milks me like a prize heifer. Hungry for my seed, Caroline opens her mouth in drooling and salacious anticipation. Although desperate to ride and unload inside her, I'm also bewitched by my whore of an aunt, and the rise and fall of her delicious breasts.

Pondering how it is possible for her to be so beautiful and elegant, yet so wickedly dirty at the same time, my breath quickens, and I grunt, "Oh, good God almighty!"

It's been a very long time since I went this long without some form of relief, and my climax breaks like a tidal wave crashing against the shore. My gentleman's relish spurts out of control across Aunt Caroline's breasts. It also easily fills her mouth, and quite unable to swallow it all, she allows the excess to spill down her chin.

She doesn't however intend to waste a drop. Before it can fall any further, she expertly gathers the escaping semen onto her fingers, and pops them into her mouth to suck them dry.

She then pushes me onto my back, and gently milks me for any remaining drops of my essence. She pulls back my foreskin and rolling her tongue around the throbbing head of my rod, she darts her tongue in and out of the eye, until finally satisfied there is nothing more to be had.

Lying down beside me she wipes her lips with the back of her hand, before kissing my cheek and smiling. "Everything I do, and every decision I make is to make you a better man, Monty. You will thank me for it, I promise you."

Still quivering with pleasure, I nestle my head into her shoulder and plant a kiss on her breast. "I'm sure I will." I nod slowly. Then closing my eyes, I allow myself a satisfied smirk. "But only time will tell."

I'm asleep again, almost before I've said the words, and Aunt Caroline extinguishes the lamp. "Sleep well, my handsome delicious young man."

Chapter Eight

The Velocipede
& The Hunt – 13 December 1898

I sleep soundly for the rest of the night and wake the following morning to the sound of someone opening the curtains. A brand-new set of driving clothes and boots identical to those worn by the duke have been laid out on the end of the bed, and Johnathan politely informs me I am expected for a light breakfast before my lesson.

After a quick wash up, the young valet helps me on with the boots, before handing me a flat cap. "I believe the duke has gauntlets and driving goggles for you, sir. Good luck with your lesson."

Johnathan takes his leave, and I'm suddenly apprehensive about meeting the duke again. Last night has somewhat cleared the air with Aunt Caroline, but I'm yet to get an explanation from our host. I nervously make my way down to the dining room, where I'm surprised to find my aunt dining alone.

Carefully putting down her coffee cup, she looks up and smiles. "Good morning, darling. Did you sleep well?"

"Um, yes. I did, thank you. Will the duke be joining us for breakfast?"

"The duke has business in Berlin again," she says. "Sit down and eat. You must be famished."

I am, but I'm also annoyed, and make no effort to hide it. "Well that's just typical of these bloody foreigners. The duke plans a driving lesson for me, then he swans off to Berlin, leaving me here, all dressed up and nowhere to go."

I don't notice the newcomer enter the room until she speaks. "Oh, I wouldn't quite say that, Montague."

The princess is dressed from head to toe in a rather fetching black leather one-piece driving suit. Her long hair is tied back in a tight bun, and there is a white silken scarf draped elegantly across her shoulders. Her face is subtly made up, and smiling sweetly she touches my arm and asks, "Am I a disappointment to you?"

I'm burning up with embarrassment and can barely bluster a response before Eleonore giggles and tells me to sit down. "I'm just teasing you. Now do as Lady Caroline tells you. It's a long time until lunch, and I'm as hard a taskmaster as the duke."

I'm wondering if there might be a hidden meaning in her words, but mindful of the earlier warnings about playing with fire, I shrug off the thought and eat my breakfast in silence. The princess nibbles daintily on a small piece of toast over polite conversation with my aunt.

She does though appear preoccupied and keen to get on with my lesson. As soon as I put down my cutlery, she gets to her feet and asks, "Are you ready, Montague? Only I think it might rain later. We should probably get going."

The question hardly needs asking, and the princess is already halfway through the door as I get to my feet. Conscious that my eyes have been following the magnificent contours of her buttocks encased in the shiny leather rather too closely, I blush again, and Aunt Caroline loudly tuts, "You will do well to remember who she is, Monty. And to remember it's a driving lesson, and nothing more. Is that understood?"

"It is," I mumble unconvincingly. "It's just a driving lesson, and nothing more."

I'm about to climb into the passenger seat when the princess coughs politely, and hands me a dark cast iron crank, "You're not strictly a passenger today, Montague, and before you can learn how to drive, you first need to learn how to start this thing."

I stand for a moment, looking rather clueless before Eleonore points toward the front chassis. "Push the long end into there, and give it a couple of turns to start the internal combustion engine."

My first attempt is a miserable failure, and I'm taken by surprise at the strength required to turn the crank. Undeterred, I lean in and take a deep breath before spinning the crank for a second time. A loud pop precedes a puff of smoke from the exhaust, and my efforts are rewarded with a soft purr from the engine as it splutters to life.

The smiling princess nods her appreciation and offers a hand to help me up. "That usually takes me at least three or four attempts. It would appear, though, that you are a natural."

I'm desperately trying to heed the warnings from my aunt, but I can't help but feel this beautiful woman is flirting with me. Matters are not made any easier by her insistence, I sit closer. "Come come, it's a sunny morning, but there is still a chill in the air."

I awkwardly shuffle closer, and the princess reaches across to tuck one side of a thick woollen blanket under my legs. The side of her neck is so close, I can smell the freshness of her cologne, and it is all I can do to stop myself from leaning closer and inhaling loudly.

Thankfully, my blushes go unnoticed, as the princess straightens up and smiles. "Are you comfortable?"

"Thank you, yes. Very comfortable." I nod.

The princess's gloved left hand playfully squeezes my upper thigh. "Good, because there is nothing to it, really."

Pointing to several levers and the wheel she says, "That one is the hand brake, the pedal on the floor is the accelerator, and this is the steering wheel. It's a double pivot system. Any questions?"

I'm stunned there isn't more to it, and I ask, "That's it?"

My question elicits a smile that could melt the heart of the hardest of men, and Eleonore cheekily raises an eyebrow. "That's all the likes of you and I need to know. The mechanics look after everything else."

She then thinks for a moment before adding, "Oh, but Ernst did tell me Herr Benz is currently working on a system for something he calls gear ratios. I do though find the technical details all rather tiresome."

This time, the hand on my thigh lingers a moment longer than strictly necessary, and the words and smile are a definite test of my resolve. "I'm happy just to drive the thing, or to ride with good company. What about you, Montague?"

There is something of a glint in the princess's eye, and she is definitely weighing my reaction. Determined not to be the one to break, I clear my throat, and stammer, "Um, quite right, Princess. Let's leave the technical stuff to the mechanics and to—"

I stop myself mid-sentence and Eleonore prompts, "It's okay. You can say it, Monty." She giggles. "My husband is rather a bore. But then I suspect you knew that already."

Her hand squeezes my thigh for a third time, and this time there is no meaningful attempt to hide the intent in her words. "Thankfully for you, I am not. And I rather think you are going to enjoy today's lesson."

I'm now burning up, but not with embarrassment. If my suspicions are correct, I'm going to be ploughing this Germanic beauty sometime soon, and I shuffle awkwardly in my seat to hide my rapidly swelling manhood.

The smiling princess nods knowingly and gestures to my side. "Give that a tug, and we can get going."

"Um, I'm sorry. Give what a tug?" I nervously stutter.

"The handbrake," she says giggling again. "Pull on that lever to release the brakes."

I release the lever, and the princess lightly pushes down on the accelerator. "Now remember, there really is nothing to it. I'll drive out, and you can drive us back."

* * * * * * * *

We drive for almost an hour and despite the princess's earlier expectation of rain, the sky remains clear and uncharacteristically sunny for the time of year. I'm also kept warm by the nearness of the princess's leather clad body, and perhaps the prospect of an imminent rutting.

Conversation however is kept to a minimum due to the noise of the engine, and I'm unsure how much longer we will be driving. Just a few minutes later I get my answer, when the princess steers the velocipede off the road and down a forest track toward a shimmering blue lake.

We park beside a small lodge at the lakeside, where Eleonore climbs down to shut off the engine. Taking this as my cue, I join her and ask, "What is this place?"

"Just a place I like to come to for some peace and quiet," she replies removing her gloves, cap, and goggles.

I hadn't noticed before, but her eyes are now ringed panda like with fine dark circles from the velocipedes exhaust. I point this out, and the princess nods and smiles. "We are a matching pair. Come, we can wash up inside."

Thinking the lodge unoccupied, I'm surprised when the door opens as we approach. A middle-aged man I recognize as a stable hand from the duke's hunting lodge welcomes us inside and shows us into a drawing room. A fire is burning in the hearth and bowls of warm water and towels are set out on the table.

"Will there be anything else?" the servant asks.

"No, you can leave us," the princess replies. "Oh, and Hans, make sure we are not disturbed."

The servant nods respectfully, before taking his leave. "Very good, m'lady. As you wish." The door closes, and Eleonore crosses the room to fumble with the buttons on my driving jacket. "Let me help you with those, they can be quite tricky sometimes."

Taken aback, I blush slightly and look toward the door. "What if?"

"Oh, don't worry about, Hans." Eleonore laughs. "He is the model of discretion when it comes to me. And besides, what do you think we are doing here?"

Feeling rather foolish, I'm still apologising when she helps me off with my jacket, and smirks before handing me a towel. "You look like a chimney sweep, and I don't fuck chimney sweeps. Here take this and clean yourself up."

Now caught between my promise to Caroline and the dull ache of desire in my loins, I wash my face barely able to concentrate on the job at hand. Beside me, the princess has lowered her driving suit to her waist, and her breasts now hang heavy in a thin linen blouse as she leans over to wash her face. I wonder if she can also see the erection throbbing in my breeches.

We both finish and turn to face each other in silence, before the princess frowns. "You look a tad frightened, Monty. Don't you want to plough me?"

"Um, well, it's not that. It's more to do with—"

"It's okay. I understand. You prefer rooting Lady Caroline's lady's maid?" she playfully suggests.

"No, not at all." I chuckle, shaking my head. "I've actually been dreaming about this since the moment I first met you. It's just, well I've made a promise to my aunt, and I'm a little worried about—"

"About what my husband will do to you, if he finds out." Eleonore sneers before pointing to my face. "Look in the mirror, and ask yourself who is responsible for those bruises?"

Moving closer she tenderly brushes a hand across one of my bruised cheeks. "I expect Lady Caroline told you it was for the best. She did, didn't she? And don't you want to punish my husband for what he has put you through?"

I do want to punish him, but in a quandary, I remain silent and the princess places one of my hands across her breasts. "Punish my husband, Montague. Punish him, by punishing me."

Before I can react, she suddenly tears open her blouse and her heaving breasts spill out from under the flimsy material. Abandoning all pretence, I allow her to lead me toward what looks like a storeroom.

Inside, I'm shocked to see heavy iron rings and a system of pulleys hanging from the ceiling. More iron rings are fixed firmly into the stone floor.

And we are not alone. Hans has been waiting here patiently for his mistress. He now helps her strip completely naked, and quite unsure of exactly what I'm seeing, I watch in spellbound silence as the manservant expertly trusses her wrists and ankles to the iron rings.

Before he leaves, he pulls down on one of the pulleys to stretch his mistress toward the ceiling. A second pulley tugs on her ankles leaving her cunny wide open and wickedly exposed.

Eleonore waits for the door to close before ordering me in front of her. "And take off your shirt, this is going to be warm work."

Her skin is as smooth as silk. Her vaginal mound is luxuriantly topped with a thick down of dark black hair. For not the first time, I stare open-mouthed and drooling at this vision of erotic beauty.

"Try not to look quite so shocked," the princess says. "Would you believe me if I said I got a taste for this in London?"

"Unlikely." I laugh. "This is not how women of noble birth behave in London, Princess."

"Oh, you would be surprised." Eleonore grins. "There are some interesting private members clubs in Soho."

I am of course aware of the reputation of Soho, but have yet to be introduced to its delights, and still unsure what is about to happen, I nervously ask, "And what exactly is – *this?*"

The princess gestures to a riding crop on a table in the corner of the room. "It's exactly what I said it is. It's punishment for what my husband has done to you. First, you are going to interfere with me. Then you are going to thrash me until I bleed. Then you are going to ride me without mercy."

Although something is decidedly odd about all this, I'm not sure I have ever been quite as turned on as I am right now. Brushing aside any remaining misgivings, I kiss the side of her neck and whisper, "Just tell me if you want me to stop, or if it gets to be too much?"

I then roughly thrust two fingers deep inside her.

Her response is to snarl and thrust her hips forward to bury my fingers to the knuckle, "I said punish me, you English bastard."

I don't need any further encouragement. I pull on the back of her hair and smash my knuckles against her sopping wet and now engorged lips. Three times I bring her to the brink of climax, and three times I pull away, and throw cold water over her to dampen her ardour.

Each time she begs me to continue. On the third occasion, I slap her face and scream, "Beg harder, you filthy trollop!"

I'm so aroused myself, it's hard to concentrate on inflicting humiliation without allowing myself a little satisfaction of my own. I soon find a compromise and loosen the pulley securing Eleonore's wrists.

I lower her down so that her head is now at waist height. I then lower my breeches so that my maypole is standing rigid just inches from her face.

Wrenching painfully on her hair, I order, "Open your mouth, slut!"

My slave obediently does as she is told, and I thrust forward until my rod is pressing against the back of her throat. Saliva drools from the sides of her mouth and froths up, as I gently plough her mouth and gradually build my speed and intensity.

Now beautifully lubricated with her spittle, I take a twisted delight at the sound of her gagging each time I bury my tool deep inside her noble throat.

"That's it, take it all you filthy whore."

Close to blowing my load, I pull out and unceremoniously wipe my precum across her cheeks. Her eyes now have the look of the devil, and she begs, "Now lift me back up, and thrash me."

I'm slightly hesitant and she angrily orders again, "Pick up the riding crop and thrash my behind you maggot."

Her taunt is deliberate and designed to elicit a reaction. I haul up my breeches, and roughly wrench on the pulley causing Eleonore to scream out as the ropes tear at her wrists and ankles. Ignoring her moan's, I reach for the riding crop and step behind her.

Her ass and back, although smooth and creamy, also bear the faint tell-tale marks that I'm not the first to treat her in such a way. Slightly reassured she can handle it, I raise my arm and bring the crop down across her shoulders.

"Harder," she hisses. "I thought you were a man?"

I strike her again, but this time much harder. A vicious red welt forms between her shoulder blades, and she whimpers pitifully, "Yes, harder. I must be punished."

I work my way methodically down her back, each time striking harder than the last, until I reach the top of her plump buttocks. They are so deliciously beautiful, I'm a little sad to be inflicting pain upon them. But I know this is what she wants.

Taking a deep breath, I slash away until the first spots of blood appear, and the princess finally screams for me to stop, "No, no more please, I beg of you."

I'm already perspiring heavily, so am pleased she has had enough. I gladly drop the riding crop, before reaching over her shoulder to loosen the pulleys.

"No." Eleonore moans. "Leave them. We are not done yet, and your honour is not yet restored. You must have me."

It's what I have wanted all along of course, but the princess is now bloodied and somewhat pitiful. She repeats her plea, and although unsure of myself, I am also still hard as a rock.

I mull my dilemma for just a second, before muttering to myself, "Oh, well. Carpe diem. Seize the day, Monty old man."

Biting the bullet, I pull my bloated phallus from the top of my breeches and reach around with my other hand to open her up.

"No, not there," she simpers quietly. "You must punish me properly."

Confused, I lean in closer, "Um, I'm not quite sure what you mean?"

Tilting her head back, the princess's cheek presses against mine and she whispers, "I want you to bugger me, Monty."

Completely taken by surprise, I almost choke on my words, "I'm— um I'm, you want what?"

"I want you to plough my asshole!" the princess demands with growing insistence. "Do it now, or my husband shall hear about how you forced yourself upon me."

My fingers are sticky with Eleonore's juices, and angered by her threat, I roughly jam an index finger deep into her rectum, and bite down on her neck, "Is this what you want, whore? Is this good?"

"Oh god, yes." She moans. "Oh god, that is so good."

Without waiting for any further invitation, I line up the head of my tool at the puckered entrance to her ass and push forward. It's tighter than any cunny I've experienced thus far, but inch by inch it gradually envelopes my meat like a well-fitting glove.

Completely at my mercy, Eleonore pushes back and clenches her muscles. "Now rut me like a common tart, Monty. Rut me and reclaim your honour."

Not one to disappoint a lady, I reach around to tug hard on her engorged and distended nipples, whilst I aggressively smash my hips repeatedly into her ass cheeks. By the time I'm ready to cum, we are both a bloody mess and dripping with sweat.

Eleonore is panting heavily, but whether she is close to her own climax is of no concern of mine under these circumstances.

All I'm interested in now is inflicting one final humiliation on the duke's wife, and therefore by extension on the duke himself.

Gripping tightly to her hips, to stop her pulling away, I make my final thrusts, before I loudly grunt and unload my semen deep inside her asshole. My knees trembling, I pull out and look upon my handiwork with more than a little satisfaction.

My creamy seed dribbles from her regal hole, and plops unceremoniously onto the stone floor. The princess herself is bathed in sweat and trembling uncontrollably. When I untie her bonds, she almost falls into my arms, and it takes a moment for her to steady herself.

She is however smiling, and I can't help wondering if she did in fact climax. It was rather hard to tell amongst all the blood, sweat and screaming.

Now steady again, she hands me my shirt and almost businesslike points to the door, "You should go and clean up again. Hans will help me to get dressed."

Right on cue, the door opens, and Hans comes in carrying a bowl of warm water and fresh towels. The door is left open as a subtle invitation, and I leave to find my jacket in the drawing room. When the princess hasn't made an appearance after ten minutes, I step outside for some fresh air.

She eventually joins me after another fifteen minutes, looking completely unflustered by her recent ordeal. Other than a very slight mark on her cheek, she looks as fresh as a daisy, and smiling she casually offers me a cigarette.

"I do enjoy a puff after a good ride." She grins cheekily. "Here, take one?"

We smoke our cigarettes in silence beside the velocipede, before Eleonore stubs the remainder of hers out and passes me the crank. "Will you do the honours please?"

She then smirks and adds, "If you still have the strength, of course?"

"More than enough." I laugh. "Stand back and watch a man at work."

Despite my boast, it does in fact take half a dozen cranks before the engine fires and splutters to life. Looking slightly sheepish I help the princess into her seat before I take my own.

Now approaching midday, the sky is still cloudless and sunny when I pull on my gauntlets and innocently comment, "I think you were wrong about that rain, princess."

"Maybe so," she says nodding slowly. She then mischievously raises an eyebrow. "But all the same, I did get rather wet, didn't I? Shall we go?"

* * * * * * * *

We arrive back at the duke's lodge just in time to join Aunt Caroline for a light luncheon and drinks on the terrace. Conversation is polite and cordial, but I can sense a growing undercurrent of frustration and impatience from my aunt. As expected, her inquisition begins the moment the princess excuses herself and is out of earshot.

"Well?" Caroline demands. "What really happened? And don't give me any—"

"I really don't know what you mean." I cut in with a shrug. "It was as the princess said. She was trying to start the motor when the crank—"

"Yes, yes, it hit her on the cheek," Caroline interrupts clearly unconvinced, before sarcastically adding, "She was very lucky it didn't do her more damage."

I know perfectly well what she means, but I feign indignation and ask, "Meaning what exactly?"

"Meaning — it looks more like the result of a slap. Which is exactly the kind of kink these continental royals enjoy. Oh, and don't come all innocent with me, Montague Finch-Morton the Third. You've turned into a randy little bastard, and it's patently obvious you've been wanting to plough Eleonore since we first got here."

I slowly nod my concurrence. "Yes, well, you're right, of course. But ask yourself — whose fault is it that I've turned into a randy little bastard?"

"That is beside the point," Caroline snaps. "I warned you more than once the princess was off limits."

"And so, she is." I nod sympathetically. "And so, she is."

Then safe in the knowledge I'm not exactly lying to her, I reach for my aunt's hand. "You have my word on it. I did not plough the princess's cunny."

Clearly more interested in getting to the truth, Aunt Caroline uncharacteristically chooses to overlook my use of vulgarity at the table, and instead emotionally implores, "Swear on it, Monty. Swear it on your mother's life."

Doing my best to reassure her, I tenderly squeeze her hand and smile. "I swear on my mother's life. I did not plough that woman's cunny."

Still somewhat sceptical, Caroline straightens up and pulls her hand away. "So, you're telling me, all you did for more than three hours was drive that Motorwagen?"

"That's it." I nod. "We were having so much fun, the time just got away from us. In fact, we would have driven for longer if we hadn't been running short of fuel."

Now seemingly assured, a half-smile appears on her face, and Caroline quietly says, "That's good, because Princess Eleonore can be quite the blabbermouth, and I would so hate for there to be any tension during our last couple of days here."

I'm still trying to digest that last statement and am deep within my own thoughts when my aunt suddenly excuses herself from the table.

More than a little disturbed by the possibility for repercussions, I'm thinking to myself, "Surely the princess wouldn't be so foolish or indiscrete?"

Noting my distraction, Caroline lightly touches my shoulder. "I said, I'm going up to my room to rest and freshen up before this evening. You should do the same."

"Yes, of course." I nod. "I'll be along shortly."

"Good." She smiles. "The hunting party will assemble in the drawing room at six this evening. Rest well, darling."

* * * * * * * *

The black leather riding boots provided by the duke are a little on the tight side, but everything else fits perfectly. Once fully dressed, I take a moment to admire myself in front of a full-length mirror. Pleased with the overall look I turn toward Johnathan. "Do you know if this is what everyone else will be wearing this evening?"

My outfit comprises a pair of white breeches, a scarlet jacket, a dark green felt cap, and a billowy white cashmere scarf. Although the young valet looks me up and down with obvious appreciation, he also shakes his head. "I'm not sure, but you do look very much the dashing huntsman, sir."

"Yes, yes, I do," I concur. "Thank you, Johnathan, that will be all."

I give myself a final once over, before picking up my riding crop and opening the bedroom door. The hubbub from downstairs is evident even before I reach the top of the stairs.

In the drawing room itself, I'm a little surprised to find I'm one of the last to arrive, and that the room is filled with more than a dozen other huntsman and their female companions all chattering away.

In the corner of the room a gramophone is playing something typically Germanic and operatic. I find out later, it is The Ride of the Valkyries, by the German composer Richard Wagner.

None of my fellow huntsmen are dressed in scarlet but all are wearing brightly coloured jackets in various colours and shades. Otherwise, they are all similarly dressed to myself.

The women, including my aunt, are luxuriously garbed in magnificent ballgowns, and are heavily bedecked in obscene amounts of opulent jewellery.

The one notable exception to this is Princess Eleonore herself.

The princess is fully outfitted to participate in the hunt and is standing proudly beside the duke. Noting my arrival, the duke beckons me to join them before he calls to a servant, "Quickly, a large schnapps for my nephew."

The rest of the nobles quickly gather round for the pre-hunt toast. It is given mostly in German, but I understand enough to know I was mentioned in the context of wishing me success on my first hunt in Germany.

Momentarily forgetting my earlier concerns, I casually glance over to Eleonore and wickedly think to myself, "Actually, Duke. I rather think I've had a little success in that direction already."

The toast quickly dies down, and I turn to our host. "Your Grace, may I ask what exactly we will be hunting this evening? Only I haven't yet been told if it's to be a fox or a stag?"

The duke and several of the other guest's guffaw with laughter at my comment, before he turns to his trophy wall and points to a magnificent boar's head. "This is tonight's quarry, Montague. The Eurasian wild boar."

The huge skull mounted on a dark wooden shield is at least three times the size of my own and is set off by a fearsome set of tusks perhaps seven or eight inches long.

"One of the offspring of this specimen has been terrorising the local farmers for the last five years," the duke says. "It's a beast of a creature, at least five feet long from snout to tail, and perhaps two-hundred and fifty pounds in weight."

"Or more," the princess says.

"Easily more," another of the guests suggests. "I've seen the beast myself, and I'd say it's well over three hundred pounds." Then pointing to the trophy wall, the hunter adds, "It's at least four feet tall, and its tusks make those look small by comparison."

I'm wondering if the duke and his companions might perhaps be exaggerating the beast's dimensions in the hope of scaring me.

I'm still no nearer to getting a definitive answer when one of the servants sounds a brass gong, and the duke puffs his chest to loudly announce, "Gentlemen, if you would all assemble in the courtyard, please."

We all duly oblige and follow the duke to where the stable hands are waiting with the horses and our weapons. Fully expecting to be given a hunting rifle, I'm a little taken aback when the duke himself hands me a long steel-tipped spear, and a short stabbing cutlass.

"Don't look so surprised, Nephew. We're a little more sporting here in Germany." Then pointing to the tip of the spear, "You've heard of pig-sticking, I presume? Well, this is what we stick it with." He chuckles.

"It's unlikely you will be on your own when we flush it out, anyway. But if you are, you need to finish it off quickly with your cutlass."

The duke then leans towards me and cautions with unusual emphasis, "A wounded boar will fight like *buggery* to free itself. If you know what I mean, Montague?"

He doesn't wait for a response. Instead, the duke leaves me to select his own weapon, whilst one of the grooms helps me into my saddle. The other huntsmen are mounted on fine sturdy looking steeds ideally suited for a prolonged hunt over rough terrain.

My horse, by comparison, is wiry to the point of being skinny. It is also at least four hands shorter than the others, and I wonder if somebody might be making a joke at my expense. Brushing aside my annoyance, I search for Caroline amongst the throng of women assembled to see us off.

At first glance, she looks a little upset and preoccupied, but as I approach, her frown quickly turns to a smile, and she tucks a white silk handkerchief into the top of one of my boots.

"For luck, and to keep you safe." She smiles. "God speed, and good hunting, Monty." Then suddenly a little forlorn again, "Go safe, my darling boy."

Before I'm able to enquire the source of her concern, two sharp blasts on a horn signal the start of the hunt, and Aunt Caroline turns toward the house. I watch her out of sight, before I turn my horse and follow the other riders.

The first twenty minutes are an easy trot across a series of open fields, followed by a gentle canter as we get closer to the forest. Despite my earlier misgivings, my mount gives a good account of itself. We reach the edge of the forest in one group just as the sun finally drops below the skyline and are met by half a dozen of the duke's estate workers.

Each man is holding tightly to a thick brown leather leash restraining a huge snarling mastiff. The duke briefly speaks to his men before he gathers us together. When he speaks, he can barely contain his excitement. "My men inform me the dogs have picked up the scent, so we should now split into two groups."

I'm placed in a group with the princess, and the duke instructs her, "Take your hunters to the far side of the forest. When you get there, blast once on your horn, and we shall drive the beast towards you."

Then to me, "Do as my wife tells you, Nephew. She is an experienced boar hunter."

The princess leads us toward the left flank of the forest, and we move painfully slowly so as not to alert the boar to our presence. By the time we reach our final position, I am thankful for the light of a full moon in the otherwise now pitch-black forest.

"Spread out. Fifty feet apart," the princess orders. "Montague, move to the middle of the line, and be ready. If it comes, it will be coming fast."

The forest is so thick, I soon lose sight of the riders to my left and right. Thankfully a comforting blast on the horn close by reminds me I am not alone. And then we play the waiting game. For what seems like an eternity, all I can hear is the sound of my own breathing, and the occasional dull thud of an ironclad hoof on the forest floor.

But then, slowly but surely, the silence is gradually disturbed by the unmistakable sound of dogs, and the toot of distant horns carried effortlessly on the crisp night air. Suddenly feeling alert but vulnerable, the hairs rise on the back of my neck, and my senses come alive for any sign, or sound of danger ahead.

The first real indicator comes from my mount. Suddenly skittish, it whinny's and shuffles nervously forcing me to rein it in. "Steady girl. What is it? Do you hear something?"

Although faint, something is definitely now moving towards us at speed. Squinting to focus my eyes, I'm struggling to understand if it is a boar, a dog, or a horse. My question is answered in dramatic fashion when suddenly, a huge snarling beast crashes through a thicket of young saplings to my front.

Barely thirty feet away, the boar is even larger than was described. More frighteningly, all four hundred pounds of it is now barrelling towards me at nearly fifteen miles per hour. Almost dumb struck with fear, I fumble with the heavy spear. At the same time, I struggle to hold my panicked mount in position.

Now just a few feet away, the terrified and obviously inexperienced horse makes a fatal error in trying to turn away. The boar's massive skull crashes into its underbelly and splinters its ribs with a gut rending wrench. One of the razor-sharp tusks pierces its heart, and my mount topples to the ground.

With my leg trapped below the dying animal, I cry out for help, and fumble in the darkness for my dropped spear. All the while I'm silently praying the boar will move on, or my companions will arrive before it tears me to pieces. I'm mildly comforted to hear the toot of the horns close by and the fast approach of horses and dogs.

Now panicked and disorientated, the massive hog turns desperately in all directions searching for a way to escape. To my relief it finds an opening, and is almost thirty feet away, when suddenly spooked again it lurches to a halt and turns back.

At that exact moment, a glint of moonlight glances off my spear tip, and the hunter now becomes the hunted. Fixated on me with its cruel dark eyes, the beast slowly and purposefully drags a huge hoof across the forest floor, before it snarls, and makes its last desperate charge.

With my companions bizarrely and seemingly no closer, I now resign myself to going it alone. Grasping the shaft of the spear firmly with both hands, I wedge the end into the forest floor for more leverage and brace myself for the inevitable impact.

When it comes, the boar is so huge it would be nigh on impossible for me to miss. The tip of the spear easily pierces the centre of its armoured ribcage. But it doesn't stop there. Squealing horrifically, the gigantic monster thrashes wildly, and the spear sinks deeper into its flesh until the tip can be seen protruding from its back.

And still, it fights on in its desperation to get to me. Its tusks are now just six inches from my face, and panic stricken, I remember the duke's advice, and let go of the spear with one hand to fumble for the cutlass. When my hand settles on an empty scabbard, my heart sinks.

Somehow during the impact, or perhaps on the ride in, I have lost it. Whatever the reason, I am out of options, and the boar's head is now so close, I can smell its rancid breath. Sensing victory, it finds renewed strength and pushes forward gnashing and snarling.

Unwilling to accept this as my end, I frantically punch and claw at the beast's dark beady eyes. Fading fast, my strength is almost completely spent when I see movement to my right. A split second later the forest is lit up by a bright flash and a deafening boom.

A heavy calibre lead slug passes over my head, and effortlessly slices through the front of the boar's thick skull. It then continues on and smashes a huge hole on its way back out, leaving me spattered with blood, brains, and fragments of bone. The boar itself is quite dead even before it slumps lifeless to the ground.

Just moments later, the forest miraculously comes alive with activity as the rest of the hunters find us. Figures hurriedly gather round, and a lamp is held to my face, "Geht es Ihnen gut, mein Herr?"

Quickly correcting himself when he recognises me, the dog handler asks again in broken English, "You are okay, sir?"

Dazzled by the lamp light, I can't see clearly who is asking, but I nod gratefully. "I am now. Thanks to whoever fired that weapon."

Shielding my eyes from the light, I squint and ask, "Was that you?"

"No, that was not me," the voice replies. "But we should get you out from under there."

While three or four men work to free me from under my horse, more lamps are lit, and I see the princess and the duke approaching on horseback. They dismount, and both help to sit me down on a tree stump, before politely enquiring after my health.

Other than a badly bruised leg, I assure them truthfully the only other injury is to my pride. "I must admit though to a little confusion as to why it took so long for—"

"Good," the duke interrupts, before turning away seemingly uninterested in whatever point I was about to make. Gesturing toward the boars now steaming carcass, he comments, "It looks like you had a damned lucky escape, Nephew. That must surely be the biggest boar we've ever seen on this estate. And that was a damn fine job you did sticking it like that."

Beside the duke, another of the nobles is now holding up my bloodied spear. He inspects it, then points to the tip looking a little confused. "And with a normal spear by God. Why the hell didn't he have a boar spear, Ernst?"

The duke suddenly looks embarrassed and is momentarily lost for words, until Eleonore steps in to save his blushes. "The duke's nephew requested something a little more challenging for his first hunt, Count Von Hallstatt."

"More challenging." The count roars with laughter. "Why the boy must have balls of steel."

Offering me his own spear for inspection he helpfully points out the steel wings on either side of the socket where the blade joins the wooden shaft. "These can be a lifesaver if you don't kill the blighter outright on your first lunge. They are designed to stop the boar pushing further onto the shaft and tearing you asunder."

He then affectionately pats me on the shoulder, "Damn brave fellow, and balls of steel," he repeats before howling with laughter again. "And a perfect target on that crock of a horse, with that scarf and crimson jacket. It's little wonder the beast set his sights on you."

The count has inadvertently answered my unfinished question, and I now believe I know why it took so long for help to reach me.

The duke somehow already knows about my dalliance with Eleonore, and preferring not to kill me himself, he was relying on the boar to do his dirty work for him.

I turn to my hosts in the hope of some sign or indicator that might give them away or confirm my suspicion. Although slightly flushed, they otherwise both remain perfectly calm and composed, and I think, "Perhaps, I'm mistaken. Perhaps I'm thinking too much into it. I was in the centre of the line after all."

With no real desire or stomach to challenge my uncle so publicly, I opt instead to give the benefit of the doubt for now, and look up to calmly reassure him again. "Thank you for your kind words, Uncle. But I was very lucky to escape with little more than a few scratches and bruises after what happened to my horse."

Looking him directly in the eye, I pause before adding, "That beast would have certainly had me, if it wasn't for one of the others getting to me and blasting it into oblivion."

Turning towards the other huntsmen, I ask, "Do you know who that was, Uncle? I should very much like to thank him."

For a moment, the duke looks me up and down with something bordering on indifference. He then turns and nods toward the hunting rifle nestled in the leather sleeve strapped to the side of Eleonore's stallion. "You can thank my wife for that, Montague. She is quite a dab hand with that thing. As soon as she set her sights on it, that boar never stood a chance."

Just when I'm thinking Ernst innocent of any ill intent toward me, he suddenly points to the rifle again. "Ja, you would quite literally have been *buggered* if she hadn't brought that with her."

Then completely calm and without the slightest hint of malice in his voice, he helps me to my feet, "Come, Nephew, let us return to the lodge for refreshments. The ladies will I'm sure be keen to hear of your exploits."

"Yes, of course. But my horse is–"

"You can ride with me," Eleonore interrupts with a sweet smile. Then turning to her husband, she innocently asks, "Is that okay, darling?"

Before I can properly assess his facial expression, the duke turns away to reach for the reins of his horse. While mounting up he mutters under his breath, "Ja ja, alle ist gut." Then in English, "I will ride ahead to the lodge and prepare for your arrival. I will expect you both shortly."

Without another word the duke gallops away, and I ask Eleonore, "Is the duke, okay? Only, he seemed a little annoyed by something?"

I'm hoping of course to find out if Ernst knows anything about us, but the princess either doesn't realise my intent, or she doesn't take the bait.

"No, no. Not at all. That is just his way sometimes," she insists, before a cheeky smile spreads across her face. "I do though think perhaps he might be a little jealous of you."

Now fully expecting confirmation of my suspicions, I nervously ask, "Jealous of me? What do you mean?"

The princess turns to where the duke's dog handlers are working to remove the boar's head from its torso. "Your kill, Montague. It is far larger than the one Ernst currently has on his wall."

"Oh, yes." I nod, both relieved and disappointed at the same time. "But in fairness, it was as much your kill as it was mine. And I haven't thanked you yet for saving my–"

In what is clearly something of a family trait, the princess deliberately ignores my attempt to thank her, and instead mounts up and offers a hand. "Come, let's not give my husband any more reason for jealousy."

I climb up behind her and wrap an arm tightly around her waist before leaning in to whisper, "I owe you a great debt of gratitude, Princess. You saved my life tonight, and I shall not forget that."

She doesn't turn to respond, but there is a slight backward movement of her hips toward mine when she says, "Nor shall I, Montague. And sometime soon, I shall expect some suitable recompense."

* * * * * * * *

Despite the duke's reassurance that my injuries are only very minor, the news of my close brush with death leaves Aunt Caroline frantic with worry. She declines the offer to come inside to warm up, and instead anxiously paces up and down in front of the entrance to the lodge in anticipation of my arrival.

When I dismount from the princess's horse, the sight of me covered in blood and limping is more than she can take. She rushes to embrace me, and tearfully wails, "Oh, Monty. I am so sorry. Are you okay?"

"I'm fine," I assure her. "The blood isn't mine, and my leg is just a little bruised."

Clearly not satisfied with my assurance, she frantically checks the front of my body before turning me around to check for other injuries. Relieved to find I'm telling the truth, she wipes her eyes and ushers me inside to the drawing room.

Whilst the huntsmen gather to congratulate me on my kill, Caroline angrily demands one of the servants bring me a drink. "Quickly, my nephew is half frozen to death."

She then clears the crowd from around the fireplace and hands me the glass of schnapps. "Sit there, and drink this. Once you are warm, I want to know exactly what happened."

The strong liquor is exactly what I needed and is a source of instant relief. I drain half the glass, and ensuring no one is within earshot, I lean forward and ask, "What did you mean outside when you said you were sorry? Sorry for what exactly?"

Annoyed by the obvious undertone in my question, Aunt Caroline shakes her head. "You really are something, Montague. I was sorry that you got hurt, of course. What else would you think I meant?"

Rather more cautiously now, I quietly reply, "That perhaps you might have known something of what was to happen this evening?"

My question is enough for Caroline to lose her temper and she angrily demands, "What does that mean? Explain yourself now?"

I wait for her anger to abate, then spend the next ten minutes describing the hunt, and my suspicions. Whilst I speak, Aunt Caroline mostly listens in silence. Occasionally she frowns or shakes her head in disbelief.

I finish my tale and am about to ask what she thinks when she shakes her head again and makes her disdain for me perfectly clear. "So you lied to me, Monty. You did sleep with the princess?"

Caught on the hop, I nervously stutter, "Well, yes, but it was the princess herself that initiated it. I was—"

"You were what?" Caroline barks angrily. "You were too spineless to say no? You were too weak willed to keep your todger in your breeches? By God, Monty, you really are a chip off the old block."

Before I'm able to respond further, she lowers her voice and says, "You swore on your poor mother's life. And even worse, you think I knew about this, and what — you think I would allow the duke to have you killed? Is that what you really think of me?"

Now burning with shame and embarrassment, I stutter an apology, "I'm so sorry, Caroline. That really isn't what I meant at all. There just seemed to be too many oddities with the spear, the horse, and some of the things the duke said. And you did say the princess can be quite the blabbermouth."

During my earlier explanation to my aunt, and for somewhat obvious reasons, I have chosen to omit the mention of the word buggery. I reason this non-essential to setting the scene of my suspicions, and that it is sufficient enough to simply know sexual relations did in fact take place.

Thankfully, she is more interested in protecting her own reputation and doesn't now ask what was said by the duke. "Well, I can assure you, if the duke does know about you and the princess, I am most certainly not privy to that information. And if I was, and if I thought he was planning to harm you, don't you think I would try to dissuade him, or at the least give you a warning of some kind?"

While she talks, my mind wanders to her apparent distraction before the start of the hunt, but trusting her fully and accepting her assurances, I choose not to mention it and instead offer, "Yes, of course, and again, I'm very sorry for upsetting you."

Brushing aside my apology and understandably still annoyed, Caroline angrily shakes her head. "But if he was planning to have you killed, I can't say I could particularly blame him. You're a bloody fool, Monty, and I warned you more than once, Ernst Ludwig Albrecht is not a man to be taken lightly."

Now much calmer, she leans in again and frowns. "The whole bloody thing is preposterous, anyway. Ernst has arranged a wonderful dinner to mark your birthday tomorrow. Why would he do that if he was so intent on killing you today?"

It's hard to argue with her logic, and I couldn't even if I had wanted to. Before I can say anything else, the band strikes up a lively waltz, and the duke turns purposefully toward us.

Intent on whisking Aunt Caroline away, he kisses her hand and sharply clicks his heels together. "Please excuse the interruption,

Nephew, but your beautiful aunt has been promising me a dance since she got here."

Turning back toward her, he bows slightly and firmly adds, "And I would now like for her to make good on that promise."

"But of course." She nods gracefully while taking his hand. "Nothing would give me greater pleasure, Ernst."

They leave, and just moments later, I'm joined by Eleonore who by now has changed into something much more befitting a post-hunt ball. I, of course, am still dressed in my soiled and bloodied hunting attire, and the princess looks genuinely disappointed to find me so dishevelled.

"I was going to ask you to dance." She frowns. "But perhaps another time?"

"Or not," I sarcastically mutter between slurps of schnapps. "I'm starting to think perhaps my associating with you might be rather detrimental to my health. What do you think, Princess?"

"I think, if you are a typical Englishman, then Englishmen must all be rather dramatic." She giggles. "But do I surmise from your tone that you believe my husband knows what you did to me, and was therefore somehow planning to do you harm this evening?"

"Am I wrong?" I ask. "And are you saying the duke doesn't know about us?"

I can almost see the cogs spinning in her head, as the princess carefully considers her response. Moving closer her expression changes to something serious and she quietly says, "Firstly, let me be clear, there is no us, Montague. What we had this morning was a moment of light relief, and nothing more. But in answer to your question, of course my husband knows. We have no secrets."

I almost choke at the matter-of-fact way in which she explains herself. "You – you told him?"

"Of course, I did. He asked about my morning. And I never lie to my husband."

Suddenly paranoid, I turn to check we are not being watched before I nervously ask, "And does he know exactly—"

The smiling princess pre-empts, finishes, and answers my question. "Does my husband know exactly what you did to me? Oh yes, Montague. Every detail, up to and including the buggery. He was particularly interested in that aspect of our liaison."

I've thought it already, but this confirms it. These people are stark raving mad. Now more concerned than ever for my safety, I finish my drink and get to my feet. "I think it better that our relationship should remain entirely platonic for the remainder of my stay here, Princess."

"You're concerned my husband may try to harm you?" Eleonore asks.

"That has crossed my mind," I confess. "And I think you know exactly what I mean when I say that?"

The princess looks innocently on, and I'm forced to remind her of the conversation with Count Von Hallstatt and my entirely unsuitable hunting equipment.

"Just a bit of harmless sporting fun." She titters again shrugging her shoulders. "You really mustn't take it so much to heart."

Disbelieving, I shake my head and angrily remind her, "I nearly died because of that bloody useless spear."

When Eleonore remains unmoved by my words, and speaks again, it quickly becomes clear that I'm dealing with a lunatic. Completely calm and composed she lightly touches my hand. "Oh, Montague darling. You were never in any real danger. I was right there watching over you all the time."

I've now heard more than enough to confirm my suspicions, and unsure how much longer I can keep a lid on my temper, I get to my feet and kiss Eleonore's hand. "Princess, you are an enchanting woman, but we have less than two days remaining here, and I would very much like to leave Munich in one piece. Therefore, I should like to excuse myself to retire for the evening."

Although disappointed, the princess politely nods. "But, of course. Sleep well, Montague."

As I walk away, she mutters to herself deliberately loud enough for me to hear, "You'll be back for more, Montague. Mark my words, they all come back for more, eventually."

Chapter Nine

The Bürgerbräukeller – 14 December 1898

Exhausted, bruised and battered, I politely decline the offer of breakfast, and it is almost midday before Johnathan returns a second time to wake me. This time he simply throws open the curtains, and cheerily pipes, "Good afternoon, sir. I trust you are feeling a little better now?"

"It's the afternoon already?" I groan sleepily.

"No, not exactly, sir. But not far off it. It's a quarter to twelve."

Worried that Caroline might have taken offence at my absence from breakfast, I gingerly ask the question and am mightily relieved when Johnathan reassures, "No, sir. She was fine. As were the duke and the princess. They all thought it best you rest longer after last night's exertions."

"You heard what happened?" I ask him.

"Oh yes, sir. It was the talk of the house, but I could scarcely believe it until I saw them bringing the bleeding thing in through the kitchens."

I shake my head, slightly unsure of his meaning. "The thing?"

"Why yes, sir. The hogs head. I've never seen such a beast. And you killed that all by yourself?"

Too tired to go into details, I simply nod, before I suddenly remember the gaping hole in the back of its skull. "Well, what I mean is, it was me that managed to stick the blighter first with my spear. It was another of the huntsmen who finished it off with his rifle."

Accepting my explanation without question, the young valet nods, and smiles. "Still, though. You must be very proud, sir. The duke's household staff were saying it's the biggest trophy head any of them have ever seen."

Momentarily forgetting the concerns for my safety, I childishly snigger to myself. "I can think of a bigger prize."

"Sorry?" Johnathan says. "I didn't quite catch that."

"Oh, it was nothing," I reply. Then quickly changing the subject, "Do you know where Lady Caroline is now?"

Suddenly sheepish, Johnathan reaches into his waistcoat and hands me a wax sealed envelope. "Lady Caroline left an hour ago in one of the motor cars with the duke and the princess. But she left you this?"

His tone is somewhat off, and alert to his discomfort I sit up and ask, "Left for where, Johnathan? What are you not telling me?"

Blushing slightly, he points to the envelope. "I'm sorry, sir. I really don't know. Perhaps there may be an explanation in the letter."

The handwriting on the front of the envelope is unmistakeably my aunts. The wax seal however is the crest of the Albrecht family. Intrigued, I dismiss Johnathan and ask him to wait outside. Unable to find a letter opener, I break open the seal, and carefully slide out the single folded sheet of paper.

Like the envelope, the handwriting on the paper belongs to my aunt, and in her typically abrupt style she wastes no time in getting to the point.

December 14, 1898

My dearest Monty,

  I do hope you slept well and are feeling a little better on this your eighteenth birthday. I say this in all sincerity, because although it was my heartfelt desire to spend this special day with you, this will sadly not now be possible.

  This morning, Ernst has requested I accompany him and the princess on some unexpected but important business in Berlin, and we won't unfortunately return until the early hours of the morning.

  I can of course fully appreciate the disappointment you must be feeling, but there is no reason for you not to celebrate your birthday still.

  Ernst has kindly offered you the use of the second Motorwagen and has suggested you might take a drive into Munich and visit some of the wonderful beer halls.

  I also think it would be rather nice, if you were to take Betsy and Johnathan along with you. They have worked so hard thus far on our journey. If you are agreeable, I believe it would be a rather splendid treat for them.

  I will however leave the final decision to you. Whatever you decide, please watch out for yourself, and stay safe.

Happy birthday, darling.

Your loving aunt
Caroline x

I read the letter for a second time, before angry and disgusted I screw it up and toss it aside. It's bad enough there will be no formal celebration to mark my coming of age, but to be abandoned by my own flesh and blood on such an auspicious day is a particularly bitter pill to swallow.

My mind is also now working overtime, and I'm wondering what further surprises might be in store for me today. Although it was never implicitly said, the princess did more or less confirm I was set up for failure on the hunt.

And if Ernst really is the kind of man Aunt Caroline says he is, he must surely have been disappointed at my lack of any significant injury.

"And was that a hidden warning at the end of the letter?" I think.

Straightening out the crumpled sheet of paper, I read the last part aloud, "Whatever you decide, please watch out for yourself, and stay safe."

If it's not a warning, it's certainly a rather unusual turn of phrase.

I read the letter for a third time before my eyes settle on the fourth paragraph, and I mutter knowingly, "It's the Motorwagen isn't it you sneaky sausage eating bastard. You've cut the bloody brakes, haven't you?"

"But he loves his velocipede more than he loves his own wife," I reason to myself. "He might kill me, but his beloved Motorwagen would almost certainly be destroyed, and that makes no sense."

Confused and frustrated, I place the letter down and slowly shake my head. "Well, Monty old boy, this isn't quite how you imagined your eighteenth birthday is it?"

Then suddenly defiant, "But what the hell. It is my birthday, and I shall damn well celebrate it regardless of what Ernst von Albrecht has up his sleeve. He has underestimated me on one too many occasions already, and I've taken everything he has thrown at me."

Leaping from the bed, I stand proudly in front of the mirror and pompously declare, "You are Montague Finch-Morton the Third, and God help any man who crosses you today."

Snatching the letter from atop the bedspread I turn to the door and shout, "Johnathan, get in here please. Quickly now."

He joins me just moments later slightly out of breath. "Is everything okay, sir?"

"More than okay," I reply confidently holding up the letter. "Do you know what this says?"

It's a stupid question of course, and met with a blank expression, I quickly add, "No, of course you don't. And why would you? But bare with me please, Johnathan."

I read the letter from start to finish, and then repeat the part concerning himself and Betsy. "I also think it would be rather nice if you were to take Betsy and Johnathan along with you."

"And so do I," I say with a reassuring smile. "It would be rather fun, don't you think?"

Clearly unsure of himself, it is a moment before a faint smile creeps slowly across the young valet's face, and he enthusiastically nods. "Yes, sir, I would like that very much. I'm sure Miss Betsy would too."

"Good, that's settled," I exclaim. "Spruce yourself up and tell Betsy to put her glad rags on. Party or not, it's my birthday today, and we shall damn well celebrate it."

"Very good, sir." Johnathan nods politely.

Before taking his leave, he smiles and adds, "Happy birthday, sir. I'm sure we shall have a most wonderful time."

* * * * * * * *

Deciding against the more practical driving outfit, I instead opt for a tailored suit, with a red silk cravat and Father's top hat. I complete my look with my silver-topped cane, and a pair of black leather gloves. Feeling altogether rather dashing, I join my traveling companions, and am pleased to see they have both made a considerable effort with their appearance.

Johnathan is clean shaven and is smartly dressed in his Sunday best. His hair is neatly combed back, and his shoes have been buffed to a high gloss shine that would put a guardsman to shame.

Beside him, Betsy is wearing her best frock below her winter coat. Her hair has been tied up in a neat bun beneath a pretty bonnet secured below her chin by a blue silk ribbon. Although not needed, her striking jawline, and plump lips have been further accentuated by the subtle application of powder and rouge.

As I assist her into the rear seat of the velocipede, my nostrils fill with the fresh scent of soap, and what I suspect might be a dab of my aunt's cologne.

"Good for you," I think to myself. "I hope you used the whole bally bottle."

I'm also thinking about how I might take another turn on this foxy young strumpet later today. "A tumble with Miss Betsy is just the kind of birthday present I deserve."

Shaking off my distraction, I briefly instruct Johnathan on the workings of the piston engine and the hand crank. I then leave him to it while I reacquaint myself with the steering column and brakes. After just two turns of the handle, the engine starts, and the young man climbs up beside me.

My only concession to driving attire is the goggles. I pull a set over my own eyes, and hand a set each to my companions. "Well then. Shall we get going?"

Both nod excitedly, and Johnathan asks, "You know the way, sir?"

"It's a piece of cake." I nod confidently. "I've spoken to one of the duke's mechanics. He says we should take a right out of the estate until we hit the main road and the sign for Munich. From there we follow the road downhill and barring any mishap we should reach the city in just less than an hour."

And by mishap, I mean any failure of the brakes on what I remember from our journey in as a series of rather steep inclines. But no need to concern my companions with such trivial details as brake failure, or their possible impending deaths.

Smiling, I playfully toot the horn and shout, "Tallyho!" as I release the handbrake, and gently press down on the accelerator.

By the time we reach the main road, and the directional sign for Munich, my driving ability and confidence is such we are cruising along at top speed.

Just a few minutes later, however, we reach the brow of the first hill, and suddenly hesitant, I slow to almost a complete halt and quietly mutter, "This is it, Monty. Time to say your prayers and hold on to your balls."

"Is something wrong?" Johnathan asks.

We are already moving forward again when I reply. Although my heart is almost beating out of my chest, I do my best to remain calm and assure him, "Nothing at all, old man. I was just taking a moment to admire the view."

We crest the hill and rapidly pick up speed. Now struggling to contain my inner terror, I silently pray for salvation and gingerly push down on the foot brake to slow our descent.

To my enormous relief, the brakes work exactly as they should, and as we level out, I casually turn away to wipe the sweat from my brow. My companions remain blissfully unaware of my recent terror, and thankfully the remainder of our journey passes off without incident.

As predicted, we arrive on the outskirts of the city in just fifty-five minutes. It is however, a further thirty minutes, and at least half a dozen wrong turns before we finally make it to the district of Munich famous for hosting the annual October beer festival, the Theresienwiese.

Although the festival has long since finished for the year, the duke's mechanic has recommended we start here. And it's not difficult to see why. The main square is ringed with colourful, and brightly lit bierkellers, halls, and bars, and whilst it's still only late afternoon, most appear to be doing a brisk trade.

I park beside the only other motor vehicle in the square and assist Betsy down onto the cobbles. Johnathan joins us, looking almost as mystified as I feel. "Where now, sir? There are so many to choose from."

He's not wrong, but not wishing to look indecisive in front of the hired help, I confidently gesture to one of the closest bars. "Let's start there."

I lead off completely unaware of how out of place we look. Or more precisely, of how out of place I look.

Betsy and Johnathan's attire is not completely dissimilar to everyone else we pass, but my shiny top hat, cravat, and silver-topped cane stick out like a bulldog's bollocks. With any numbers of eyes gawking at this strangely mismatched trio, I confidently stride up to the bar and order in my best German, "Drei grose Biere bitte – und ein–"

Part way through, my language skills suddenly fail me, and slightly embarrassed, I nervously stammer the rest in English, "I mean – um, well do you also have some light refreshments?"

The barman clearly hasn't the first idea what I've just said and looking puzzled he turns and speaks briefly to one of the older barmaids.

"Do you mean, you would like some food with your beer's?" she asks.

"Yes, that's it." I smile. "Thank you for your help."

Although her face has long since seen better days, she still has a deliciously full bosom, and my eyes fixate on her plump behind as she leads us to an empty table close to where a brass band are quietly playing.

"Wait here, and I will bring your drinks," she orders sternly.

Not completely unexpected given the circumstances, we sit in relative silence until the barmaid returns a few moments later clutching tightly to three incredibly large glasses of beer.

Betsy noticeably gasps, and to ease the tension, I playfully tease, "Too big for you to manage, Miss Betsy?"

Knowing already how feisty she is, it is no real surprise when she lifts the enormous glass with both hands and giggles cheekily. "I've had bigger, sir."

Both Johnathan and I snigger at her joke, and with the ice broken, I raise my glass. "Okay, to my birthday, and to no more calling me sir. Well, not for today anyway." I laugh.

"But seriously. To my new friends, Johnathan, and Betsy, who for today at least will call me Monty."

We clink glasses and each take a large gulp of the seriously frosty beer.

"That is a damn fine drop of ale," Johnathan says before contentedly licking his lips and downing another large chug.

"Thirsty?" I ask with a raised eyebrow and a grin.

"You could say that." The valet laughs. "It's been a while."

After this the conversation flows easily between the three of us, and I have almost forgotten about the food until the veteran barmaid returns with a hefty platter of sausages, sauerkraut, and mustard.

"More beers?" she suggests looking to the almost empty glasses.

I'm visibly impressed that Betsy has kept up with the men, and without needing to be asked again, she cheekily looks me in the eye and slides her glass across the table. "Yes, please, Monty. I'm just getting started."

"That saucy little minx is teasing me," I think to myself.

In the hope of playing her at her own game, I smirk and point to the largest sausage on the platter. "Big enough for you, Betsy?"

The wily young maid is more than a match for me. Reaching for a fork she expertly spears the sausage and holds it up to the light to make a show of inspecting it. Pouting her lips sadly, she then shakes her head, before dismissively tossing the sausage back down onto the platter, "No, no, no. This won't do at all, Monty."

"Oh yes. And why is that?" I ask. "It looks like a perfectly good sausage to me."

"Then you still have much to learn about sausages," Betsy replies, sounding rather more educated than I have previously given her credit for.

"My personal preference is for a banger with significantly greater girth, and at least four additional inches of length."

While Johnathan almost chokes on his beer, I nod appreciatively and think to myself, "Touché, Betsy. Well played."

I'm also thinking, "And play your cards right, girl, and I can almost guarantee you something tasty, full bodied and English to get your mouth around this evening."

Just in the nick of time to dampen my ardour, the fresh drinks arrive, and already boisterous we noisily clink them together. "Chin chin, and down the hatch," I urge. "The night is young and there are plenty more where these came from."

* * * * * * * *

With four beers each under our belts, I return from the bathroom and check the time on my pocket watch. "Right folks, it's just after seven. I think let's call it a day here, and try somewhere else, shall we?"

Although we are all now on friendly terms, my companions are also still Lady Caroline's servants, and are therefore unlikely to disagree with my suggestion. They get to their feet without question, and I help Betsy on with her coat.

Outside, the temperature has dropped to just below freezing, and stamping our feet to keep warm, I ask, "Any suggestions for where next?"

Quick as a flash, Betsy points to a large brightly lit sign on the other side of the square. "I heard that place was quite fun, Monty."

"Really?" I ask a little surprised. "And pray tell who the source of this information was?"

Looking a little uncomfortable, Betsy nervously replies, "Um, it was the duke's housekeeper. When I told her we were going to Munich, she told me abou—"

"Well, that's good enough for me," I interrupt. "And don't look so damned worried, old girl. I wasn't testing you. The Bürgerbräukeller it is."

* * * * * * * *

The interior of the Bürgerbräukeller is much larger than one might expect of its outward appearance, which is just as well given how busy it is. Initially unable to find a place amongst the long rows of sturdy oak tables and benches, our dilemma is quickly resolved by the greasing of a palm with a large German banknote, and a burly hand to eject those that have overstayed their welcome.

Looking duly impressed, Betsy shuffles along the bench and asks, "How much did you give him?"

"I actually have no idea." I chuckle. "It seemed to do the trick though."

When the barmaid arrives to take our order, I'm already struggling to hear above the volume of chatter in the hall. When the Oompah band strikes up mid-sentence, I give up completely and raise my hands in surrender.

Thankfully, the customers here are wonderfully predictable, and with a somewhat limited menu anyway, the barmaid returns moments later to unceremoniously dump three glasses of beer onto the table.

She leaves without a word and grinning sarcastically, I raise my glass to my friends. "Welcome to the Ritz."

Unlike the previous bar, in the Bürgerbräukeller we are sharing a table, and over the course of an hour numerous people have come and gone. Although most have been German, alcohol is a great leveller, and all three of us are now happily chatting away with strangers.

On the opposite side of the table, two buxom but not particularly attractive young women ask Johnathan, "You will buy some beers for us?"

He looks to me, and already quite tipsy, I nod. "Why not?"

I then get to my feet slightly unsteadily and shout for a barmaid. "In fact, more beers for the whole table. And schnapps. Lots of schnapps."

The arrival of the drinks is unsurprisingly met with a round of applause and hoorahs, and my generosity is toasted with numerous glasses of schnapps. When our newfound companions later find out it is my birthday, even more drinks are called for, and we are joined by more young women keen to join the fun.

With our impromptu gathering growing more and more raucous, my bladder is now full to bursting. Excusing myself to use the bathroom, I carefully remove the hand that has been pawing at my groin for the last ten minutes.

I've barely been gone for five minutes, but when I stumble back toward our table, the dynamic has changed dramatically.

Aside from the pair of harpies previously fighting over Johnathan, the other women have all left, and have been replaced by three rough looking and obviously drunk sailors wearing the uniform of the Imperial German Navy.

One of them is wearing my hat, whilst another is closely inspecting the silver top of my cane. Worse still, the third and roughest looking of the bunch has an arm wrapped tightly around Betsy's waist. She doesn't look at all happy about it, and Johnathan looks fit to explode.

He only relaxes slightly, when he sees me approaching and the burly mariner removes his arm from Betsy's waist and stands to sarcastically raise his glass.

His English, although slurred, is surprisingly good. "Look men, his lordship has returned from the powder room."

Then directly to me, "And will his lordship be buying a round of drinks for the men of the Kaiser's navy?" He then places a hand on Betsy's shoulder in a deliberate act of provocation and adds, "Or does he prefer to save his generosity for his whores?"

Catching Johnathan's eye, I very slightly shake my head for him to stand down, before I calmly turn back to answer the question. "I'd be delighted to buy a round of drinks for you. It is though time for us to be leaving."

Reaching into my pocket, I dismissively toss a handful of banknotes onto the table. "I trust this will be sufficient for a round of beers, and a bottle of schnapps?"

My question is, of course, rhetorical, and without waiting for a reply, I nod toward the other mariners and my belongings in their possession. "I believe those are mine, gentlemen?"

At first there is no attempt to return them, but then the obvious leader of the group retakes his seat and nods to his comrades. "Give the little prince his crown, and his little stick before he gets upset and soils himself."

Ignoring this renewed provocation and keeping a lid on my growing anger, I take my things, before reaching for Betsy's hand to help her out. The sailor sitting beside her makes no attempt to move, and she is forced to awkwardly slide across his lap to get past.

Johnathan is so angry it is all I can do to push him away from the table and toward the door, "Another time, my friend. Maybe when the odds are better stacked in our favour."

We are almost at the exit when Betsy suddenly stops and blurts an apology. "Oh hell, Monty. I'm sorry, but I'm bloody bursting." Then clearly worried about walking back through the bar alone, she asks, "Will you walk me to the bathroom please, Johnathan?"

As they leave together, I call after them, "I'll go ahead, and start the Motorwagen."

I'm almost there when I hear the hurried approach of footsteps from behind, and an angry voice snarls, "Hey, Englander. That was very rude of you to leave like that."

Knowing exactly who it is, I slowly turn to face my aggressor, and am immediately hit in the chest by the handful of now screwed up banknotes. "And don't think you can buy us off with your money."

Conscious I'm outnumbered three to one, I gingerly look beyond my adversaries for any sign of my companions. Knowing exactly what I'm doing the lead sailor laughs, and sneers, "Don't bother, little prince. There is no one coming to help you. That has been seen to."

Wondering what he could possibly mean, I think as fast as my brain will allow. Although I can't possibly beat all three of them, I'm determined to inflict as much damage on them as possible.

Masking my nerves, I casually point to my top hat. "Would you mind awfully if I put this down? It's very expensive and it would be such a shame if it was to get damaged."

Clearly thinking me mad, the sailor looks to his companions and shakes his head in disbelief before he turns back and theatrically bows. "Of course, your lordship, please go ahead."

When I turn to place the hat on the backseat of the velocipede, I also remove my leather gloves, and casually reach for the crank.

Unfortunately, it knocks against the chassis, and with the element of surprise gone, a voice screams, "Get him."

All three men launch themselves at me, and with just a split second to spare, I turn and hurl the crank at the nearest of my attackers.

At such close range it is impossible to miss, and the heavy length of cast iron splits open his skull with a sickening crump. Blood gushes from a gaping hole, and the stunned seaman drops unconscious to the floor.

His companions, although now less sure of themselves, cautiously circle me like hungry lions, whilst I swing and jab with my cane in the hope of keeping them at arm's length long enough for help to arrive.

Unfortunately, it is the cane that is my undoing. Biding their time for just the right moment, a burly hand grabs for the silver top and drags me forward and onto the receiving end of a huge right hook.

Spun completely around, my head glances off the chassis, before a rough hand pulls me back around, and my tormentor snarls, "Don't be passing out on us now. We are just getting started."

Both men wade in, and for every punch I manage to land, I take at least three or four to my ribs and face. When another huge right knocks me off my feet, and strong thighs straddle and pin me down, a familiar voice suddenly screams, "Do something. Quickly before they kill him?"

One further jab strikes my jaw before a punch from seemingly out of nowhere sends my captor toppling to the side. Groggy and half-conscious with swollen and puffy eyes, my recollection of what happens next is vague to say the least.

It's confirmed to me later, that both my attackers are quickly and efficiently beaten into submission. They are then sent away battered and bruised carrying their still unconscious friend.

When all is quiet again, I hear that same familiar sweet voice, "I've found it, but it's covered in blood. Here you can use my handkerchief to clean it."

Moments later, the crank goes to work, and the combustion engine purrs to life before an out of breath Johnathan puts his arms under my torso and says, "Take his legs, and help me get him onto the back seat."

They place me down, and Betsy carefully covers me with a blanket as the Motorwagen pulls away. Thinking me fully unconscious she tenderly brushes a hand through my hair. "I'm so sorry, Monty. This isn't how it was meant to happen. Honestly, it wasn't."

* * * * * * * *

By the time we reach the lodge, I've recovered enough to walk unaided. Even so, both of my companions help me to my room, and Betsy insists on drawing me a bath. "Believe me, sir. You will feel a lot better afterwards."

Conceding to her request, she leaves to fetch the hot water, while I spend a few moments assessing my injuries and washing my face. With the dried blood gone, and the swelling around my eyes lessening, I don't look half as bad as I feel. I am though feeling tired and lay down to rest until Betsy returns.

In reality, I've slept for less than ten minutes, but it feels like far longer when soft and nimble hands skilfully unbutton my breeches, and Betsy whispers, "Your bath is ready, sir?"

When I open my eyes, I'm pleasantly surprised to find the petite young nymph has let her hair down and is completely naked. Smiling sweetly, she expertly removes the rest of my clothes and purposefully leads me into the next room.

Steam is rising from the tin bathtub, but I'm shocked to find we are not alone. Momentarily taken aback, I self-consciously place a hand across my manhood, and bluster, "Um – what is this?"

"Oh, don't be shy," Betsy says. "We are all friends now, and we thought you might like to keep the birthday celebration going."

Suddenly giggly, she lifts a bottle of champagne from the ice bucket on the dressing table. "If it helps, Johnathan liberated this from the duke's wine cellar."

Pleased at this deliberate affront to the duke, I nod my approval and smile. "Well, in that case, I hope there is enough room in that tub for the three of us."

It's a little snug of course, but with Johnathan at one end, and myself at the other, there is just enough room for the petite young woman to shimmy her delicious curves in between us.

Placing a hand on each of our thighs, she cheekily grins and asks, "So then, gentlemen. Are you ready to get this party started?"

Although I'm as randy as hell already, there is something much more pressing on my mind that needs attending to first. Considering how best to approach it, I take a long slow sip of my champagne, before I turn to Betsy and ask, "When you said, this isn't how it was meant to happen, what did you mean?"

Shocked at the realisation I was conscious and fully aware, she suddenly looks worried, and I rephrase my question, "What I mean is, was I meant to get a beating today, just not as bad as it actually was?"

Understandably reluctant to confirm my suspicions, Betsy looks away embarrassed, and I try to reassure her, "Whatever you tell me, I promise I won't be angry with you."

Still nervous, she slowly nods, and I quietly ask, "And do I have the duke to thank for this evening's surprise?"

"Yes, sir," she replies, suddenly teary. "I'm so sorry, but we didn't have a choice. They said we were to make sure you went into that bar, and we weren't to help when those men attacked you. But I swear to God, they said it would only be a minor scuffle."

"Who is they?" I demand. "The duke and the princess?"

"Not the princess," Betsy replies shaking her head. "It was the duke and Lady Caroline."

Noting my shock, Johnathan comments, "It's true, sir. And it's true we didn't have any choice, other than to go along with this. Lady Caroline threatened to abandon us in Munich without a penny, or any means of getting home."

Still slightly tearful, Betsy sniffles, "But we couldn't do it. When we saw what those men were doing to you, we had to step in – well what I mean is, it was when Johnathan stepped in."

"That was you?" I ask slightly stunned. "That was some impressive work, Johnathan, and it would appear I owe you a great debt of thanks."

Looking slighting embarrassed, the young valet mumbles modestly, "It was nothing, sir. But if you want someone to thank, you can thank my father and my older brother. They were both fairground fighters with a penchant for violence in and out of the ring. As you might well imagine, growing up around men like that toughens you up and teaches you a thing or two about fighting."

Reserving my growing disdain for the duke and my aunt, I assure Johnathan and Betsy they are not to blame for what has happened this evening. I then raise my glass and smile. "And thank God for Johnathan, and his prize fighting kin."

"Oh, and what was that you were saying about keeping the celebration going?" I ask pulling Betsy closer toward me. "It's still my birthday for at least two more hours, don't you know."

"Oh, really?" She giggles playfully pushing me away. "Then perhaps you ought to lay back, relax and enjoy the show."

Doing exactly as I'm told, I take a sip of champagne and quietly look on in lustful anticipation as Betsy takes charge and orders Johnathan to his feet.

Although not yet fully erect, his rod is thick and meaty, with the heavenly promise of much more to come. Moving onto her knees, the young maids hand looks tiny as it tightly coils around the valets rapidly swelling serpent.

Her other hand drops to squeeze firmly on his weighty balls, causing the young man to gasp and tremble under her touch. Looking me in the eye, Betsy winks, and drools onto the head of his shaft before she rhythmically works Johnathan to his full and impressive potential.

Now standing firm and proud against the backdrop of his rippling stomach muscles, his pole is just a little longer than my own. It is, however, a good deal thicker, and I quite unintentionally find myself salivating.

I also quite unashamedly reach for my own aching phallus, and slowly begin to stroke it up and down.

Catching my eye, Betsy smiles and winks again, before she turns back and lowers her head. Her tongue flickers back and forth like a puff-adder, causing Johnathan to close his eyes and shudder.

She then hungrily laps at his pre-cum, before without warning, her mouth opens like a sword swallower, and his entire length disappears down the back of her throat. While Johnathan noisily grunts his pleasure, I can barely contain my excitement. "My God, that is impressive." I groan between strokes.

Suddenly reaching behind her, Betsy disengages from the job at hand, and pulls me forward onto my knees. Clearly in her element, the beautiful young woman smiles and places one of my hands around Johnathan's swollen tool. "Go on," she encourages. "I know you want to."

Then giggling to herself, "And I know it's not your first time."

She is of course correct, and like my own experience with Monsieur Lavigne, at this point Johnathan is so far gone with pleasure, it is of no real consequence who gets him off.

To confirm this assumption, he firmly cups the back of my head with the strong hands of a man used to manual labour, and impatiently pulls me closer. The tip of his shaft is moist and glistening with a mix of his manly sap and Betsy's saliva.

Moving closer, she lowers her head and playfully wags her tongue. "Go on, Monty. Don't be shy."

Slowly extending my own tongue, I slide it across Johnathan's engorged mushroom, being careful not to miss any of his delicious nectar. Then, growing in confidence, I slowly lick the length of his shaft, before my mouth opens to swallow the first couple of thick meaty inches.

All the while, Betsy has moved behind me, and is now probing at my asshole with a soapy finger. Her other hand reaches around for my pulsating manhood.

Perfectly in rhythm, my slobbering mouth and tongue work Johnathan into a climatic frenzy, as Betsy energetically finger ploughs me, and pumps away on my shaft.

The pleasure is so intense, and I'm so distracted, I don't notice any of the physical or audible signals until it is already too late, and Johnathan roughly forces his meat further down my throat. Filled to bursting point, I'm barely able to breathe, and can almost feel the eruption before it happens.

Bucking wildly the young valet offloads his vast creamy cargo into the back of my throat. At that exact same moment, Betsy sinks her index finger deep into my ass, and my own seed spurts across Johnathan's legs, and drips down into the bathtub.

Keen that not a drop of cum be wasted, Betsy quickly orders me to my feet. She then drops to her knees to milk us both of every last drop. We are only allowed to sit back down when she is completely satisfied we are dry.

Like myself, Johnathan is flushed, panting and out of breath.

Betsy however is only just getting started. Reaching for the champagne bottle, she tops us up and smiles wickedly before raising her glass. "Drink up, and gather your strength, boys. It's my turn next, and I have rather a hankering for a spit-roast."

Raising an eyebrow, she then grins and looks down to her own firm ripe breasts, "But for now, why don't you boys slide over and take care of these."

* * * * * * * * *

The following morning, I dress as a gentleman should and give myself a final once over in the mirror, before I head downstairs for breakfast. Aside from a split lip, and some minor bruises and swelling around my eyes, I'm pleased to see I have otherwise escaped any serious, or lasting injury.

Pondering the duke's possible reaction to my lucky escape, I pause a moment at the entrance to the dining room to steady my nerves. I then take a deep breath, and arrogantly barge in fully prepared for a confrontation.

I'm naturally disappointed then to find Aunt Caroline dining alone. Looking up from her breakfast, she briefly looks me up and down before saying, "Good morning, Monty. You look well given–"

"Given I was meant to look a damn sight worse today?" I angrily interject.

Ignoring my outburst, Caroline calmly gestures for me to take a seat before she turns to the maid, "Some coffee and breakfast for my nephew please."

While the maid goes about her business, we both patiently hold our tongues. As soon as she leaves, it is a race to see who can speak first.

"Well, then?" I blurt. "What have you to say for yourself?"

Still calm, Aunt Caroline slowly shakes her head. "You should be thanking me, Monty. If I hadn't talked Ernst down to a beating, you would most likely have been dead by now. He wanted to have you shot."

"So, you don't deny it?" I sneer. "You don't deny conspiring with that bastard to have me beaten nearly half to death?"

"Not at all," she replies. "But what have I told you about being so dramatic. It's not befitting of a gentleman, and let's face it, you are hardly knocking on death's door today."

"No thanks' to you," I scream. "Those thugs were out for blood. And if it hadn't been for—"

Not wishing to drop Betsy or Johnathan in it, I abruptly stop myself mid-sentence, but Aunt Caroline is already two steps ahead of me. "I know exactly what happened yesterday evening, and whilst it was unfortunate those men overstepped their remit, I knew deep down that Johnathan wouldn't abandon you."

Almost sounding proud of me, she then adds, "And you didn't exactly go down without a fight, did you?"

"Meaning?"

"Meaning, that chap you walloped with the lump of iron is going to be seeing stars for at least a week."

Caroline's comment slightly eases the tension, and I ask, "And what about the hunt, were you also in on that?"

"No, of course not," she insists. "Ernst only took me into his confidence at the hunt ball. And mark my words, Monty, after the princess stepped in to save you from being mauled by that boar, he was adamant the only way to restore his honour was by having you killed. It took all my charm and persuasion to talk him out of it."

My blood runs cold, and shaking my head, I ask, "He was really that aggrieved at my ploughing his wife?"

Suddenly incredulous, Caroline angrily exclaims, "Seriously? When are you going to grow up and take accountability for your actions?"

"You didn't plough the princess," she screams. "You whipped her with a riding crop, and then you buggered her arse! It's no bloody surprise the man feels aggrieved."

Unaccustomed to hearing my aunt use any kind of profanity, and realising I've been caught out again, I reach for my coffee cup to mask my growing discomfort.

"Yes, you might well look embarrassed," Caroline barks. "Not only did you dishonour one of my close friends, but you also lied to my face yet again."

I try to offer an apology, but am quickly closed down. "No, Monty. Enough is enough. In just a couple of weeks' time we will return home, and I can't stress strongly enough how important it is for you to be ready for what comes next."

"I understand." I nod sheepishly. "And I'm sorry for—"

"Do you really understand?" Caroline snipes. "Because I'm not sure you do. And simply looking like a gentleman is not enough. Your mother and I now need you to step up and start acting like one."

Nodding again, I quietly try to excuse my behaviour. "I know, and I'm sorry. It was just that — well what I mean is, in Paris everything seemed to have a purpose, but here in Munich the only purpose seems to have been to break me?"

"That wasn't the purpose at all," Caroline angrily replies. "The purpose of sending you to the academy wasn't to break you. It was to make you. It was to toughen you up, and looking at you now, and knowing what you have endured these past weeks, I think it has done exactly that."

Smiling appreciatively at my chest and arms, she then adds, "You've also put on some extra muscle, I believe."

Blushing slightly, I thank her for the explanation, and sarcastically steer the conversation back toward the duke. "He must have been disappointed I wasn't more badly beaten?"

"Yes, he was," Caroline smirks. "But his honour has been satisfied."

"You're quite sure about that?" I ask.

"Oh yes," Caroline replies confidently. "In fact, before he departed this morning, he left you a belated birthday gift."

The small polished wooden chest she is pointing to has an intricate hunting scene carved into its lid, and the sides are inlaid with silver and delicate mother-of-pearl.

I've been wondering about it since I sat down and am now intrigued to find out what's inside. Before I lift the lid, I smirk and ask, "Is this thing likely to explode in my face?"

"That would be no more than you deserve." Caroline frowns. "But no, I think you are safe enough."

Despite her assurance, I still lift the lid carefully. Inside, the box is lined with plush green velvet, but I'm more than a little puzzled by its contents.

"You like them?" Caroline asks.

"What's not to like?" I reply. "They are quite magnificent, but are they meant to be a challenge, or a warning of what is still to come? I mean, why else would Ernst gift me such a fine pair of vintage flintlock duelling pistols?"

Slowly shaking her head, Caroline says, "Reading between the lines, I would say they are a warning of what is to come if you ever touch the Princess Eleonore again."

"That's not bloody likely." I scowl. "That woman is even more bonkers than her husband. Quite frankly I'll be glad to see the back of both of them."

"Good, because the next time, I don't think I will be able to sway Ernst from his intended course of action."

Caroline then pauses before adding, "And to my knowledge, Ernst has never lost a duel."

Noting my sudden silence, and doing her best to conceal a grin, my aunt points to my breakfast plate. "You should eat some of that.

You're suddenly looking rather pale, and we shall soon be leaving for the station."

Pleased for the opportunity to change the subject, I look up from the table, "Speaking of which, did I hear you correctly when you said we would be returning home within a couple of weeks?"

"Or less." Caroline nods. "I'm sorry, Monty, but circumstances have taken an unfortunate turn for the worse at home. We will therefore have to cancel some of our plans and cut short our journey."

"What do you mean a turn for the worse?" I ask with obvious concern. "Has something happened to my mother?"

Aunt Caroline reaches for my hand. "No, no, nothing like that. Your mother is safe and well. She has, though, sent a telegram to say your fathers bank in London has sent the first notice of foreclosure on his estates."

Struggling to comprehend, I nervously stutter, "But – but I thought we had more time? How long do we have before they foreclose?"

"According to your mother, we have until the tenth of April next year."

"That's not even four months away," I exclaim. "How on earth am I to find a suitably wealthy spouse in such a short space of time?"

Then suddenly doubting myself, "Am I even ready or up to the task?"

"You're more than ready," Caroline calmly assures me. "I admit to having had my doubts, of course, and there are times when you infuriate me. But despite everything you have changed dramatically for the better since leaving England. Both physically and mentally."

Tenderly squeezing my hand, she then says, "You are going to make your mother very proud."

Suddenly frowning she then lightly scolds, "You just need to listen to good advice when it is given, and trust that every decision I make is in the best interest of you and your mother. Do that, and you won't go far wrong."

Unsure, if she is expecting a reply or some comment, I'm thankful when the decision is taken out of my hands and Caroline speaks again, "Oh and on the subject of having adequate time to find a spouse, four months should be more than enough time, thanks to your mother."

Unsure of her meaning, I ask her to explain.

"You don't think my sister has been sitting idly waiting for us to return, do you? No, no, no, that is not the way of your mother at all. No, Monty, Charlotte has been hard at work compiling a list of all the most eligible young women in the United Kingdom. And I must say, she has done rather well."

To illustrate her point, Aunt Caroline hands me the telegram. "Look for yourself, she mentions it in the second line."

The words on the paper clearly confirm her assessment of Mother's endeavours, "As of now, I have identified eleven young women. All are from good families of excellent financial standing. They are, unfortunately, located as far afield as Southampton and Edinburgh. Therefore, time is of the essence."

That, and the wolves knocking at the door," I think as I hand back the telegram. "So, what now?"

Opening her diary, Aunt Caroline carefully unfolds a small map of Europe, and points to the lightly pencilled markings highlighting our original intended route. "I haven't shown you this before, but from here our next stops were planned for Vienna, St Petersburg, and Moscow.

"Unfortunately, with time now against us, we will instead leave today for a short stop in Rome. Afterward, and again time allowing, we will either make a stop to visit a dear friend of mine in Marseilles, or we will proceed directly to Paris, before our final journey home in time for Christmas."

This is the longest I've been away from England, and although I'm slightly homesick, I'm also feeling a little apprehensive at the thought of what awaits me at home. Doubting myself again, I start to ask, "But what if—?"

"You are ready," Aunt Caroline affirms. "And four months is more than enough for you to marry and save your family estates. Now finish your breakfast. Ernst has arranged for two of his mechanics to drive us to the station.

Chapter Ten

The Piazza Navona
& Marseille – 16 December 1898

We overnight on the train and arrive at our accommodations in Rome a little after midday. Despite the short notice, Monsieur Lavigne has once more excelled himself in arranging for us to stay in a magnificent four storey Baroque style town house which overlooks the Piazza Navona.

Which is just as well. Because despite sleeping well enough last night, the rigours of train travel have left my aunt and I feeling somewhat weary, and in need of rest. Thankfully, the sun is shining and the view from the fourth-floor balcony is just the tonic we need.

While I sit back and bask in the late autumn sunshine, the housemaid pours two glasses of ice water and places a slice of lemon in each before excusing herself. As soon as she is gone, Aunt Caroline asks, "Is everything alright, Monty?"

"Yes, of course," I reply. "Why, do I look worried about something?"

Grinning, Caroline says, "Not worried, but that young woman was just your type, and you barely gave her a second look."

"My type, Caroline? And what would that be?" I smirk.

Not usually known as one for making jokes, we both chuckle at her response. "On recent form, it would appear anything with breasts and an arse, Nephew."

Our laughter dies down, and she adds more seriously, "Anyway, there is precious little time for such tomfoolery. We have less than a week in Rome in which you must fully immerse yourself in the culture of this great city."

Misreading the change in mood, I foolishly joke, "Didn't Roman culture die out at around the same time as the Roman empire?"

Unamused, Caroline gets to her feet and points to the magnificent granite centrepiece in the square below. "That is the Fontana dei Quattro Fiumi. The fountain of the four rivers. And those two are the Fontana del Moro, and the Fontana de Neptune. Why, this square alone contains more history and culture than most of the towns and cities in England combined."

She then turns to face me, "Rome is a city awash with history, the arts and culture. And you must learn it all."

"Yes, of course." I nod. "I shall do my very best."

"Yes, I'm sure you will, Monty. But for now, there is something I should like you to do for me."

Only too keen to be of assistance, I'm about to stand when Caroline places a hand on my shoulder. "No, finish your drink first and then come to my room."

She leaves without another word, and I'm left wondering exactly what she might be expecting of me.

I have my suspicions of course and considering we haven't been intimate since our tumble on the Orient Express, I arrogantly assume she must be craving another dose of Montague Finch-Morton the Third.

* * * * * * * *

The bedroom door is slightly ajar, but not wishing to assume anything, I knock lightly and ask, "May I come in?"

"I will be very disappointed if you don't," Caroline replies softly. "Come in and close the door behind you."

Inside the room, the drapes have been closed and the only light is coming from half a dozen candles dotted around the room. The air is filled with the sweet scent of burning incense, and unsurprisingly, I find the object of my current lust face down on her bed completely naked.

Her full rounded buttocks are wonderfully illuminated by the flickering candles and are oddly reminiscent of a pair of smooth but featureless globes. On the table beside her, I see a selection of fragrant oils in small glass bottles.

Approaching the bed, I slowly run a finger down Caroline's spine and quietly ask, "Am I to assume you would like me to massage you?"

Turning her head, she looks up and replies, "You assume correctly, Nephew. Mademoiselle Béatrice Aguillard seemed to be most appreciative of your massage skills, and I myself am now quite intrigued to sample them for myself."

"That's right," I tut loudly. "You were spying on me through that bloody mirror, weren't you?"

"Not spying, Monty. I told you before, Eric and I were assessing your performance."

"It was still a bloody gross intrusion of my privacy," I mutter.

"It is also ancient history." Caroline frowns. "But enough of that. Unlike you, it's been rather a long time since my last climax. So, instead of moaning, why don't you reach for one of those bottles, and show your aunt just how much you appreciate her."

In Aunt Caroline's world anything longer than twenty-four hours might reasonably be considered a long time between climaxes.

Ignoring my desire to enquire what she got up to in Munich, I wisely keep my thoughts to myself and obediently remove the stopper from one of the bottles.

After warming the oil in my hands, I gently work it into Caroline's back, before I press my fingers and thumbs more firmly into her shoulders. Shuddering slightly, she softly moans, "Oh, that is so good, darling."

Leaning forward to kiss the side of her neck, I whisper in her ear, "I know, and I'm very glad to be of service."

Done with her shoulders and arms, I move further down the bed and trickle more oil onto the lower part of her legs. Up to now, other than the occasional soft groan of pleasure, her breathing has remained calm and shallow.

All that is about to change when my hands move higher to firmly knead her buttocks, and I lightly brush an oily index finger between her lips and across her clitoris.

"Oh, you absolute bastard." She groans. Her arse lifts a few inches into the air, and I look down with smug satisfaction at her obvious arousal. Carefully probing her moisture, two fingers slowly disappear inside, whilst my thumb lightly flickers across her bullet-hard nub.

Dangerously aroused and desperate for more, Caroline pushes backward onto my fingers. "Oh, God. Oh my God. Yes, Monty, yes, that is so—"

Relishing my moment of control, I abruptly remove my oily digits from her sopping wet cunny and firmly order, "Turn over."

She obeys without question, and her legs spread in obvious anticipation of my finishing what I've started. For a moment, I silently relish the sight of her lustrous glistening bush, and her nipples standing hard and proud.

Deliberately ignoring her pleas for completion, I instead smile and pour more oil into my hands to massage her firm and bountiful breasts. I work her nipples as hard as I did with Princess Eleonore. When there is no complaint, I lift my hands to her throat and gently squeeze.

"Oh, Monty. Where did you learn that?" she gasps. "Nobody has ever done that to—"

Her words falter under an immense wave of pleasure, as a finger and thumb reacquaint themselves with her glistening button. Panting heavily, she breathlessly moans, "Yes, my darling, take me to heaven."

At the same time, she fumbles for the buttons on my breeches and demands, "Get it out. Get it out and play with it while you plough my holes."

For the last ten-minutes, my rod has felt like a hunting dog straining at the leash. Naturally then, it is a great relief to finally release him into the fresh air.

Smiling wickedly, Caroline firmly squeezes my balls, before she lets go, and snarls again, "Now fuck my holes, you dirty bastard."

The first time I was unsure if I had heard correctly. The second time is confirmation enough, and I willingly spread my fingers to simultaneously assault both of her heavenly chambers.

Still vigorously working her clitoris with my thumb, I alternate between stroking myself with my other hand, and roughly twisting her engorged nipples. Like the Princess Eleonore, the pain appears to be a massive turn on.

Caroline is soon gasping for air, and her pubic mound smashes relentlessly against my knuckles to signal the onset of her orgasm.

"Don't you dare stop." She gasps. "Don't you bloody dare stop."

I couldn't even if I had wanted to. Mesmerized by the naked goddess writhing on the bed, I now want her to cum even more desperately than she wants it for herself.

Knowing exactly what to say to take her over the precipice, I look her in the eye and whisper, "Cum for me, Aunt Caroline. Cum for your nephew Monty."

Shuddering uncontrollably, her juices flood across my fingers, and I lean forward and sneer, "That's it, you filthy whore. Don't hold anything back. I want it all."

All the while, I'm still furiously pumping on my meaty shaft. When my own breathing suddenly picks up speed, Caroline rolls to the side and demands, "In my mouth. Quickly, before it's too late."

With barely enough time to react, her lip's part just as my first eruption spurts across her face. The second is right on target and she takes a moment to swirl it around in her mouth, before she hungrily swallows it down.

The remainder she slowly savours by gently squeezing on my shaft to expel any remaining morsels of my climax before lapping them up with the tip of her tongue. With the job complete, Caroline grins her satisfaction and tenderly plants a kiss on the end of my rod.

She then looks up and nods her appreciation. "I was right what I said yesterday. Your mother is going to be very proud of you."

Her eyes slowly lower to my groin and her smile changes to a smirk. "And of the fine, and upstanding gentleman you have become."

I'm still buttoning my breeches when Caroline pulls a blanket across herself, and subtly indicates for me to leave. "You should take some rest now, darling. This evening we shall dine at one of the fine restaurants on the Piazza."

* * * * * * * *

The venue of choice for dinner is on the far side of the Piazza and is just a few minutes' walk from our accommodation. Typically, Rome in its design and décor, it is also extremely busy. Unfortunately, we don't have a reservation.

The head waiter is genuinely apologetic and politely suggests we try again in an hour. "I think by then, we may have a table available."

I'm about to reach for my wallet when Caroline discretely whispers, "Let me handle this, Monty."

She then smiles sweetly, and points to the waiter's ledger. "Thank you, that would be wonderful. The reservation will be for three guests and will be in the name of Montague Finch-Morton the Third, Eighth Earl of Benfleet, and Lady Caroline Winstanley."

My aunt is as smart as she is beautiful. She is also a master of manipulation and knows only too well how to impress. The waiter now looks slightly awestruck, but before he can say anything, Caroline plays her ace card.

"And our guest this evening is the Contessa Francesca da Carrara."

Suddenly pale, the waiter blusters an apology before he calls for a colleague and frantically mutters something unintelligible. Equally stunned, the second waiter scurries away to prepare our table, while the first continues to nervously apologise. "Once again, I am so sorry. If I had known who you were, and that you were with the Contessa, I would—"

"That's quite alright," Caroline interrupts. "Is our table ready?"

"Yes, of course," the waiter replies stepping aside. "Welcome to the Ristorante Piperno."

Our table has a prime position close to the fire, and as soon as the waiter leaves, I turn to Caroline and nod appreciatively. "That was most impressive."

"It was nothing," she replies. "The Italian's are as easily impressed by money and titles as anyone else. And why have a title if you're not going to use it to your advantage?"

She is right, of course, and I nod my agreement. "I shall remember that."

"And if that doesn't work, and all else fails, well that's when you reach for your wallet." Caroline giggles.

Moments later, the still sheepish looking head waiter returns carrying a large bottle of Chianti. Doing his best to remain calm, he politely lowers his head. "With the compliments of the house. May I pour, sir?"

Never one to turn down a free drink, I nod and gesture to Caroline's glass. "Yes, of course, ladies first."

He pours our wine, before nervously excusing himself. "Please enjoy, I shall return shortly with the menus."

"You have left that man quite terrified." I chuckle.

"Not me." Caroline smirks. "It was the mention of the contessa and the thought of upsetting her, that has him quaking in his boots."

"Is she really that intimidating?" I ask.

"Not particularly." Caroline smiles. "But she is from an extremely wealthy and influential Roman family. In addition to their interests in agriculture, industry, and banking, they also own many high-profile properties here in the city."

There is a momentary pause, before she smiles again and casually adds, "Including the Ristorante Piperno."

"Christ all mighty. It's no wonder the man is so petrified." I chuckle. "Then why didn't you just tell him that at the—"

Behind us there is a sudden low murmur from the other diners, and I turn to see what all the fuss is about. A strikingly tall, well-dressed woman is slowly making her way through the restaurant in a subtle and understated way that says she owns the place—without actually saying it.

Her hair is dark and lustrous. Her eyes are the deepest chocolate brown, and although in her late forties, the contessa's complexion is as smooth and flawless as a woman half her age.

The head waiter is anxiously shuffling along behind her tightly clutching the menus. Before she reaches our table, I lean across and whisper, "It's a shame she is not a little younger. She is quite stunning, and with all that money and property, she sounds just my type."

"Think again." Caroline giggles. "Francesca is far too smart for you, darling. She would also eat you alive, and let's just say, well, I don't think—in fact, I know she is not your type."

Before I can ask her to explain herself, the Contessa joins us, and we both stand to meet her. While she enthusiastically hugs and kisses my aunt, I mentally note how much more breathtaking she is up close.

When she turns to me, I firmly maintain eye contact, as I softly plant a kiss on her outstretched hand. "My very great pleasure to meet you, Contessa."

"And I you," she replies smiling. "I have heard so much about you from Lady Caroline. And please, call me Francesca."

Wondering exactly what she might have heard, I cover my blushes by helping her to her seat. "Thank you, Montague. That is very kind." She smiles again.

The waiter is still hovering and after pouring a glass of Chianti for the Contessa, he nervously asks, "Would you like to see the menus now?"

"Nonsense," she snaps dismissively. "You know what I like, Lorenzo. We shall have the Artichokes alla Giudia, and the salt cod."

My aunt was right, Francesca Da Carrara is clearly a woman in control. But is she so powerful as to be beyond my reach?

I think not. I'm a Finch-Morton man after all, and I haven't failed yet. Ignoring my aunts earlier warning, I look across the table and smile. "I hope you don't think me too forward, Francesca, but I would be failing in my duty as a gentleman if I didn't compliment you on your beauty."

While Caroline frowns, and Francesca looks on with a mix of bemusement and expectation, I continue by saying, "Of all the women I have met thus far on our journey, you really are quite the most beautiful of them all."

Completely unmoved, the contessa reaches for Caroline's hand. "Thank you, Montague. But I think you do Lady Caroline a grave injustice. Surely, she is the most beautiful woman in the room this evening?"

Knowing I'm being tested, I look appreciatively to each of the women in turn before raising my glass. "Contessa, you have me at a disadvantage. I am delighted however to be in the company of the two most beautiful women in Europe."

Seemingly pleased with my response, Francesca raises her own glass. "You were right, Caroline, he is something of a charmer isn't he?"

"Something like that," Caroline replies unconvincingly. "My nephew is indeed becoming quite the man about town."

* * * * * * * *

An hour into the meal, I excuse myself to use the bathroom. When I return, the ladies abruptly stop talking and suddenly suspicious, I ask, "Oh yes, and what were you two ladies just talking about?"

Looking altogether mischievous, Francesca smirks at Aunt Caroline before saying, "Actually, we were just discussing your reasons for making this journey, and of course your success thus far."

Now even more intrigued to know exactly what they were discussing, I frown and ask, "Thus far?"

"Yes." Francesca smiles. "Your success in turning yourself into an eligible young gentleman. But in particular your success in seducing one Mademoiselle Béatrice Aguillard. Your aunt would have me understand you left quite the impression on her?"

I'm slightly lost for words, and Francesca is quick to cheekily take advantage. "When exactly will you be taking her to Buckingham Palace, Montague?"

To my side, Caroline sniggers at my discomfort. Knowing Francesca has got the better of me, I shrug and raise my glass again. "Well played, Contessa. Well played."

Returning the compliment, she nods politely and then catches me completely off guard. "And do you consider me as easily seduced as that young woman?"

Already stunned by the directness of her question, the next comment leaves me embarrassed and slightly mortified. "And is it right you consider me, *just your type?*"

"Really?" I scowl at Caroline. "Is nothing sacred anymore?"

Before she can reply, Francesca giggles and touches my hand. "There are no secrets here, Montague. Caroline and I are both very good friends of Monsieur Lavigne and have known each other a very long time."

She then leans across the table and lowers her voice, "And speaking of secrets, I should very much like to hear more about your escapades with Princess Eleonore when you have the time."

Believing her interest in my sexual encounters to be an indicator of her interest in me, I'm about to start regaling her with all the juicy details when she suddenly places a hand across my own. "But not now. It is getting late, and I understand you have an early start in the morning."

Right on cue, Lorenzo appears with our overcoats. Expecting to part ways, I'm surprised when the contessa insists on escorting us back across the Piazza to our accommodation.

More surprising is finding she has her own key and is fully familiar with the layout. Noting my astonishment she smiles and asks, "I trust you are finding my home to your liking, Montague?"

"It is most comfortable." I nod. "Most comfortable indeed."

She then turns toward the staircase with the same look of mischief I saw earlier. "Come, it is getting late. We should all sleep now."

Suddenly hopeful of a ménage à trois, I excitedly follow the two women toward the second-floor landing. Caroline's bedroom is opposite to mine, and my hopes rise further when she opens the door and invites us both in.

Francesca is the first to enter the room. I, however, am barely through the door when Caroline shakes her head and tells me to stop. "That is far enough, Monty."

She then says, "You must have been wondering what exactly I meant when I said Francesca was not your type?"

There is barely enough time for me to think of a response, before I'm stunned to silence when Caroline pulls her friend toward her and kisses her directly on the lips.

Smiling sympathetically, Francesca quietly says, "Try not to take it too personally, Montague. You may not be my type. But nor then is any man."

To illustrate her point, she places a hand across Caroline's bosom, and the two women kiss passionately. Still naively hopeful of an invitation to join, I quietly watch them, looking and feeling somewhat awkward.

When they do finally break their embrace, Francesca looks down to the rapidly growing bulge in the front of my breeches.

"My my." She grins "That is quite the compliment. And it would be such a shame for it to go to waste."

Taking this as my cue, I excitedly reach for my top button and Aunt Caroline suddenly giggles. "Whoa, not so fast, Monty. Francesca means you might want to tug yourself off tonight."

To make the point perfectly clear, the two women kiss again, before Francesca lays down on the bed, and Caroline somewhat dismissively points to the door. "Please make sure you close that properly on your way out."

I leave feeling slightly humiliated. I'm also feeling as randy as a dog in heat but have no bloody intention of bashing the bishop tonight.

Not giving a damn who hears me, I lean over the staircase handrail and yell from the top of my voice, "Betsy, get your pretty little arse up here."

* * * * * * * *

The next four days are not completely dissimilar to my educational tour of Paris. I do of course have considerably less time, and therefore the time spent in each location is much less than one would have ordinarily desired.

I am however escorted by an excellent and highly knowledgeable English-speaking guide who does his best to ensure we experience as much as possible of this great city in the time available.

Starting with the Capitoline museums, we also visit all the major galleries and marvel at the works of Caravaggio, Michelangelo, and Botticelli. On one of the evenings, I'm fortunate to attend a performance of the opera Rigoletto by Giuseppe Verdi in the famous Teatro Argentina.

On my final day with my guide, we visit the iconic Roman Colosseum in the morning. We then spend a wonderful afternoon roaming the Vatican City.

We finish the day enjoying dinner in a quaint taverna with marvellous views over the Tiber River, and Saint Peter's Basilica.

* * * * * * * *

By the time I arrive home, it is almost 10 pm, and I'm surprised to find Johnathan waiting patiently in the hallway to meet me. After helping me remove my overcoat, he turns toward the staircase. "Lady Caroline and the contessa are expecting you for drinks on the fourth-floor balcony, sir."

Mildly suspicious, I ask him, "Just drinks, Johnathan?"

His expression remains stoic. His reply gives nothing away. "That's what they said, sir."

After Munich and the threat of abandonment, it is unlikely he would defy his mistress a second time. Regardless, I don't press him further, and I climb the stairs expecting nothing more than a drink.

Although the room is in darkness, the voices and laughter from the balcony are evident as soon as I open the door. When it loudly clicks shut behind me, I hear Caroline say, "Quickly. That must be him now."

A moment later the laughter dies down, and she shouts, "Monty dear, is that you? Come outside. We have a nice surprise waiting for you."

What greets me on the balcony is something akin to a medieval orgy, or perhaps more appropriately given our current location—a Roman orgy. I am however the only man present.

My aunt and Francesca are seated beside each other on a long rattan sofa. Both are topless, and both have their skirts hitched high above the waist. Betsy is also topless and is on her knees vigorously tonguing the contessa's quim. Caroline is noisily suckling on one of her friend's enormous breasts.

My own surprise is facing away from me. Francesca's housemaid is completely naked, and her wrists have been tightly bound to an iron rail secured to the top of the balcony handrail.

Briefly looking up from her suckling, Aunt Caroline struggles to suppress her grin. "She is a late birthday present from me, as well as a farewell gift from Francesca. Enjoy my dear."

Slightly apprehensive, I turn to the contessa, "Are you absolutely sure she is okay with this?"

"More than okay." Francesca smiles. "Giovanna has been looking forward to it since the moment I let her in on our plan."

As if to confirm her mistress's words, the young woman leans further forward and spreads her legs invitingly.

"Go on," Caroline urges. She then salaciously wiggles her tongue. "Betsy has done a nice job warming her up for you."

I'm already as hard as a rock, and now satisfied she is a willing participant, I excitedly step forward to inspect my gift.

Giovanna's breasts are bigger than I had imagined, and they now hang down like delicious milky udders. Her areolae are as dark as burnished copper and are as large as saucers. Her nipples quickly stiffen under my touch, and she trembles gently from a heady mix of excitement and the late evening chill.

Gently lifting her head, I kiss her on the cheek and ask, "How badly do you want me to fuck you, Giovanna?"

Her English is basic at best, but she understands exactly what I'm asking.

"Yes, sir. Very much, sir."

"That's good. That's very good," I mutter whilst reaching down to unbutton myself. The release of my bloated shaft close to her face causes Giovanna to gasp and leaves her wide eyed and salivating. Behind us, one of the women laughs, and I hear Francesca mutter, "I don't think she was quite expecting that."

"Too big for her?" Caroline giggles.

"Well." Francesca laughs again. "Let's just say her husband is not exactly blessed in that department."

Suddenly feeling empowered, I lift Giovanna's head again, and sneer, "Is that true? Does your husband have the penis of a woman?"

This time I might as well be speaking Mandarin Chinese. But it's of no consequence to me. Understanding or not, this young woman is going to get it. And she is going to get it hard.

Moving behind her, I use my feet to splay her legs further apart. Her buttocks are soft and round. Her bush is thick, dark, and luxurious.

Although shimmeringly obvious, I spread her cheeks wide apart to confirm her arousal for myself with a finger. Her slit is moist and slippery, and groaning my satisfaction, I mumble to no one in particular, "You were right, Betsy has done a marvellous job."

Thinking I'm talking to her, Giovanna slightly turns her head. "I sorry, I do not understand."

"And why would you?" I mumble while lining myself up at the entrance to her honeypot, "I'm sure you will understand this though?"

I slowly push forward, and the young woman gasps as her lips are forced apart by the first few inches of my meat. Allowing her just a moment to catch her breath, I gently rock back and forth to lubricate myself. I then penetrate her a little deeper, and Giovanna softly moans, "Oh, Cosi Grande, Cosi Grande."

"You think this is big." I snigger. "I've barely even got started."

Pulling myself out to the tip, I push forward again to the halfway point, and take a firm hold on Giovanna's hair, "This is it, girl. Time to say your prayers."

Without further warm up or warning, I sink myself to the hilt, and suddenly fluent in English again, the young woman breathlessly screams, "Oh, fuck. Oh yes."

Behind us, the ladies have paused their own fun to watch the show. Slightly unnerved by the silence, I turn my head and a smiling Aunt Caroline playfully waves me away. "Oh don't mind us, dear. You just carry on as if we weren't here."

With no intention of minding anyone but myself, I turn back and reach for Giovanna's drooping breasts. I squeeze them hard, and then hammer my hips into her pudgy ass cheeks.

It's been nearly a week since my last climax, and heavy with seed, my balls slap noisily against her puffy lips as I relentlessly batter her without mercy or remorse. The increasing intensity of her moans spurs me on, and in turn I increase the speed and ferocity of my hammering. Conscious also of my partner's needs, I reach below to squeeze and fondle her moist swollen nub.

It is soon apparent we are both close to climax, and from behind Francesca orders, "Inside her. Cum inside her."

That had been my plan all along, but happy to oblige our host, I noisily grunt and discharge my oversized load deep inside Giovanna's belly. Just moments later her own body shudders and her vaginal muscles noticeably tighten around my rod as she noisily reaches her peak.

Reluctant to break away, but suddenly aware of how cold it is, I carefully pull out, hitch up my breeches, and reach forward to untie Giovanna's restraints.

I'm about to wrap my jacket around her shoulders when her mistress sits up to intervene, "Thank you, Montague. That is very gallant of you, but the jacket won't be necessary."

She then smiles and uses a hand to roughly spread Caroline's legs. "Giovanna's work is not yet done for the day. Isn't that, right?" she asks her housemaid.

In response, the young woman drop to her knees beside Betsy. While both servants diligently go about their work, Aunt Caroline looks up and smiles. "That will be all for this evening, Monty."

Beside her, Francesca nods her concurrence and breathlessly adds, "Yes, and a belated happy birthday, Montague. Sleep well."

Outside, I stop for a moment on the landing, and shake my head at the utter absurdity of it all. "Has the whole world gone completely mad?" I ask myself. "And if it has, then why do I find it so damn exhilarating?"

* * * * * * * *

The distance from Rome to Paris by rail is a little under nine-hundred miles all in. It is then a very great relief when Caroline confirms there is enough time for a short detour and stopover on our way.

As the train approaches the station, I turn to her and ask, "Tell me again, what is so important about Marseille? I mean, it's not exactly brimming with culture now, is it?"

"And nor was I expecting it to be," Caroline tuts. "And if you were to pay more attention to me every now and then, you would already know we are here for me to meet an old friend."

Her smiles give away her real intent, and I ask knowingly, "Oh, yes, and who exactly is this old friend of yours?"

"See for yourself," she replies, pointing through the window.

At the end of the platform, a tall broad-shouldered gentleman in the uniform of a major of the French Foreign Legion is waiting patiently for the train to come to a halt.

Failing miserably to hide my disapproval, I moodily ask, "Oh yes, and how is it you know this Froggie?"

"Well, not that it's really any of your business," Caroline replies. "But Charles is as English as you or I. He was also a very good friend of my dear departed husband. They served together in the guards."

The train slows to a complete stop and spotting us through the window the immaculately attired officer smiles and doffs his Kepi. He then opens the carriage door and climbs aboard.

Unlike Caroline's other male friends, this chap appears rather less cultured. Or perhaps he has simply spent too many years tramping around in the desert.

Whatever the reason, he ignores the usual social graces, and instead throws his arms around her in a tight bear hug and loudly declares, "My God, Caroline. You don't know how bloody good it is to see you again."

He then plants a slobbery kiss on each of her cheeks, before putting her down. Although a little take aback, Caroline still smiles sweetly. "Thank you Charles, it's also good to see you again. It's been far too long."

"It has." He nods. "But you are here now."

He then turns to me and thrusts out a hand. "You must be Montague?"

Without waiting for my response, he instead proceeds to introduce himself. "Major Charles Boxhall, Adjutant third regiment of the French

Foreign Legion. Formally a lieutenant of the Grenadier Guards. Delighted to meet you, old man."

Suddenly impatient, he turns back and takes Aunt Caroline by the hand. "Well then, I think we should get going. The champagne is on ice, and I'm due back on duty tomorrow morning. So, let's not waste a minute of our time together."

I'm about to reach for my jacket when Caroline shakes her head and Charles holds up a strong weathered hand. "I'm sorry, Montague, but what I have in mind for this evening is more along the lines of a party just for two."

"Don't look so disappointed," Caroline consoles. "The dining car will remain open all night, and if you get really bored, I seem to remember there are one or two bars just outside the station entrance."

She then grins and adds, "And if all else fails, I'm sure Betsy and Johnathan would be happy to keep you company."

To her side, a smug looking Boxhall smirks, "Chin up, old man. I shall be taking very good care of your aunt, and I'll have her back in good time in the morning."

"I bloody bet you will," I think to myself.

Before they leave, he cautions, "Oh and I wouldn't particularly recommend either of those bars if you know what's good for you. I think probably better you stick with the dining car."

They leave together, and I petulantly mumble under my breath, "The bloody cheek of the man. What the hell would he know about what is good for me?"

* * * * * * * *

As expected, very few other passengers are staying on board overnight, and barring a couple of bored looking stewards, the dining car is otherwise completely deserted.

Determined to make the best of a bad situation, I order a light supper and wash it down with two large glasses of scotch.

By the time one of the stewards offers me a third, I'm as mind numbingly bored as he is, and I politely refuse.

"I'm sure those bars must be a damn site more interesting than this," I think. "And what's the worst that can happen, anyway?"

I return to the cabin to fetch my overcoat and collect my pocket watch. It's just after 9 pm, and I calculate if I have two or three more drinks, I can be back on board and asleep by midnight at the latest. Happy with my plan, I alight the train, and leave the station in search of some excitement.

As alluded too, both bars are within easy spitting distance of the station entrance. Ordinarily I might have needed a moment to decide which of them to visit first, but on this particular evening, there is no need for me to think for myself.

Recently burnt out, the heavy scent of charred timber still hangs heavy in the air, as I pass the ruins of the first bar. The second bar although still standing, looks only slightly less salubrious than the first.

Outside, two sailors are brawling and a third violently vomits onto the pavement just a few yards from my feet. I gingerly peer through the grubby windows and can see the clientele inside are almost entirely male.

Most appear to be sailors or are wearing uniforms similar to the one worn by Major Boxhall. All appear drunk or are otherwise lively and boisterous.

Remembering his warning, I briefly consider returning to the train before my bravado gets the better of me and I place a hand on the door. Inside, the noisy chatter ceases almost as soon as the door closes behind me. Behind the bar, a giant of a man in a grubby striped apron stops pouring a beer and turns to me with a scowl. All others in the room look me up and down with barely concealed contempt.

I'm already feeling I've made a mistake in coming here when the barman noisily grunts, "Monsieur, I think you must be lost, yes? This bar is for legionnaires, sailors, and fishermen only."

His wiry moustache is as greasy as the last remaining wisps of hair on his head, and determined not to be intimidated, I smile and point to his shiny dome. "I think the only thing lost in here is your hair, Monsieur."

My joke causes a general ripple of laughter from all but the barman himself who looks fit to explode. Flushed with anger, he reaches below the counter for a vicious looking club. He is almost upon me when I produce one of the gold sovereigns gifted to me by Monsieur Lavigne for use in the event of an emergency.

Considering my impending death to more than qualify as an emergency, I hurriedly shout, "Drink's all round, barman. And keep them coming until this is done."

Stopped in his tracks by my unexpected offer, the ogre is caught between his obvious desire to bludgeon me to death, and his other desire to take my gold. In the end, and to my very great relief, his greed gets the better of him. With all watching on, he rudely snatches the coin from my hand, and skulks back to the bar.

I wait until everyone else has a drink in hand. I then take a glass of cognac for myself, and casually turn to survey my fellow drinkers. Most in the room have lost interest in me and have gone back to whatever they were doing before. One of the sailors is now blasting out a lively tune on a battered accordion.

Feeling the legionnaires are in the majority and hoping to build on the good will of my recent generosity, I raise my glass and loudly toast, "Vive la Légion."

My words are met with obvious approval, and to a man the legionnaires get to their feet and return the toast. Content that any possible danger to my wellbeing has passed for now, I turn back to the barman and ask for a large beer. Still clearly unimpressed with me, he pours it without a word, and I take it to the only unoccupied table in the room.

I've barely had time to take a seat when I'm approached by a heavily made-up tart in her mid to late fifties. Clearly a woman of business, she wastes no time in sliding along the bench beside me to pout. "Allo, mon chérie. It makes me so sad, to see such a handsome man sitting all alone."

"Oh, really." I nod somewhat sarcastically. "And what do you propose to do about it – I'm sorry, I didn't catch your name?"

"It is Céline, Monsieur." She purrs and places a hand on my thigh. "Perhaps you might enjoy the company of a lady?"

Feeling mischievous, I decide to tease her. "That's a splendid suggestion, Céline. And please be sure to let me know when the ladies arrive."

My humour is wasted on a woman much more interested in the contents of my wallet. Completely emotionless, she slides her hand across my appendage and whispers, "For the right price, it will be my pleasure to keep you company, my darling."

In all honestly, she is as rough as the calloused on a blacksmith's hands, but my libido is rapidly rising under her touch, and with scant else likely to be on offer this evening, I ask, "And how much will it cost me for the pleasure of your company?"

Giggling like a schoolgirl, she whispers in my ear, "It is not polite to put a price on my services, but if you insist, it will be one-hundred-francs for the evening."

Clearly dazzled by my expensive attire and earlier act of generosity, the quoted price is nothing if not outrageous. Stifling my desire to laugh, I instead whisper back, "And how much for a quick knee trembler outside?"

Feigning offence Céline abruptly pulls away, and loudly exclaims, "Monsieur, what kind of woman do you take me for?"

When I open my wallet, her eyes light up, and she quickly answers her own question. "But how much will you offer me for this thing you ask for?"

I don't have francs, but my wallet is stuffed with German and Italian banknotes. I take out half a dozen and casually hand them over. "Is this enough?"

I have no idea if I've overpaid, but the notes swiftly disappear down the front of Céline's blouse, and she offers me a hand. "Come, Monsieur, I know of a quiet place close by where we won't be disturbed."

She leads me outside and we immediately turn down an alley at the side of the bar until we reach a small storage yard. It is filled with filthy stacks of wooden beer crates, and the air is heavy with the pungent scent of vomit and stale urine.

Concealing my disgust, we find a space beside a wall, and reluctant to spend too long out here, I tell Céline, "Forget about the knee trembler. You can pleasure me with your mouth instead."

She nods and obediently drops to her knees to unbutton me. "As you wish, Monsieur."

I'm already somewhat hard, and after a few deft strokes of her wrist the tart giggles and mutters to herself, "Mon Dieu, Monsieur, it is a monster."

Braced for her lips to engulf me, I tilt my head and close my eyes in expectation. A moment later something hard prods between my shoulder blades, and a gruff voice snarls, "Turn around, and don't do anything stupid."

Shocked but conscious of my continued exposure, I nervously ask, "Is it okay if I button myself up first?"

"Quickly," the voice growls. "And no funny business."

I slowly turn and find myself staring at three tough looking legionnaires. The older one in the middle is pointing a revolver and has three chevrons on his arm.

"You, get out of here," He barks at Céline.

The whore doesn't need telling twice. She quickly scurries away while the three men silently weigh me up. Hopelessly outnumbered and hopelessly outgunned, I dismiss the option of violence in favour of tact and diplomacy.

"I don't know what this is, but you should know I am a very good friend of Major Charles Boxhall, adjutant of the third regiment."

The three men look to each other, before the sergeant turns back and nods agreeably. He then lowers his weapon. "Well why didn't you say so?"

His accent has a strong hint of Spanish, and slightly more relaxed, I smile and ask, "You know Major Boxhall?"

"Do we?" the sergeant asks his colleagues. Both men nod and I'm about to step forward to introduce myself when I'm ordered back, and the revolver is jabbed into my chest.

"We all know Major Boxhall," the legionnaire snarls. "The man is a bastard. Now enough of this time wasting, give us all your money, and that shiny gold watch I see in your pocket."

I'm slightly hesitant, and to assert how serious they are the sergeant lifts the revolver under my chin. "Unless you want to die in this piss-soaked hovel, you shouldn't keep us waiting."

I willingly hand over my wallet but am understandably hesitant to part with my watch. At a nod from the sergeant, one of his men steps forward and roughly yanks it from my pocket. Hopeful this will satisfy them enough to leave. I'm surprised when the sergeant points to my belt. "And the rest?"

Hoping to bluff it out, I frown and raise my hands. "You already have everything."

A fist slams into the side of my head and I'm sent reeling backward into the wall. The sergeant then hands his revolver to the man closest to him and kneels beside me to unbuckle my belt. Yanking on the end of it, he grunts, "That was for lying to me."

With the belt now rolled up in his hand, he turns to his men and orders, "Give this Englishman a beating and send him on his way."

The order is met with smiles of approval from the legionnaires, and both roughly seize an arm to yank me back to my feet. The first of them is poised to pummel my face when the sergeant suddenly turns back and shouts, "Wait!"

Jabbing at the inscription on the back of the pocket watch he then thrusts it under my nose and demands, "How do you know Eric Lavigne?"

Slightly taken aback by the question, I bluster, "He's, um, a good friend of both myself, and my aunt Lady Caroline Winstanley."

Suddenly calm the sergeant of legionnaires orders his men to release me. Then looking slightly embarrassed he steps forward to straighten my jacket, and as he pats me down, I ask, "Are you also an acquaintance of Monsieur Lavigne?"

"Not Monsieur Lavigne." The sergeant chuckles. "Captain Lavigne was my commanding officer in Algeria and Morocco many years ago. He is a very great man. A very great man indeed."

Taking my arm the veteran sergeant says, "Come, we must celebrate this chance encounter with a drink."

Back inside the bar a table is quickly cleared for us, and the sergeant orders the barman, "Cognac, beer, and absinthe for my friends. And get a move on you hideously ugly bastard."

Although disgruntled, the barman is no fool and knows he is no match for the grizzled military man. Wisely choosing to hold his tongue, he turns away to fetch the drinks, and I take the opportunity to introduce myself to the men around the table.

The sergeant then introduces himself as Matías. "And this pair of rogues are Thomas and Francis."

Surprisingly, both men have unmistakable English west country accents, and now fully acquainted with my assailants, I discretely point to the pocket watch still in the sergeant's hand. "Do you think I could get that back, Matías?"

"Yes, of course." He nods and hands it over along with my wallet.

The wallet is somewhat lighter than it was previously, but I choose not to mention it. I do though enquire after my belt.

This time there is a slight delay as Matías considers his response. When he is ready, he smiles and places the belt onto the table.

Five sovereigns remain inside the hidden compartment, and while I look on, he takes out three and hands one to each of his men. The third disappears into his own pocket.

Slowly nodding, he says, "I would say you got off rather lightly all things considered. And a sovereign each is no price at all for saving you, wouldn't you say?"

Obviously confused, I shake my head and ask, "For saving me?"

"Saving you from Mademoiselle Céline." He suddenly roars with laughter. "That woman is riddled with the pox, and a dose from her would have cost you far more than three gold sovereigns my friend."

The drinks arrive, and Matías enthusiastically slaps me on the back. "Now drink up, Montague, and tell me everything you know about Capitaine Lavigne."

Chapter Eleven

Return to Paris – 22 December 1898

My recollection of saying farewell to my new friends and returning to the train is hazy to say the least. The only things I vaguely recall are the sun starting to rise, and my taking a rather long piss on the station platform. Beyond that, everything else is somewhat of a blur.

In fact, the only two things I know with absolute certainty are number one – I had a jolly good time last night. And number two – I am now paying the price for it.

Already thoroughly nauseous, my sudden awareness of the train carriage swaying from side to side has me gulping for fresh air to prevent myself from emptying my stomach onto the floor. At the same time, the incessant hammering on my cabin door is a mocking accompaniment to the incessant hammering in my head.

Desperate to shut out the noise, I bury my head into a pillow and shout, "Whoever that is, bloody well bugger off and leave me alone."

In reality, my shout is barely more than a croak. Even if it wasn't, it is unlikely Johnathan would have listened to me anyway. With orders from his mistress and a key from the senior conductor, he lets himself in and enthusiastically throws open the curtains.

"Time to get up, sir. Lady Caroline is insistent you join her for dinner."

The mention of the word dinner leaves me confused, and I slowly lift my head from the pillow. "What in God's name are you talking about, Johnathan? It's still light outside. What happened to breakfast and lunch?"

The young valet struggles to suppress a grin as he points to the watch hanging by its chain from my pocket. "It's nearly five in the afternoon, sir. You've been sleeping all day."

Suddenly bolt upright, I fumble for the watch with one hand and rub the sleep from my eyes with the other. "What, no that can't be right?"

When I realise it really is that time, I leap from the bed and look through the window. "Where the hell are we?"

Johnathan's reply is as calm as ever. "Just under halfway to Paris, sir." He then casually passes comment, "The countryside is quite beautiful. It looks a lot like England don't you think?"

He's probably right, but much as I would like to stand and admire the scenery of France, my mouth has suddenly filled with saliva, and I now have something much more pressing to attend to.

Desperately lunging for the bathroom door, I barely make it to the WC before last nights alcohol spews from my mouth in a violent torrent of all that is foul and unpleasant.

Johnathan patiently waits for me to finish and compose myself, but when I'm still intermittently chundering five minutes later, he hands me a towel and quietly says, "I'll let Lady Caroline know you are awake, and that you will be joining her for dinner, sir."

Before excusing himself, he suggests, "Dinner is not until seven-thirty. I don't suggest you go back to sleep though. Stay awake and freshen up. You will feel much better for it, sir."

I thank him with a backward wave of my hand. A moment later the bathroom door closes behind me, and I noisily return to the business of heaving my guts up.

* * * * * * * *

Although I'm feeling far less nauseous than earlier, I still have the shakes and my forehead is covered in a light film of perspiration. Looking up from her newspaper, Aunt Caroline smiles and passes me her handkerchief.

"I think there is no need for me to ask if you had a good night. You look positively dreadful, Monty."

Ordinarily, I would reply to a comment like that with something equally insulting or sarcastic. This evening, however, it is all I can do to nod an acknowledgement and remain standing. Forcing a smile of my own, I take my seat and ask her to pass the water jug.

"Actually." She frowns. "I was thinking something a little stronger might help and have taken the liberty of ordering for you."

Moment's later a steward arrives with an extremely large tumbler of scotch, and noisily places it down on the table. Just looking at it makes me want to wretch, but Caroline insists I take a drink. "Just small sips. I promise it will help to level you out. Your father and uncle used to swear by it. They rather bizarrely called it the hair of the dog. Although I never fully understood why."

"It sounds delicious," I snipe sarcastically. "And who wouldn't want bloody dog hair down the back of their throat when they are feeling like death warmed up?"

Patiently waiting for me to finish my rant, Aunt Caroline then carefully pushes the glass closer. "Go on, take a sip."

The first sip burns all the way down to my stomach, and I gag slightly on the acrid taste of acid in the back of my throat. She is right, though. By the fourth sip the alcohol has started to work its magic and I am soon feeling well enough to eat a little bread.

I'm also feeling a little more chatty, and after asking and finding out very little about Caroline's evening, I take a few minutes to tell her about my own. When I've finished, she nods politely. "It sounds like you had an interesting evening and a lucky escape."

"Yes, you can say that again," I enthuse. "If it hadn't been for the inscription on my pocket watch, I would surely have taken one hell of a beating from Matias's men."

"I wasn't referring to that." Caroline quietly giggles. "I was referring to your lucky escape from that ghastly woman Céline. Your sergeant friend was quite right, Monty. Three gold sovereigns is a small price to pay for avoiding a dose of the clap."

With something else on her mind, she then leans across the table and takes my hand. After checking we can't be overheard, she smiles cheekily and whispers, "He was also right about Major Boxhall. The man is a total bastard—but that's why I like him."

"So, you did have a good night?" I ask her somewhat knowingly.

"A woman never discusses such things," Caroline replies with mock indignation. "And a lady of breeding would certainly never be so indiscrete."

She then looks away and nods to the approaching steward. "Ah that must be our oysters."

I've barely got over my hangover, and whilst the whisky has helped slightly, the arrival of the aromatic fleshy molluscs turns my stomach once again. Visibly disgusted, I push the platter across the table toward Caroline. "Help yourself. They are all yours"

"Really?" she teases. "The steward assures me they were freshly caught in Marseille this morning." To tease me further, she lifts one of the oysters by its shell and waves it under my nose. "Are you sure, Monty? They are wonderfully plump – and fishy."

Suddenly pale and heavily perspiring, I get to my feet and excuse myself. Despite my assurance to return within a few minutes, Caroline knows perfectly well she won't be seeing hide nor hair of me again this evening.

Smiling sweetly, she says, "Of course you will. But in case you don't make it back, I will see you for an early breakfast before we arrive in Paris. Sleep well, my darling."

Resisting the urge to run, I wish her a good night, and turn to leave as fast as decorum will allow me. I'm almost at the door to the dining car when decorum is no longer an option.

Clasping a hand across my mouth, I bolt for my cabin with all the grace of a clapped-out pit pony. My retching continues well into the night, and long after my stomach is emptied of all but its lining.

Strangely though, and considering my fragile condition, by the time I finally collapse into bed, all I can think about is what Eric will have planned for the final night of our journey.

"I'm sure it will be something quite marvellous," I say to myself. "I'm also sure it will involve a splendid magnum of Pétrus or two."

Excited to be returning to Paris, I roll over and sleep soundly for the rest of the night.

* * * * * * * *

I wake the following morning fully refreshed, but ravenous. In the dining car, I cheerily greet Aunt Caroline and order myself a hearty breakfast of toasted bread, ham, and eggs.

When this first round fails to hit the spot, I repeat the order and am still eating as the train makes its final approach to the Gare du Nord.

"You should leave the rest," Caroline suggests. "If you are still hungry, I'm sure Eric's housekeeper will be able to rustle up something to keep you going until lunch."

I cram down a last piece of toast, and follow my aunt into the corridor, where she hands Johnathan a small slip of paper and a banknote. "This is the address of Monsieur Lavigne's residence on the Boulevard Saint-Germain. Find a hansom cab and go ahead with Betsy and the luggage please."

"Very good, ma'am." Johnathan nods. "Will there be anything else?"

"No, that's all," Caroline replies before turning to me. "Come, Monty. Lets not keep Eric waiting. Apparently he has a surprise for us."

Intrigued, and fully expecting to find Eric waiting for us on the station platform, I'm surprised to find he is not. "That's odd. You would think he would be on time to meet us today? Particularly when you consider how damn chilly it is this morning."

"Eric is never late," Caroline playfully scolds. "And I am sure he will be exactly where he said he would be."

She continues on to the station entrance where we find a small crowd of excited onlookers all keen to get a glimpse of the shiny new Motorcar parked beside the pavement.

In his driving clothes I could almost be looking at Ernst Albrecht, but when Eric spots us, his smile is unmistakable. Standing up in his seat, he excitedly toots the horn and shouts, "All aboard for the Boulevard Saint-Germain."

He then jumps down to assist myself and Aunt Caroline into the back seat, before returning to his own. "Have you ever seen such a beautiful piece of engineering?" He grins. "She arrived yesterday from the factory in Germany, and is the first of her kind in Paris."

Caroline nods her approval and I politely concur, "It's quite superb, Eric. What kind of motorcar is it?"

"It's a Benz velocipede," he declares proudly. "The Germans are not usually good for very much, but I must hand it to them, they do make a damn fine motorcar."

Just before pulling away from the station, he turns and says, "It's a damn shame you are not staying longer, Montague. I think you would have enjoyed taking her out for a spin."

"I'm sure I would." I nod innocently. "Perhaps the next time I visit."

For the rest of the short drive to Eric's home, he enthusiastically extols the virtues of the velocipede. We listen without interruption, and neither of us have the heart to tell him the Grand Duke of Hesse has two of them. Nor do we tell him I am more than familiar with how to drive one.

* * * * * * * *

After settling into our rooms and freshening up, we join our host in his conservatory for an early lunch. Still glowing with happiness at our return, Eric kisses Caroline's hand once again, before he turns and places his hands on my shoulders.

"Stand still and let me get a good look at you."

He looks me up and down, as proudly as a father might look upon his favorite son before saying, "My God, how is such a change possible in such a short space of time? Why, I can almost see your muscles through the fabric of that expensive suit you are wearing. And your whiskers are now almost as magnificent as my own."

"But not quite," he adds with a grin and a chuckle. "Come, sit down and tell me all about your time in Munich and Rome."

We talk for almost two hours, after which Eric slowly shakes his head. "I'm sure you must have wanted to kill the duke for what he put you through, but it does sound like you also have a lot to thank him for. It has certainly toughened you up, and has put some much needed extra flesh on your bones."

He then chuckles again. "And the gift from the contessa must have been quite a surprise on your last night in Rome?"

"Yes, you could say that." I smirk. But not as surprising as my time with the princess or our night in Marseille.

Unaware until now of our stopover, Eric turns to Caroline with feigned suspicion. "Have you been keeping secrets from me, my dear?"

"Not at all," Caroline replies sweetly. "It was just a short detour to break the tedium of our journey. It was, though, rather eventful for Monty. Isn't that so, darling?"

Eric listens intently as I regale him with the tale of my time with the legionnaires. When I tell him about the grizzled old sergeant he nearly falls off his chair. "Don't tell me that old rogue Matías is still alive?

"Still alive and still serving with the third regiment," I confirm.

"And still up to his old tricks." Eric laughs. "By God, it's nothing short of a miracle he is not hanging by his neck from a rope yet. The man is a bloody good soldier though."

When I mention the sovereigns, Aunt Caroline tries to apologize. "I'm sorry, Eric. I know it wasn't strictly an emergency, but—"

"Nonsense," our host cuts in. "It sounds like an emergency to me. And that blaggard would have cut Montagues throat if he had tried to get them back. Anyway, don't you worry yourself. I shall have the missing coins replaced before you leave in the morning."

We both know there is no use arguing with Eric on matters of finance or his generosity, so we don't even try. Instead, we thank him and enquire how he has been since we left.

With so much to discuss, it is soon late afternoon and after checking the time, Eric stands to excuse himself. "Please forgive my leaving you, but there are still one or two arrangements to be made ahead of this evening."

As interested to know as I am, Caroline asks, "May we know the plan for this evening, Eric?"

Raising an eyebrow, he replies with a smile, "Back to the Folies Bergères. Only tonight, I have booked the entirety of the place for a quite special private performance."

"Really Eric, that is too generous," Caroline gushes.

"Maybe so." Eric nods. "But it is also entirely appropriate to mark both the culmination of your journey, and Montague's belated coming of age."

Sensing he might be getting a little emotional, Caroline tactfully diverts attention away from her friend as he leaves. "Come, Monty, we should rest before this evening. It sounds like we are in for quite the treat."

* * * * * * * *

Resplendent in our finery, we first meet for pre-dinner drinks in Eric's drawing room before making our way to the Folies Bergères a little after eight. When we arrive, I'm shocked by the size and volume of the crowd milling around the entrance.

"Didn't you say it was a private—"

"It is," Eric assures me. "And don't look so worried. The Folies rarely, if ever, closes for a private event. This lot obviously didn't get the telegram." Chuckling at his own joke, he then puts a protective arm around Aunt Caroline and uses his cane to force a path through the crowd.

The concierge immediately recognises him and lifts the rope barrier to allow us through. "Monsieur Lavigne please accept my apologies for this inconvenience. Many of those waiting are regulars and refuse to believe we are closed this evening."

"That is quite alright, Pascal," Eric reassures him. "Is everything as I requested?"

"Exactly as you requested," the concierge nods.

"Good. And the rest of my guests, are they all here?"

"They are," Pascal confirms. "Please let me escort you inside."

* * * * * * * *

Aside from one large table in the centre of the room, all others have been removed and have been replaced by two rows of chairs arranged theatre style in front of the stage. As we approach the table, Eric's guests politely stand up to greet us. If either Eric or Caroline are surprised by the presence of any of the guests around the table, they certainly don't show it.

I, however, am a little taken aback as Eric makes the introductions. "Montague, I believe you know most of those present, but let me recap for the benefit of everyone else. Ladies and gentlemen, please allow me to introduce Monsieur Henri de Toulouse Lautrec, his good friend Monsieur Bruno Allard, and my very good friend Madame Cecille Moreau.

"Next, we have Mademoiselle Betsy Cooper, Monsieur Johnathan Wade and Monsieur Jean-Claude Dupont—"

It is surprising enough to see Betsy and Johnathan at the table, but it is the remaining pair of guests who are the biggest surprise.

"And finally, Montague, please allow me to introduce Mademoiselle Béatrice Aguillard, and her fiancé Major Bernard Chastain of the Fourth Dragoons."

Béatrice looks almost embarrassed to see me, but her fiancé can barely contain his disdain as he shakes my hand. "A pleasure to finally meet you, Montague. My fiancée has told me how you looked after her the last time you were in Paris."

If looks could kill, I would be dead already, but before I can say anything the major calmly retakes his seat and strikes up a conversation with Jean-Claude."

"What the hell?" I whisper to Eric. "Is there something I should know?"

"All in good time," Eric mutters. "Let us first sample this wonderful Pétrus eighty-seven. There are very few bottles remaining of this fine vintage."

It might well be in short supply, but the presence of three full magnums on the table is an obvious testament to the power of Eric's wealth and influence.

Knowing he is not a man to be hurried, I patiently wait until he refills my glass before I ask again, "So, are you going to tell me why you have invited Béatrice Aguillard here this evening? And why her fiancé, if indeed he really is her fiancé, keeps glaring at me as though he wants to kill me?"

"That is because he does," Eric smirks. "And yes, he is her fiancé. Apparently, he proposed just after returning from his last deployment."

Thankfully, the stage show has started and is loud enough to mask our discussion and my rapidly rising blood pressure. "And you somehow think this is funny, Eric? Christ, am I to assume that Béatrice has told him about—"

"Yes, there was a rumour," Eric interrupts. "A rumour that reached the ears of the gallant major shortly after his proposal. By all accounts, he confronted his fiancée and fearful of losing him, she told him everything of your plying her with alcohol, and of your subsequent seduction."

"She bloody what?" I bluster.

Touching my leg, Eric loudly chuckles to himself. "Oh, don't look so hard done by. Isn't that what happened?"

On the other side of the table, Major Chastain briefly turns and scowls before he catches my eye and quickly looks back to the show.

Lowering my voice slightly, I ask, "And how do you know all of this, and more to the point, why the hell are they here this evening?"

"Because, Monty, it pays me to know exactly what is happening in my city. I have eyes and ears everywhere, and word has recently reached me that Chastain was bad-mouthing you to anyone who would listen. He has sworn to kill you—"

I'm suddenly pale, and Eric places a hand onto my shoulder and leans in. "He has sworn to kill you, which is why I have invited him here this evening to clear the air."

"Clear the air? But how, Eric? The man looks angrier by the second."

Pointing to the stage, our host chuckles to himself again. "He's probably not a great lover of theatre. And who could blame him, the acts are dreadful this evening."

"But seriously," he adds. "Relax and enjoy your dinner. Trust me, you have nothing to worry about, and all will become clear after the show."

Relaxing under these circumstances is easier said than done. I barely touch my meal or make eye contact with my potential killer and his fiancée. When I do, both struggle to hide their growing contempt.

The other guests, including Aunt Caroline, continue on as though everything is perfectly normal. If any of them have the slightest inkling of my concerns, or Eric's plan for reconciliation, then they are all doing a damn fine job of concealing it.

* * * * * * * *

When the curtain finally drops at the end of the stage show, Eric gets to his feet, and my heart almost skips a beat. "Ladies and gentlemen, please now follow me and take your seat in front of the stage for the next performance."

My fellow guests obediently take their seats, and I'm about to sit down beside Aunt Caroline when Bruno suddenly takes me by the arm. "Not you, Montague. I would like you and Major Chastain to join me on the stage please."

Unsure of exactly what is happening, I turn toward my Parisienne mentor. "Go with Bruno." He nods. "Trust me, everything will be fine."

Trusting him is another easier said than done. Particularly when I see the heavy cavalry sabre hanging from the major's belt.

I do though trust him completely, and despite my nerves, I follow Bruno and Chastain onto the stage. Toulouse's friend then positions us on either side, before he returns to the middle to address the audience.

"Ladies and gentlemen, this next performance has been arranged by our host, Monsieur Eric Lavigne, for the purpose of settling a dispute between two men of honour—"

Before he can continue, the curtain rises behind us, and my jaw drops at the site of the elaborately carved wooden chest sitting on top of a small table. Inside it are the pistols gifted to me by the duke.

"A duel?" I stammer. "A bloody duel?"

"I knew the man was a coward," Chastain sneers. "I knew it the moment I saw him."

Ignoring the insult, I nervously appeal to Bruno. "Is this even legal in France?"

"Not since the seventeenth century," he replies quite casually. "But this is a matter of honour between gentlemen, and be assured, Montague, no court in Paris would convict under such circumstances."

"He's a bloody coward," Chastain taunts again. "It is almost beneath me to dispatch such a man."

Conscious that any decision I make tonight will mark me out for the kind of man I am for the rest of my life, I take a breath to compose myself, before I look to my aunt and blow a kiss.

I then turn back to Bruno and mask my nerves with an arrogant sneer. "Let's get on with it then. There is still a rather fine drop of Pétrus I should like to get back to."

Calling us back together, Bruno points to the pistol case. "Gentlemen, please choose your weapons."

Chastain selects first, and Bruno hands me the remaining pistol. "Now gentlemen, please stand back-to-back, and cock your weapons."

The noisy cocking of the weapons is a stark reminder of how serious this is, and I wonder if my opponent is as nervous as I am.

Before I can decide one way or the other, Bruno issues his final instruction, "At my command you will both walk ten paces, turn, and fire. Is that clear, gentlemen?"

We both nod, and with the audience now deathly quiet, Bruno says, "Very well, gentlemen – proceed!"

My legs are trembling, but I count the paces and turn as casually as I am able. Chastain turns slightly ahead of me. He raises his pistol, but he holds his nerve and doesn't immediately fire. Wrongly assuming him to be wavering, I raise my own weapon, centre it on his chest and squeeze the trigger.

When the smoke clears, I am stunned to see my adversary still standing. He is completely unscathed, and worst still, he is now grinning from ear to ear. He slowly raises his pistol higher until it is level with my forehead. Chastain is so confident of his aim; he looks toward his fiancée and smiles smugly as he fires his weapon.

Like my own shot, the noise of the explosion reverberates throughout the theatre and thick black smoke belches from the end of the pistols barrel.

But there is no impact. Nor do I feel any shot passing my head.

I am still trying to figure out how it is possible for both of us to miss at such close range when Chastain angrily storms toward Bruno. "What is the meaning of this? I could never miss such an easy target. I demand a rematch."

Bruno does his best to placate the major, and calmly assures him, "Please allow me to check and reload the weapons. But while I do this, I might suggest you both re-join the rest of the guests for a few moments?"

Chastain is reluctant to leave the stage, but when I hand my pistol to Bruno, he grudgingly does the same. At the bottom of the stairs, Eric is waiting for us with two cloudy glasses of Absinthe. "A little something to steady the nerves, gentlemen?"

We both reach for the glasses at the same time, but Eric pulls the tray away and shakes his head. "No, not for you, Montague. Your glass is on the table. These two are for Major Chastain and his beautiful fiancée."

Clearly still frustrated by his failure to kill me, Chastain takes the drinks without a word and leaves to join his beloved Béatrice. While they reunite, Eric leads me back to the table, where I am met with a flurry of knowing nods and smiles of admiration.

"Here," he says handing me my drink. "Get this down you, my boy. Things are about to get interesting."

"Really?" I exclaim. "Can they get any more interesting?"

My question is laughed off and I quietly ask, "Were those pistols loaded properly?"

"Of course, they were." Eric nods. "I personally supervised the loading of the powder and—"

Feigning realisation, he suddenly stops himself mid-sentence and shakes his head. "Oh Eric, you stupid man. You forgot to load the ball didn't you. It's no wonder those blasted popguns didn't work."

Serious again, he leans closer and whispers, "But you proved yourself to be a man with a fine backbone, Montague. And that was the real point of tonight."

Now more confused than ever, I slowly shake my head. "But how has this settled things? Chastain is itching for another chance to kill me."

"I don't think so." Eric casually nods to the other side of the table. "In fact, the good major looks quite placid don't you think?"

Clearly under the influence of something stronger than absinthe, Chastain and his lover are now lazily slumped backward in their chairs. Both have glazed vacant expressions, and both appear to be dribbling.

Before I can ask what they have been given, Eric glances across the table to Aunt Caroline, who in turn looks to her servants. "Betsy, Johnathan, the major and his fiancée look a little under the weather. Take them to get freshened up please."

I'm fully expecting them to be led toward the bathrooms, but on a night of surprises, it's no real surprise when they are taken onto the stage and led behind the curtains. Taking this as their cue, the remaining guests retake their seats in front of the stage.

They leave the centre seats open for Eric, Caroline, and my good self.

* * * * * * * * *

For the next five minutes, Eric steadfastly refuses to answer any more questions about what is happening next. I am still none the wiser when the curtains finally rise to reveal a large four poster bed positioned in the centre of the stage.

Toulouse excitedly whoops his delight, but I'm initially dumbstruck and gasp, "What in God's name is this?"

Major Chastain and Béatrice are on their knees on either side of the bed. Both are naked from the waist down and both are wearing thick leather collars around their necks. Betsy is standing behind the major holding tightly onto his leash. Johnathan is doing the same for Béatrice.

In what seems like a well-rehearsed performance, Aunt Caroline nods and both servants tug on the leashes and order their charges onto the bed. Clearly heavily drugged, both lovers comply without question, and Johnathan turns them to face the audience.

By now, the air is heavy with anticipation, and there is more than one gasp of appreciation when Johnathan releases his swollen meat from the tight confines of his breeches. One or two of the men in the audience shamelessly unbutton themselves much to the delight of Madame Cecille who is only too eager to offer a hand.

Taunting the major, Johnathan slowly waves his thick rod in front of the man's face, before he climbs onto the bed and drops to his knees behind Béatrice. Using a strong hand to lift her arse higher, he then lines himself up ready for the off, and looks to his mistress for guidance. Like the Romans of antiquity, Aunt Caroline theatrically raises a thumb into the air before she smiles and slowly turns it downward.

His orders now perfectly clear, Johnathan grips tightly to Béatrice's hips, and unceremoniously ploughs his full length deep into her cunny. In that moment, the young man is transformed into a wild beast, and ignoring the major's slurred cries of protest, he hammers her with enthusiastic abandon.

Suddenly jumping to his feet, and seemingly indignant, Toulouse excitedly points to the major and shouts, "What about him? This is not fair. Is there nothing for him?"

The questions are of course entirely rhetorical, as by now it is perfectly clear to all that Toulouse is fully aware of the details of Eric's plan. His shock then is feigned and almost hysterical when Betsy lowers her bloomers to reveal the large wooden phallus hanging heavily between her legs.

Kneeling beside Johnathan she reaches between Béatrice's legs to lubricate her fingers, which in turn she uses to lubricate the head of the phallus.

Despite this small consideration, I can't help but feel a little sorry for the man. At its widest point, the wood is at least as thick as the rod currently pounding away at Béatrice, and I shudder slightly at the thought of what it will do to him.

The major however is so far gone, he has no idea what is knocking at his back door, until Betsy starts to nudge her way inside. Suddenly wide eyed, he squeals like a frightened piglet until Betsy finds her rhythm, and pleasure takes over from the pain.

Perfectly in time, the servants match each other stroke for stroke. To their front, the drugged-up lovers have long since given up the fight, and both now grunt their satisfaction.

Close to his climax, Jonathan winks to Betsy and increases the intensity of his thrusts. Betsy does the same and reaches under her ride to fumble for Chastain's flapping erection.

The major is the first to blow. His seed spurts across the bedcovers, and exhausted he slumps forward taking Betsy with him. Still impaled on the hefty length of wood, she continues to rut him while Johnathan noisily grunts and finishes himself off deep inside Béatrice.

Behind me, Bruno and Jean-Claude are also nosily finished off by the skilful hands of Cecille.

With the performance over, I'm left feeling somewhat shocked and confused. My friends, however, all rise to their feet to deliver a thunderous round of applause. As excited and animated as ever, Toulouse claps the loudest and shouts, "Bravo, Eric. Bravo. That was quite spectacular."

Our host playfully pats my leg and asks with a wink, "Do you agree?"

I'm really not quite sure what to think, but I nod anyway. "Yes, Eric. That was quite spectacular. But how is this meant to settle things between myself, and Major Chastain? Surely, they will both remember this when the effects of whatever you have given them wears off?"

"Unlikely," Eric replies. "That was a powerful sedative. But even if they do, neither of them will want the proof of this being made public. They both have far too much to lose."

Noting my continued mystified expression, Eric smiles and loudly clicks his fingers toward the stage. Moments later, a well-dressed young man previously unseen emerges from one of the wings. He is carrying a tall wooden tripod and one of those newfangled camera things.

When the penny finally drops, Eric nods and smiles again. "Yes, Montague. Please allow me to introduce Monsieur François Blanchet. François is one of the finest photographers in France."

The young man politely nods his thanks, and Eric asks, "Did you get everything I asked for, François?"

"Everything," he replies. "I will have the pictures and negatives delivered to your home tomorrow morning, Monsieur Lavigne."

"Excellent, excellent." Eric nods. He then turns back and reassuringly places a hand on my shoulder. "So, as you can see, Montague, this little misunderstanding between yourself and Major Chastain is now settled."

Without waiting for my reaction or response, he turns to the others and roars, "Come now, my friends. There is still a full magnum of the Pétrus eighty-seven on the table, and it damn well won't drink itself."

Chapter Twelve

Homeward Bound – 24 December 1898

We finally call it a night in the early hours of the morning, but any thoughts of sleep I might be entertaining are quickly dispelled by the sound of light footsteps tiptoeing toward my bed.

Thinking I'm asleep already, Betsy carefully lifts the bedcovers and climbs in beside me. An arm tenderly wraps around my waist, and I can feel her breasts pushing into my back through the thin material of her cotton nightdress. For a moment she lays there quietly, but then she kisses the side of my neck and whispers, "Monty, are you awake?"

"If I say no, will you leave and allow me to sleep?" I reply sarcastically.

My clear and ungroggy response easily gives away the fact I have been awake all this time. Lifting her head, Betsy playfully rolls me over to face her. "Oh, Monty, you are such a tease. You heard me come in, didn't you?"

"Maybe." I smirk. "And why did you? Is there some kind of emergency I can help you with? Perhaps a raging bush fire that needs extinguishing?"

My last question is filled with innuendo, but I'm surprised to see Betsy suddenly looking apprehensive and a little nervous. "What is it?" I ask. "Why so forlorn all of a sudden?"

Reluctant to answer, she wraps her arms tightly around my body and buries her head into my chest. A small tear slowly snakes its way down her cheek, and I can feel her trembling slightly.

"What is it?" I ask again with obvious concern. "You can tell me."

"You will think I'm being silly," she says quietly.

"Maybe so," I reply lightly stroking her hair. "But I would still like to know what has made you so upset?"

Lifting her head from my chest, Betsy wipes the tear from her cheek, and says, "I know it's silly, but I think we have become good friends during these last months travelling together."

"We have." I smile. "Very good friends, but why so upset?"

Slightly teary and emotional, the young maid sniffles. "Because tomorrow we will return to England, and it makes me sad to think I might never see you again."

"What are you talking about? Of course, you will see me again," I try to reassure her. "Why would you think otherwise?"

"Well, because you will return to Morton Hall, and I will return home with Lady Caroline. And because—"

Hesitant to finish the sentence, Betsy nervously looks to me for approval.

"Go, on," I urge her. "You can say whatever is on your mind. I promise I won't get angry or upset."

Suddenly bashful, she lowers her eyes. "Well, because you are soon to be married. And when you do, I don't think you will ever think of me again."

I had no idea that Betsy might have feelings for me and caught completely unawares I'm now blushing almost as hard as she is. I'm also lost for words, and am thankful when she adds, "I just wanted to spend this last night with you. Is that ok, Monty?"

That is perfectly ok with me of course, and eager to divert attention away from my embarrassment, I smirk and point to Betsy's groin. "Only if you promise you haven't still got that bloody great log between your legs?"

My joke instantly eases the tension, and we both relax. To answer my question, Betsy grins and lifts her nightdress. "Of course not, but feel free to check for yourself?"

I'm relieved to find the wooden phallus gone. I am, however, left spellbound by what I do find, "You, you—"

"Yes, sir." Betsy smiles. "I shaved it just like Mademoiselle Béatrice. I do hope you like it. It's ever so smooth."

Without waiting for a response, she takes one of my hands and places it over her mound, "Go on, feel for yourself."

"Umm, very nice," I hum softly. "Very nice indeed."

I then pull her toward me and kiss the side of her neck. "And you think I could forget you so easily, Betsy. How on earth could that ever be possible?"

"It couldn't." She giggles as she wraps a soft hand around my aching pole. "And nor could little Monty."

"Hey, less of the little," I playfully scold. "My old fella is more than big enough to make you squeal, missy.

We both stop laughing, and for a moment we stare without speaking. Betsy is the first to break the spell when she leans forward to plant a kiss on my lips. Tender at first, it quickly grows in intensity, and our tongues entwine and swirl deliciously in our mouths.

As hard and aroused as I have ever been, my desire to be inside her is like nothing I have ever felt before. Lifting the nightdress over her head, I gently push her down onto the bed and part her legs.

Savouring her anticipation, I smile and lower my head to slowly run my tongue along her moist slit. Her rich sweet aroma is even more intoxicating than the very first time we were together, and now desperate for our bodies to become one, I lightly probe at the entrance to heaven with the tip of my dangerously pulsating shaft.

Betsy is seemingly, even more desperate than I am for us to be joined, and impatiently pulls on my thighs. "Please don't tease, Monty. I need you inside me now."

Pushing forward, my bulbous crown splays her lips like a beautiful pink butterfly, and her muscles relax and draw me in. Her inner warmth caresses my masculine flesh, and our bodies move as one.

Badly wanting this feeling to last, I alternate my thrusts between slow and gentle, and hard and fast. When I feel myself close to the verge, I ignore my lovers' pleas, and pull out to feast on her beautiful breasts, and that shiny pearl so resplendent in her blushing oyster.

I kiss her all over as passionately as any lover might, and only resume our lovemaking when I'm certain the danger is averted.

Hungry for her own sweet release, Betsy claws at my back, and moans softly, "Harder now, Monty. Fill me completely with your seed."

Her eyes are so deeply intense and mesmerising, I would challenge any man to deny this woman her wants and needs. Willingly obeying her request, I pull back and thrust my rod deep inside her burning cunny. This time, I pound her as hard as a blacksmith hammers his anvil, and close to the precipice, I lower my head to whisper, "Cum with me, sweet Betsy."

"Oh, sweet Jesus." She moans softly. "I can feel you about to—"

Before she can finish the sentence, her body stiffens, and a great shudder steamrolls its way across her body to culminate with a breathless gasp of unencumbered pleasure. My own climax is just moments behind and is as intense as any I have experienced.

It floods her belly and still intimately locked together, Betsy pulls me forward onto her chest. "Promise you won't forget me, Monty? And promise you will come to see me every now and then."

I couldn't lie even if I had wanted to. This saucy vixen has me well and truly under her spell. My smile and kiss on her cheek are as honest and sincere as my response. "I promise. I won't forget you, Betsy Cooper. And it would take the brigade of guards to stop me from seeing you."

"Or a jealous new wife?" She grins mischievously.

I casually brush aside the question as having no relevance. "No, not even that. And besides, we are a long way from crossing that particular bridge."

Satisfied with my assurances, Betsy carefully pushes me away and rolls onto her side. She then snuggles in behind and tightly wraps her arms around my waist. Still hot and sticky, we are both asleep within minutes.

Our second departure from Paris was no less emotional than the first. This time, however, our host insisted on personally escorting us to the station and waiting with us until the departure of our train to Calais. Obviously then, there was a good deal more hugging and fond farewells than I would ordinarily have liked or am comfortable with.

I am, of course, deeply indebted to Eric, for his friendship and all he has done for me. It's just that sometimes he is – well, a little too French in his mannerisms and displays of emotion for my liking. I was though a little sad to be leaving again and promised sincerely to return as soon as my situation would allow me. Perhaps even with my new wife.

In stark contrast to Eric's Gallic outpouring of emotion, our time on the train was unusually subdued. Concluding Aunt Caroline to also be a little sad at reaching the end of our journey, I dutifully paid respect to the silence and neither of us spoke more than a few words until we were safely on board the steamer *Castalia*.

On this occasion there will be no overnighting on board, and conscious we will be making landfall in just a few hours, I pour Caroline a glass of claret and quietly ask, "Is everything all right? Only you were unusually quiet after leaving Paris."

I'm greatly relieved when she shakes her head, and smiles. "I'm fine, darling. I have just been contemplating how far we – well how far you have come since we left England."

Nodding proudly, she takes my hand. "You have become a fine young gentleman, Monty. And I'm not just saying this because I'm your aunt. Any woman would be proud to have you as a husband."

"You really mean that?" I ask.

"Of course." She nods. "These last few weeks, I have seen a significant change in you. You have matured and grown as a man. Not just physically, but also up here," she says lightly tapping her head.

"And the way you handled yourself with Major Chastain was quite outstanding. Other than the major and his floozy, you were the only other person in the room not to know those pistols were not properly loaded. Yet despite this, you stepped up to the plate admirably. That would not have been the case at the start of this journey."

She is right, of course, and whilst I have a lot to thank Eric and the duke for, Aunt Caroline is undoubtedly the real reason behind the positive changes in me.

Blushing ever so slightly, I lift her hand and plant a kiss. "I could not have done this without you, Caroline. And whatever happens from this point on, I will forever be grateful for your support, guidance, and undying patience."

"Thank you, Monty. Your mother is going to be so proud when she hears of your transformation, and even more so when she sees it with her own eyes."

Nodding to herself, Caroline thinks a moment and then frowns. "You do understand however, this was the easy part? The real work begins when we reach home. Time is now against us, so there can be no further foolishness or undue delay."

I know exactly what she is alluding to, and I nod my understanding. "Yes, I do. And you have my word, I'm ready and able to do whatever it takes to marry well and wrest our estates from the clutches of Father's creditors."

"Good," Caroline says. "I knew it all along, but I wanted to hear it for myself. Now, make that your last," she says pointing to my glass of scotch. "It won't do to reunite with your mother half-cut."

* * * * * * * *

Our carriage from Dover makes good time, and we reach the main gate of the Morton Hall estate just as evening is starting to draw in on Christmas eve of 1898.

Ahead of us, the familiar tree-lined avenue lazily wends its way toward the manor house. Suddenly aware of the enormity of the task ahead of me, I abruptly tap the driver on the shoulder and ask him to stop. "Let me off here, please."

Obviously concerned, Caroline asks, "Is everything okay?"

"Yes, it is," I reply. "But if it is okay with you, I should like to walk from here. I would like to take a few moments alone to clear my head before I'm required to talk or even think about marriage again."

"Of course, darling. But try not to worry. Tomorrow is Christmas day, and my sister has assured me there will be no such talk until at least after boxing day. Take your time, Monty. I will tell Charlotte you will be along shortly."

The carriage continues on, and I turn and look toward the house. Most trees on the avenue have long since succumbed to the ravages of late autumn, but a scant few still hold on tightly to their rapidly browning leaves.

Clearing my head completely of thoughts of marriage, I take a deep breath and slowly start to walk. My thoughts then are mostly of Paris, Munich, and Rome. But they are also of Betsy. And of when I might see her again. This girl has me quite bewitched, and her image only clears when I spot Mother patiently waiting to greet me.

She is standing at the top of the grand marble steps at the entrance to our home and is partially silhouetted by the light from the hallway behind her.

As I approach, she somehow looks younger and more beautiful than I remember. She is, of course, just a few years older than her sister and is fortunate to share the same physical traits that I find so attractive in Caroline.

Even so, I'm a little surprised to find her dressed in a gown quite so revealing and risqué. Cinched at the waist, the tight lacing across her ample bosom is oddly reminiscent of the time I was drooling over Aunt Caroline on the night before our departure.

Shaking off such an immoral thought, I move closer, and my mother smiles and opens her arms. "Oh, Monty, you will never know how badly I have missed you. But it is wonderful to have you home in time for Christmas."

Breaking away, she kisses me on the cheek, then looks me up and down with an obvious and glowing maternal pride. "You are even more handsome than your father was when we married."

"And my you have grown," she says squeezing my arms.

"And those whiskers." She giggles. "My sister was right, darling. You have indeed become a fine young man."

Taking a pace backward, she looks me up and down again before nodding approvingly. "And Caroline informs me you have been a diligent student and have learned a tremendous amount during your travels. Is that true?"

"Yes, Mother. I believe it is." I nod proudly. "And I'm ready to—"

I'm quickly silenced by a finger placed on my lips.

I'm then taken by the hand, and Mother nods. "I'm sure you are, Monty. And there will be adequate time for that discussion after Christmas. For now, however, I should very much like to find out exactly what it is you have learned these past two months."

Noting my shock, she releases my hand and walks toward the door. When she turns back around to face me, a hand casually loosens the lacing across her chest and she smiles reassuringly. "Don't be shy, Monty. Come show your mother what you have learned."